THE POTS

(That Mothers Leave For Their Daughters)

Nonjabulo
Sangweni-Arahill

Black Earth Publishing

Paperback ISBN: 978-1-7355968-4-6
eBook ISBN: 978-1-7355968-9-1

Library of Congress Control Number: 2020915537

Cover Design by: Nonjabulo Arahill

Printed in the United States of America

Cover design by: Art Painter
Library of Congress Control Number: 2018675309
Printed in the United States of America

To the women who raised me.

My mother, grandmother, and late aunt.
Nozipho Princess Sangweni, Sibongile Witness
Sangweni, and Thobeka Lungile Sangweni.

Thank you for your unconditional love, your
endless wisdom, and your unwavering support.
Thank you for welcoming me into womanhood
and for always helping to guide me through.

I love and honour you.

CHAPTER 1

September 2010

On the night before she left, Mama pulled me so close I could smell the onions on her, the scent clinging to each layer of her clothing. "I wish I could take you, Makhosi, but I'll be gone all week and your father is already not happy about that." I knew that. Baba hated it when Mama and I weren't home. We missed so many local ceremonies it no longer occurred to me to want to go. This wedding was a miracle because it forced Baba to allow Mama to go. Her absence would not go unnoticed at a family ceremony and I knew he didn't want to give anybody a reason to talk. That he would never let us both go gave me a week to show what sixteen years of woman training had taught me. I nodded absently at my mother.

If I wasn't so excited about her leaving, I may have been upset at how excited she was to be leaving me. She would get to leave the dusty, brown roads that we walked on every day. For a week she would be free of our village and live like the fancy women in the township with their running water and neat houses in a row; the paved streets with street names, that didn't turn to mud every time it rained. She could enjoy all that while I played her role here. I would look after my father and older brother, Sizwe, just as well as she did. My excitement left no room to be upset.

...

Light flooded my once cave dark hut and a few seconds later Mama's face peered through. Even at five o'clock in the morning, she smelled like onions. She was gone in the next instant, but the onions remained. She'd seen me see her and that counted as waking me up. I normally got up at six o'clock and if I was woken up even a minute earlier I was demonic, but that was in my youth. Today I graciously woke up an hour earlier because Mama was leaving and I had to show her I was ready. I rubbed the sleep from my eyes and joined her in the big standalone flat that was the kitchen. It was the biggest flat in our household, even bigger than my parents' which had a little lounge area where Baba always took his food. The smallest one belonged to my brother, and I nearly never went in there. Baba and Sizwe had been systematically replacing each of the huts with the more sophisticated flats so that now only two remained in the yard; mine and the guest hut. They were evidently in no hurry to get to mine, and I didn't mind. I'd heard the roar of the rain beating up on the tin roof, and on those days I knew they all missed the gentle way it fell on my thatched roof.

"I've already started the fire, the bad water's in the kettle and the good water's in the jug. Just boil the tea when he wakes up." She shuffled across the kitchen, looking fancy in her town clothes. Fewer layers, long skirt hugging her hips, headscarf tied securely in the big dome-like way that made her look like a queen.

"Yes, Mama." I wished she wouldn't fuss, I knew how to do everything. The 'bad' water was the salty water we got from the pump which we used for bathing and washing, cooking too if it hadn't rained for a while and the storage tank was empty. The 'good' water was rainwater, re-served primarily for tea and cooking if we could manage it. I watched her scan the entire kitchen, if our household was Mama's empire then the kitchen was her headquarters. Her scanning eyes found their way to me.

"Nana, if you can't do two meals that's fine. Just cook one big pot and serve it twice." Like hell I would, if she cooked two meals a day then so would I. I nodded. "You should have enough water for-" she froze mid-sentence and wiped her hands on the checkered dishcloth hanging next to her. I'd heard it too, the bus was close and it was time to go. She pulled her bag over her shoulder and walked to the door where I was still standing. A pinch to my nose and a smile that made all her features soft conveyed all the things there was no time to say.

"I'll be back before you know it."

"I know, Mama, I'll take care of them. Ung'khonzele. Send my love."

With her free hand, she grabbed the plastic bag with the mealies sticking out. Mama didn't believe in entering someone's home empty-handed and since the only thing we had in abundance was land, our gift was always fresh produce. I watched her pause briefly at the door of their flat, I assumed to give a quick goodbye to my father before making her way to the gate. I waved until I could no longer see her through the small squares of the fence.

Sizwe always came to the kitchen in the morning and made his own tea when Mama was around, but I wasn't sure if he expected special treatment in her absence. I hovered around the kitchen waiting to see if he would come. He walked in, all bare chest and sleepy eyes, yawning as he moved around the rectangular room. A grunt perfectly timed with a nod served as my greeting. I stared back at him, offering a shrug of my right shoulder in response. He made his tea and sandwich and I did the same. Sitting at the table, we ate in the comfortable silence of two people who had perfected the art of ignoring each other. He then poured his bathwater and left. I collected the dishes he'd left on the table, dumping them into the big plastic container with the rest of the dishes I was about to wash.

...

On more than one occasion while Mama was gone, I wanted to fling myself into the wall. I had grossly underestimated just how much went into 'taking care of them' in her absence. With each new day, waking up an hour earlier lost more of its luster, and being responsible for cleaning all the dishes, all the time, took its toll. Our two huts and three flats became my enemies as I swept all of them, except my brother's, every day. By the second day, exhaustion bested my pride and I cooked one big pot of 'every vegetable I can find' stew. When I ate it, it tasted of defeat. When I served it to my father, I left before he could taste it. I didn't want to see his disappointment that it tasted nothing like Mama's food. No matter how hard I tried, I was still not a woman.

When Monday came I ran to school, happy for the escape. Every math problem made my heart dance. It forced me to not think about dishes, cooking and sweeping. The long end-of-school-day bell, twice as long as the end-of-break bell, signaled the end of my freedom and I made my way home, counting down the days until Mama's return. She had left on Saturday and by the time

Thursday came I was about to lose my mind. From the time I woke up I was counting the hours. The six o'clock bus she would be on would arrive at around seven and it couldn't come fast enough. "Shesha," hurry up, I hissed at my brother as we made our way to the bus stop. He turned to look at me before turning back to face the single-lane gravel road, putting his hands in his pocket for good measure. Sometimes my brother was a real nuisance, which was why I mostly ignored him. But today I was so happy that not even his attitude could bring me down. No longer feeling like we had to make the walk together, I ran past him all the way to the bus stop, happy to carry out Baba's instruction of "go fetch your mother." I would have gone if nobody told me to.

My run was premature so that I still had to wait a few minutes for the bus to reach me and stop. I watched Sizwe approach, unlike me he would arrive just in time, having successfully avoided being a sweaty, heaving mess. We shared everything, a mother, a father, a home and we were only separated by four years, but whenever I looked at him I couldn't imagine a person less like me. How could he act so cool when I knew he was as excited as I was to see her? When Mama stepped out of the bus I ran to cross the street that separated us, unashamedly. I reached her and then just stood there, smiling, because that's all I could think to do. She came bearing gifts.

There was a parcel on her back, carried the same way she would a baby. Four plastic bags were distributed between her hands and a passenger still in the bus carried a large funny looking thing down to the ground for her, before helping her place it carefully on her head. He then got back on and the bus and was gone.

I sensed motion and turned to see Baba coming towards us, releasing her of the burden on her head. I didn't know that he would be coming too, his presence giving me a minor, pleasant shock. His face was unreadable and I didn't look at it for too long. All he asked my mother was if she had traveled safely. My mother's gentle nod before she lowered her eyes again was the only response she would give right now. Sizwe took the plastic bags from her, gave one to me and we all walked back home in silence. I stole a glance all around me, Mama and I in the center and Sizwe and Baba a little further back, at our sides. I imagined the neighbors spying on us through their curtains as we passed and saying to each other in hushed voices, "what a handsome family, the Mthethwa's."

...

I knew I would have to wait for my turn with Mama, but I wasn't worried. Sizwe worked with my father who worked in the local court as an adviser to the chief, a job which paid mostly in reverence and whose schedule was incredibly irregular because it centered around when people had disputes. Regardless, they were always gone on Saturdays. They could stay home all week but still have somewhere to go come Saturday. I would watch them through the kitchen window after they'd had their breakfast in the morning, bathed and sparkling as they walked out the gate dressed in their best clothes. My brother in his white shirt, that had once been for school, tucked into his black pants, silver buckle shining. My father in that day's Madiba shirt, untucked, the crease of both their pants running perfectly down the middle, sharp enough to be a weapon. They would leave after breakfast and come back after lunch, most times. Tomorrow was Saturday so after breakfast I would have Mama all to myself and she could tell me all about her trip. Right now she belonged to my father. We all took the parcels first to their flat where everything new was received, stacking them neatly in the living room, later they would go to the kitchen. Sizwe and I were meticulous in our packing, every second meant information.

"What is it?"

We all knew Baba was talking about the funny looking thing, and we all leaned in closer to hear Mama's answer.

"It's an old potter's wheel," she said as she gently ran her hands over it. It wasn't that big and it wasn't that sophisticated if you just analyzed the parts. However, it was confusing that those parts were arranged like that. There were three disks arranged in a straight line, joined by a rod that cut through each of their centers. The bottom disk was the smallest, a small distance above it was the biggest disk and a greater distance above that one was the middle-sized disk. Its height was such that if someone sat naturally with it between their legs, then their hands would fall comfortably on the top disk. Having never seen anything like it before, I willed my father to ask the question I was dying to know the answer to. What is it for? However, I could tell by my father's reaction to what my mother had just said that he did in fact know what it was, now that she mentioned it. Maybe he just hadn't seen it in a long time or he hadn't seen one that looked like that, but he knew what it was for. Instead, he asked her what he was dying to know, "What are you going to do with it?"

"I'm going to learn to be a potter." Something shifted in the room. So suddenly that a crack formed in our universe. My father looked at my mother for a long time but said nothing. Still, he wore his displeasure on the outside. Something shifted in me too. My heart swelled. The room shrunk and the air slowly got heavy. Something big was happening. Mama sat looking straight ahead, her head held high, her hand on the potter's wheel. My father looked down at her from where he stood, his face in a scowl. My brother was alert, like me, taking it all in. I replayed it in my head, in her voice, how she said "I'm going to learn to be a potter," and not "I would like to learn to be a potter." There was no question. Her voice was soft, but it was firm. My brother and I locked eyes and I tried to find in his the admiration I knew was evident in mine, but his gaze was gone as quickly as it came. I thought my mother was the queen of the world. My father broke the silence by asking her a question I already knew the answer to.

"Who will teach you?"

"No one, the lady who gave it to me showed me how to use it. I just need practice now." Good Mama. The air got thicker. I made a secret vow to be extra helpful to Mama so that Baba never had reason to complain. If he was displeased he would blame it on the wheel and take it away. I gave my mother a silent smile that I hoped told her of my devotion and the brief moment passed only between us. My brother and I locked eyes again and this time it held, he felt it too, we had overstayed our welcome. There was an acute change in the air and we knew we were no longer wanted. I took the plastic bags to the kitchen to unpack the food. Sizwe made his way to his flat. I wished to be a fly on that wall.

...

I opened the plastic bags and rejoiced because Mama had outdone herself. One plastic bag was solely dedicated to scones, and concealed within them in wrapping paper was what I assumed was once the wedding cake. The rest of the plastics had things I was equally as happy to see. Things I could tell were bought by a woman; dishwashing liquid, a set of new dishcloths, washing powder, a long bar of soap, and fabric softener. Baba usually did the shopping, based on a list Mama compiled. Oftentimes the money didn't stretch far enough to cover everything and the first things cut were those that Baba deemed 'luxuries', like fabric softener. He was right that it was a luxury, but how it made the clothes smell and feel was wonderful. It made Mama and I feel rich to smell like that. So rich we made it the official measure of our wealth; with fabric softener or without.

I finished by packing away another secret delight, beef stock cubes, feeling spoiled. I poked at the coals, rearranging the logs and twigs to reignite the fire. When I blew into it, it came alive. I walked their tea to them extra carefully, double-checking to see if my tray was perfect, knowing Mama would notice. The door was open and the room was cool and quiet. It was so quiet I heard myself walk in, I heard myself put the tray down. I received softened eyes and a gentle nod as a means of gratitude before I heard myself walk-out. It wasn't clear whether they'd moved at all since Sizwe and I were last there.

I filled the kettle up, boiling enough tea for Sizwe and me, knowing he would be in the kitchen shortly to investigate the contents of the plastic bags. After tea, I warmed up the food. If for nothing else, I knew that my father and brother were happy to have Mama home because it meant they didn't have to eat my cooking anymore. They had never said that they hated it, but I knew they did. When Mama finally walked into the kitchen, she was no longer dressed in her fancy town clothes. The floor-length maroon skirt that hugged her body once again replaced by her loose brown one. She was still tying her faded green pinafore over her waist as she looked around her kitchen. I missed seeing her sparkle and wished she could have kept her nice clothes on longer, but her old clothes brought comfort.

She stirred my pot of rather watery beef curry. I was still not perfect at doubling my proportions and it showed. She removed the pot from the fire and emptied the contents into another dish before chopping up an onion and frying it in some oil. Next, she added spice mix, before she threw my stew back into the pot. I watched transfixed as she worked with the efficiency of two people, now peeling and chopping a potato before throwing it in. Lastly, she added the magic, the beef stock. In just those easy steps she had corrected my stew from a sad, runny mess to absolute deliciousness. I watched in awe, a true woman at work. It was good to have Mama home.

I finally got my time with Mama the next day. After breakfast, the two of us went to stock up on more water. We went later than the morning group to avoid the traffic. I didn't ask her questions, Mama didn't like that. I was practically hopping from foot to foot as we walked, trying to silently urge her on, knowing it would do nothing. I would simply have to wait until she chose to share.

She waited until we got to the pump and her bucket was situated underneath the spout before my patience was rewarded. There was no detail she hadn't absorbed and her words became pictures in my mind. "There's this plant that grows there," she said, pumping the water effortlessly with a vacant look in her eyes. "It's like a giant mass of leaves. If it was smaller it could be a houseplant, but it grows big, outside. It's everywhere." She stopped pumping for a second, looking at my face and talking directly at me for the first time, "It's beautiful, Ma. It's maroon, or maybe red depending on the light." She started pumping again, the spell broken. "I just love how it's everywhere there, the place is littered with them, that's the plant of Mshayazafe."

Even years after her last visit, she still remembered where to get off. She made the short walk downhill, stopping right before the sharp corner the road made so she could secretly study the house before any of them saw her. I was pumping now, Mama done and standing off to the side, lost in her details. It was in a row of houses that looked just like it. Five rooms of government housing; kitchen, dining room, two bedrooms and a bathroom, all connected by a short passage and all with running water and electricity. They had painted since she was last there, it had been a dull brown color then. Now it was vivid in bright yellow, with red trimmings around the windows and doors that made it stand out."It's beautiful, Ma. There's a garden too, at the back of the house, and a neat lawn in the front." Her speech was steady, even as she helped me mount the twenty-liter bucket on my head, and even as she did her own.

The only girls born to a family of five, Mama and Aunty Sli had grown up incredibly close. The sisters were only three years apart and when Mama said they hugged for an eternity, I knew she meant it. Aunty Sli had come to visit us twice that I could remember and each time she was like a shot of life for my mother. I'd fall asleep to their laughter drifting in from the kitchen late at night. I could picture the two of them, fresh-faced and carefree before they were mothers and wives, giggling late into the night.

When Mama arrived, Aunty Sli had put her right to work-giving her an apron and making room for Mama by her side. The wedding they were preparing for was for Aunty Sli's neighbors, who would soon welcome their new bride. They belonged to the same clan and had grown so close over the years, that they really treated each other like family. Every woman in the community was present, contributing in some way.

Some chopped and peeled and others filled the silence with the stories they shouted and the songs they sang. I pushed the gate, holding it open so Mama could walk in first, bucket securely on her head. I could almost hear the high cackling laughs of the women, enjoying the excuse to be out of their homes after dark. "Your Aunty Sli and I were amongst the last to leave." She stopped talking then, focused entirely on lowering her bucket. First down to her chest and then to the floor. I copied, adding an extra step on my knee before lowering mine to the ground.

I got started on the dishes while Mama prepared the kettle for tea, our reward for every task. She had spoken non stop all the way to the pump and all the way back. It was magic to me that she hadn't noticed how out of character she was acting. Ordinarily, a complete sentence, unprompted, from my mother was worth celebrating. I shook my hand in the silky water, creating bubbles. Dishwashing liquid was so much better than the powdered soap we had to use sometimes.

"Should I pour for you, Ma?" she asked in response to the kettle whistling. She'd already pulled up the second cup by the time I nodded, the dishes weren't going anywhere. "Your aunty had liquid milk because they have a fridge. Tea tastes so different with liquid milk."

"Yes, but it tastes better with Cremora," I added a second teaspoon of the powdered creamer to prove my point. Mama rewarded me with a smile from the other side of her cup. "Your cousins missed you, so I said next time we'll come together." If I believed her, I would have smiled from behind my own cup. Instead, I settled in and waited for her to continue. She'd shared a room with the two girls, one of them giving up her bed. Zinzi, at fourteen, was two years younger than me, while her sister Zandi was seventeen, a year older than me. They had a four-year-old brother, Musa, that I still hadn't met. "He's the cutest little thing, but he won't leave Sli's side! I don't remember you or Sizwe being like that." I wanted to comment but I couldn't think of anything. "Your Uncle Muzi, he's a good, kind man." She seemed to meditate on that sentence, her pause stretching. I vaguely remembered a kind face.

"And he can pray." I looked up at her, involuntarily. I had been expecting to hear about the next thing, something I could comment on. I didn't know anything about my uncle so I had nothing to say about this either. I waited. "They took me to their church, on Sunday, and I prayed for all of us." She beamed in a way that told me that the church had been a highlight. I knew she missed it. We didn't go to church. Still, I prayed sometimes like Mama had shown me, alone in my room.

"..poor thing, she was so scared," Mama's voice brought me back and I started to nod gently,

hoping it would urge her on so I could figure out who she was talking about. "I guess I
must have looked like her too on my wedding
day," I watched as her face went from lovingly
remembering something to sadly remembering
it. I should have been listening. I could have
steered away from this. Sometimes I could tell
what would make her sad and gently push her
in a different direction. Sometimes it worked. I
should have been paying attention.

"So that was Sunday? What did you do on
Monday?" I prompted, sometimes this worked
too, but I was too heavy-handed with the excitement and she knew what I was doing. She sipped
her tea slowly, the cup rising and lowering, "the
days were all pretty much the same after that." It
was her sad voice, the low one, lower and slower
than her usual. I nodded. "Okay, Mama," so this
was it for the day. I shouldn't complain, when she
did speak she spoke plenty, and as we sat in silence I let my mind wander back to all the details
she had offered me.

...

As we prepared dinner, she seemed to remember that she hadn't told me about her potter's
wheel and the knowledge shot sparks through
her and she became animated again. Once again
my beloved storyteller. On the day before she
came home, she went to say goodbye to the
neighbors. She found the new husband's mother

outside, spinning some clay on the wheel. "I wasn't sure what she was doing, nana, but she wasn't doing it right," Mama burst out laughing at her own joke and I burst out laughing at her, and with her. I warmed at the endearment 'nana'. Baby. I loved it when she was like this.

When the older woman saw Mama and Aunty Sli she immediately got up to wash her hands as she greeted them. "What is that, Ma?" Mama asked her, instantly intrigued.

"It's my late husband's old potter's wheel. Oh he loved to do this, he would lose entire days just creating the most beautiful pots," she let the moment linger, pausing to watch the image in her head, before slowly coming back, "but I can't even make a hole in the clay. It's been in the outside house since he passed, I put a lot of his things there. But now I've been slowly clearing the space for uSandile and his new bride. This is one of the last things I have to decide what to do with. I thought maybe if I could figure it out then I would keep it, but there is just no chance in hell of that so I guess I'll be throwing it away unless I can find someone to take it."

"Maybe you must just keep it because Sandile may want that piece of his father one day?" Aunty Sli suggested.

"I've tried and given up on that one, he says it's too messy for his taste. I tell you art is in some people and just not in others."

"I'll take it," Mama said when she said that, she

was more surprised than anybody else.

"Do you know how to use a potter's wheel, dear?"

"Not a clue, but I'll learn. If you mean what you said, then I'll be happy to take it off your hands."

The older woman hadn't argued and by the time the three women finally parted they were all a mess from trying to figure it out. It turned out that even though MaZungu had always watched her husband do it, she really had no idea what he was doing. She did, however, describe to Mama what she had seen him do, and how he had dried and then baked his pots. She even gave her the paints that he used to decorate them.

"I'm sorry I can't be more helpful, but I'm sure if you just give yourself the time you will figure it out. Good luck! It makes me so happy to know that someone will love one of his most prized possessions, it would have killed me to throw it away. Thank you."

"No, Ma, thank you," they shook dirty hands and parted ways.

CHAPTER 2

It was a whole two weeks before Mama actually tried to use her new machine and it was a disaster. On Saturday afternoon when Baba and Sizwe were out, we set to work. Normally the freedom my brother enjoyed, a freedom I couldn't dream of, annoyed me- but today I didn't care. Mama and I were having our own adventure. She had gone early in the morning to the river bank to fetch some clay and we were ready. Positioned comfortably on a low chair with the pot in front of her, she went over the instructions as they had been told to her, apparently for my benefit. I nodded after each sentence as if I understood.

"Take a big stick and start to spin it, you'll have to keep doing this when the wheel slows down. Place the lump of clay in the middle. Use small lumps, you don't need a lot and always make sure the clay is wet, adding water as you go. That is the most important. Lastly, use small movements. They have a big effect.

She looked at me as if to say, "So what do you think we should do now?" To which I could only offer a blank stare. Finally, she took a thick walking stick and used it to start the wheel moving, keeping at it until it was moving very fast. I recoiled for safety, which earned me an annoyed look from Mama so I moved back. She then took a small lump of clay, less than a handful, and covered her hands over it, pushing gently. She had a look of intense concentration and I was scared to make a sound for fear of breaking it. When she removed her hands the clay was in a perfect ball and she beamed at the accomplishment. Next, she poured a little water on it before nervously sticking her finger into the middle. In what looked to me like magic, she created a very narrow vessel. Mama beamed, I could tell she was trying to make it grow taller, but she wasn't too sure about the 'how'. The lady had said that small movements made big differences, so maybe she could stretch it by pulling it up a little bit?

Failing at getting height, Mama was now more interested in trying to make the bowl larger. I saw her put her finger inside and just touch her finger to the edge. The result was amazing, just not complete. The part where she touched stretched, but only that part so that now there was a fat bulge while the rest of it was still thin.

It reminded me of our neighbor MaSibiya, whose large upper body seemed to have been matched to somebody else's skinny legs. When I said this to Mama I couldn't help laughing. She joined me, happy to let off the steam. She said something about what a lovely woman MaSibiya was, but she couldn't help looking amused. We spent the full two hours we had in the afternoons before we had to start preparing dinner playing with the new toy. She let me do it too and it was even more magical to touch it and know that I had made those changes. I was no good, but still, I knew I was falling in love with it.

When it came time to stop we had managed to make only one very sad looking, lopsided dwarf-of-a-bowl-almost pot. I thought the top was too open to be a pot, but admittedly it was too big to be a bowl. It was a nothing, but it was a nothing I had made with Mama and a nothing we would keep, if only to remind us where we'd started. We baked the final product in a pit at the bottom of the garden, using dry cow dung and some twigs as we found them. It was another process that would take a while to master, but it was decidedly more instinctive for Mama, she understood fire. We finished and cleaned ourselves up, so well that my father and brother could have never dreamed that we had ever touched clay. Then we made dinner.

Over the next few weeks she was consistent in her growth, every Saturday like clockwork. Baba and Sizwe would disappear and we would rejoice. Alone at last, free to make our pots. Although there was no lack of effort put in, progress was slow. By all accounts my mother was still terrible, getting better each time, but still terrible. Slowly, the things she made started to look like they could potentially, one day, be something usable and I swelled with pride. She did too, in her own way, her silent way. She was happier. It was a change I knew only I would notice because on the surface she was exactly the same, which was just as well because it meant my father and brother wouldn't notice. On the list of things I'd stopped asking my mother about, because the answers weren't satisfactory, was where my father and brother went every weekend. "The courts, Makhosi, you know that," when she used my full name I knew it was a threat, to not push, to not ask anymore. So I didn't, instead picturing that my father was an important man and my brother was learning to be an important man and the court was where important people gathered. I thought it every time I saw them walk out in their nice clothes, sparkling out of the gate.

I don't think Mama really knew where they went or what they did, perhaps she didn't care. Perhaps I didn't care either, all I wanted was our private time together. I knew Mama was keeping our pottery sessions a secret. What would happen when Baba found out? It was a strange secret because it relied entirely on his negligence. We kept our supplies in the guest hut, where Baba and Sizwe never went. We never had guests and even if we did, tending to their needs was a female responsibility. But, what if Baba decided to walk in one day and find proof of our crime? I put the thought out of my mind with commendable swiftness.

It was on the third weekend since we started that Mama felt she had made something worth keeping. It was a bowl, no lid or fancy trimmings, but it had a smooth finish. She hadn't faltered once, hadn't doubted herself, and that confidence was evident in her work. "I think pottery is a judge of character that way," she'd said once as she worked, unprompted. "When you're unsure the work is weak and it shows it, and when you're strong, it is too." I nodded, not wanting to ruin the moment by saying something less impressive. She was improving steadily. I got better too. I could do the basic first steps, shaping the clay, opening it up, and even making it taller. Mama would finish it up, making it better.

As the weeks turned to months, she kept getting better. Her skills flourished to a level of near mastery. She learned to add a lid, which I thought was amazing because I just couldn't get it. By the end of autumn, she could make truly beautiful pots, with or without handles, with or without lids. She could make pouring spouts, she could do anything. She was an artist with the clay and to watch her was to witness the magic. When she was really focused, to me, she and the clay all seemed to be one thing. The entire scene was one beautiful transfer of energy. She said the clay spoke to her. I laughed then, but I believed her.

...

I remember the day when my father finally discovered the pots. He didn't really discover anything more than Mama stopped hiding it. It was Saturday afternoon after one of our sessions and the door to the guest hut, our storage room, was open. We always shut it so I assumed that Mama had forgotten to, so I closed it. Baba and Sizwe would be back soon, so I went to clean myself up and when I came back it was open again. Mama answered the question on my face firmly and softly. "Leave it." I didn't understand why, she knew it would mean a fight. The hut was getting full of pots and we had to do something with them. Perhaps that was Mama's thinking. Although Baba finding out meant a fight because of the secrecy, it also meant that he only found out when she wanted him to. When she was ready for him to. There were so many pots now, that she could better stand behind a decision to do something with them. To perhaps even sell them. I had hoped for this in my most secret thoughts, but I had not dared even whisper it out loud. Not even to Mama.

Baba had always been the sole breadwinner in our family. Although the details were hazy, he did work at the local court. In addition to the status it granted him amongst the villagers, he was also paid a small salary which took care of all the things that required money. Our schooling was free through local government schools, but there were still some fees we had to pay. His paycheck also paid for all the things that Mama couldn't grow and, twice a year, some new clothes for us. To supplement this, Mama received a government grant for each of her children because she didn't 'work' in the same way that Baba did. Even added all together and stretched as far as it could go, each month the sum was never quite enough. We were always choosing what to sacrifice; dishwashing liquid this month, beef stock cubes the next. To compensate Mama did all the work to fill the gaps. Silently and endlessly. She grew and cooked our food, she mended our broken clothes, she washed and cleaned, she cared for us.

But with the pots, we began to slowly pull away from what was normal and she was leading us. Her and not Baba. I thought back to when Mama first brought home the wheel, when I first felt the tear in our universe. I thought I could hear that tear getting deeper. I was scared and although her face was calm and collected, I knew Mama was too.

I heard shouting in the night as I tried to fall asleep. I'd been waiting for Baba's reaction since the afternoon and it had left me on edge. I sat up in my mattress. It was unlike my father to raise his voice, he preferred to wield his power silently. It was even more strange to hear it raised at night, it seemed louder. It was Baba who occasionally lost his temper so I would catch only a line before he calmed himself down again. Then there was silence, during which I could only assume Mama was making her replies which I would never hear.

"You want to go begging from house to house like we're poor?"

Silence.

"Don't I take care of you?!"

Silence.

They won't think that, would you think that?

A long silence. I assumed that Baba was now calm again.

It was a long time still before I heard the final rapture.

"ENOUGH!"

My heart threatened to break through my rib cage and I could only imagine how Mama felt. I wiped the sweat from my forehead, listening. I lay back down, convinced it was really over. Mama had done it, come what may. I wanted to comfort her, but there was nothing I could do. I was stuck where I was and so was she.

She was withdrawn on the days that followed that, and when Saturday came I thought she wouldn't work on her pots in order to smooth things over, but she didn't miss a beat. She looked so peaceful doing it that I knew she'd spent the entire week yearning for it. Her pots alone were what was able to pull her out from where she had sunken to. Nothing I tried had worked. The pots were like magic, after the first hour she was even ready to talk to me, and I offered her my undivided attention.

"Makhosi, you must be independent when you grow up. Free. There is nothing more important. Do you understand?" I didn't, but I desperately wanted to please her so I nodded. "You must never put yourself in a position where somebody else has control over what you can do. You must stand on your own two feet and be free." She looked at me, poised for a response, so again I nodded. When she spoke again it was in her sad voice, "And when you finally settle down, you must make sure that you choose a strong man. Do you know what that means?"

I looked back at her blankly, not sure whether to say yes or no. She wiped a tear that had gently rolled down the outer corner of her eye, following the tilt of her head. She cupped my face, her hand warm and covered in clay. "Of course not, how could you know? Hmm?" She let my face go with a sigh. "Just don't settle down before you know what strength is, okay?"

"Yes, Mama," she held my gaze until I got uncomfortable and turned to the ground. She looked so sad and I didn't like seeing her like that.

"We will sell our pots," she stated clearly, for no one in particular. She wasn't looking at me, but I was the only person around so she must have been saying it to me. I pushed aside the headiness I felt from her calling them 'our' pots. I knew they were really hers but it was nice to be considered a part of it, a partner. The sounds of fighting I'd heard that night filled my head, it seemed unlikely that Baba had agreed to that. "So Baba said it's okay?" I tried to be casual but it came out as desperate as I felt. "No, your father is completely against it." My heart picked up speed and I waited for her to continue on her own, certain whatever I said would be the wrong thing.

"It's not easy being a woman, I want you to know that, Ma. Not a single thing is easy and one day you'll know for yourself." She paused and the weight of that statement hung between us, heavy. "We can't let people who don't know our burdens make our decisions," her face was strained and when she finally looked up at me, she gave a quick smile that stayed on her lips. "Don't worry about your father, okay? You and I are going to make beautiful pots and we will sell them. And one day, you will become very rich and live like a princess." She pinched my nose when she said 'princess' and I offered her a quick smile of my own. I felt like she had just done to me what I always did to her, gently leading me to a different, happier topic. I let myself be led, imagining my life as a rich princess.

We worked that day, later than we normally did, giving ourselves less time to clean up before Baba and Sizwe came home. Mama wasn't bothered, she prepared and even served dinner with traces of mud still on her pinafore. I knew this was another act of silent defiance and I joined her. I served my brother his dinner-making sure that my own clay stains were visible, proud to join my mother in solidarity. Sizwe hardly noticed. It seemed like he hardly noticed anything. Surely he must feel the silent warfare happening in our home, surely he'd heard the shouting. There was no screaming that night as I finally drifted to sleep. I tried to rationalize whether this was good or bad and fell asleep without a clear answer.

...

When Mama and I started to paint the pots, I found my talent. She lacked the patience for it, declaring by the end of the first painting Saturday it was to be my job. Every so often she made suggestions, which I treated like instructions, but I was allowed artistic freedom. I worked out a system of creating 'families' as I called them. All painted the same I would have a really large pot, a slightly smaller one, and two very small ones, and then I would add a teapot and two cups along with some different sized plates. "It will encourage people to buy the whole set rather than just the singular pieces. If we give discounts for sets, it will encourage them even more." Mama was pleased and I was rewarded with more freedom.

I started with a base color for the entire pot,

waited for it to dry before adding detailing of a different color, sometimes the same color to deepen it. Then came the fun part, adding detail. First I painted a family, a springbok mother and her calf, their fawn bodies against a bright orange-yellow sunset base. "It's beautiful, nana." I'd blushed and brushed off the compliment with a mumbled "thank you, Mama" when she had admired it next to me, but I thought it was beautiful too. By far the most beautiful work that day, I eventually moved it out of sight to keep from looking at it. We started to work independently. Both of us outside, Mama creating the work and me a little way away from her decorating it. Every so often we would look up at the same time and share quiet smiles. Sometimes I would look up and catch her engrossed in her work. I smiled more then.

CHAPTER 3

It was already well into the winter when Mama finally started selling her pots. A chance encounter, so lucky that we knew we had to give thanks and Mama did just that. I had seen her go into the visitors' hut to light incense and call on our ancestors before when culture deemed it necessary; a birth, a wedding, a death. I'd seen her go privately to call on their wisdom when she felt lost and this time she requested I go with her to see her offer her sincerest thanks because she knew they must have been working in her favor to bring this to pass.

There had been a case developing in the local court about a dispute over some cattle. A farmer had found two bulls and a cow out in a clearing. The cattle were unaccompanied and unmarked and he had joined them to his herd. The brother of the local chief had come forth a few days later to report the theft and his suspicions of the farmer as his herdboys had identified the stolen cattle within his herd. The farmer insisted that the law of the land stated that unless he had been caught red-handed, the fact that the cows were unmarked and abandoned meant that they were for anyone to take.

While everybody was clear that the cattle did in fact belong to the chief's brother, the farmer was also right. He had acted in accordance with their laws, but it was an uncomfortable situation because to side with him would be to indirectly go against the chief and insult him. It was a delicate matter because the court took both justice and hierarchy seriously. Baba told us about the case as it grew and it was finally decided that in order to avoid a conflict of interest, it couldn't be judged within the chief's jurisdiction. So the case was moved to the district court. However, the members of Baba's court were allowed to attend and present their verdict as a piece of evidence.

The trip was finally set for the following Thursday, with the court dates set for Friday and Saturday and the men returning on Sunday. I could tell how proud and important Baba felt and it rubbed off on me too, no matter how hard I tried for it not too. I imagined Baba and Sizwe sparkling even more than usual, in a more important place. Over the next few days, they marched their importance everywhere. They spent the early part of the week going to see the other members of the court to discuss the travel arrangements and the case. I could see my brother's pride too, he loved my father's attention and the two of them walked with a spring in their step all week. Mama and I would laugh at them in the kitchen, her exaggerating their proud walks as she carried dishes from where they ate. It *was* ridiculous that everyone was going on like these cows were so important. But it was contagious, the happy, expectant spirit affecting all of us. Mama and I had another reason to be joyous, this meant they would be gone for four straight days. For that reward, even I could pretend to care for those cows.

The icing on the cake, the real reason this case was so opportunistic- and I suspect the real reason Mama felt she had to give thanks- was because that Friday and Saturday coincided with the grant days for our district. The government offered grants to men and women over a certain age, and recognizing their inability to travel far- their money was brought to them. This resulted in a huge monthly market day at all the various stops, with vendors competing for the old people's money as soon as they got it. Mama sometimes stopped by, mostly to socialize but even that was rare.

Located strategically on top of a hill, my school served as one of these stations. We all loved grant days because it meant we were let out early on a Friday. It was with a childlike excitement that Mama told me that was where she was going to sell our pots for the first time. On Saturday I would accompany her to the high school, which served as the grant station for the next district. Excited though I was, I knew there would be consequences. A fact both Mama and I seemed to dismiss for right now. We were brave and fearless and I didn't want to miss even one minute of it. "Mama *please* can I stay home on Friday, just this one time? So I can help you." Her face was unmoved so I backed up my pleading with logic. "The two of us will be able to carry more, so we can sell more," my sad eyes came through for me once again and I felt triumphant. Mama had caved. "Just this one time," she said, not sternly enough.

...

We left for the hill at eleven on Friday, because the government cars were set to arrive at noon. Not that we really expected them then, they were notorious for consistently being at least two hours late. People came early to socialize and see the friends they only got to see once a month. It was also a great time to window shop for the things they would buy after they received their money. Mama knew that most sales were made long before the actual transaction and she wanted to give people enough time to see her product. The school was about a fifteen-minute walk up the hill, but we would be slowed by our baggage. Mama and I each had a wheelbarrow full of pots and she had a huge sack strapped to her back with even more. I carried folded in my bag a huge black plastic sheet that would serve to mark our territory and be the display deck for our inventory. I also carried water, a packed lunch, and a grass mat so Mama and I could sit down when we got tired.

The trip took us thirty minutes and it took another twenty minutes to find a spot and get ourselves set up. Mama let me do most of the arranging, putting my favorite designs in front and the bigger pots at the back. It was a charming display that stood out from the ones around us of people selling live chickens, vegetables, and clothing. Opposite us was a woman selling large sacks of maize meal, a clearly popular stop as maize meal was a staple in every home. Yet, we were so different that people couldn't help stopping by us and asking about our pots. Mama knew most of the women and they were so shocked and impressed when she told them she'd made them herself, that I swelled with pride. "*You* did this, MaBiyela?" they asked, addressing her by her maiden name, "kazi yini enye ongay-enza esingayazi?" *We wonder what else you can do that we don't know of*. Mama laughed off all the comments, her shy pride showing. They asked for prices and she told them, and they promised to come back. When she mentioned that I painted them I flushed, prouder still. The maize lady proved to be great for pulling in customers because they would go to her out of necessity, but when they turned to leave they would spot us and come over out of curiosity.

I didn't in my wildest dreams think that we would do as well as we did. By three o'clock Mama asked me to go back home to get as many of the pots as I could fit in the wheelbarrow because we were almost out of stock. We were almost out of stock! I wished I could carry more than I did, but Mama wasn't upset. She was proud. We were finally packed and on our way as the sun was setting, carrying less than half a wheelbarrow of inventory. The walk back was quiet and unreal, free of all that weight we'd carried uphill and heady with our success.

My head was full of calculations trying to figure out our new riches. Mama was great at packing, using the big ones to form the structure and then filling the holes they created with the smaller pieces, before covering everything with a sack and securing it with rope. Each wheelbarrow must have held at least fifty of the smaller pieces and at least two of the really big ones and even more of those smaller than that. Everything we sold ranged in price from R15 to R50 for the big pots and we had sold two and a half wheelbarrows of goods. Modestly, I calculated that we had made at least R800 per empty wheelbarrow and I was dying to ask Mama if I was close.

Back home, we unpacked and had our supper and I marveled at how different things were when it was just us. We had a simple meal of bread and jam while I boiled us water for tea. Neither of us felt like cooking and it was so nice to not be expected to. The effortlessness of it made those jam sandwiches the best thing I'd ever eaten. That's when I saw the first signs of worry cross Mama's face.

"I saw Bab' Majola at the school when you were here fetching more pots. I know he saw me too and I know he will tell your father."

She was right about that. Bab' Majola would tell Baba and probably soon. He lived within walking distance of us and always made a point to stop and chat with Baba if he was home when he passed by. He was a nice man and would probably tell Baba about seeing us as means of making conversation and not necessarily to report us to him, but the result would be the same. I hadn't given any real thought to my father or my brother the entire day and the reality of their existence hit me like a train.

"What do you think Baba will do?"

She was quiet for a while, thinking, I thought. But the silence stretched and I realized she wasn't going to say anything. She was done talking for the day. We cleaned up and said goodnight and I went to bed feeling very strange; I was thrilled at what we had achieved, anxious at the possibility of not being able to carry on doing it and terrified at the thought that we could be punished for it. I focused on my excitement for tomorrow. We had another day to sell before our reckoning was inevitable. We would deal with Baba when we absolutely had to.

...

The next morning Mama told me how much we'd made, a grand total of R2,760. I stared at her and I knew from her face that she wasn't joking, just incredibly happy. She beamed and I jumped at her. That was more money than I knew a person could make in a single day. It was more than half of what Baba got for the month, a piece of information my mother shared in the height of her excitement and asked me to forget straight after. She let me hold the money, but it still didn't seem real to me. She then took it and put it away, keeping on her only a total of R150 in varying bills for change. We packed the wheelbarrows, this time she mostly packed the smaller pieces that she knew sold well and only two of the really big ones, along with ten of the middle-sized ones. This helped because we would have to take the bus to get to the high school, so what we could carry is all we could sell. We had slightly less merchandise, but almost the same in total value. We were ready.

The twelve o'clock bus got us to the school at about half-past. We set up the same way we had yesterday and were ready to start by one o'clock. Mama decided to raise the price of the smaller pieces by R5 each and since she only had two of the really big ones, she made them R80 each. It was an experiment to see if people would still pay if the price was just a little bit higher and we couldn't wait to find out. It was like reliving the day before all over and Mama had been wise to pack the way we did because people bought all of our pots. All of them. An older woman asked Mama to come again next month with one of the really big pots just for her, she even paid her a R30 deposit to secure it. Mama and I had started our very own business and we were thriving. As we waited for the bus home I wondered how much we made this time.

We made R2 990, including the R30 deposit. In just two days we had made R5 750! It was beyond comprehension for both Mama and me. There was so much to say that we didn't say anything, content with our thoughts. That evening the high finally wore off and Mama sat me down to talk about what we would tell my father. "I have to tell him, If he doesn't hear from me first he'll be even more upset."

"He'll take our money away, Mama, I know he will.' I felt that it was really *her* money, but I wanted her to know that we were in this together. "Yes, he will. That's why I can't tell him, about all of it." Her eyes found mine and she held my gaze the entire time she spoke. "We're going to say that we sold everything for half the price. Ma, do you understand?" She rubbed the back of my hand gently like she was trying to ease me into the lie. I nodded, wanting her to know that I didn't need convincing. I was happy to lie to protect our work. She relaxed in her chair, and I knew she understood my loyalty. "That way even if he takes all of the money, we still have half of it. Even half of what we made will be a huge surprise to him, it's still a huge surprise to me."

"So we'll say the little pots were all R10 and the bigger ones were R20 and the biggest ones R40?" She smiled at my cooperation. "Yes. Exactly. Make sure you don't forget that, not that I think he'll ever ask you, but this is our hard work and we have to protect it. Right?"

"I won't forget Mama, I promise." And I certainly would not.

...

Early Sunday evening when they finally arrived, Mama and I were bathed and everything was spotless. We cooked a chicken, not one of our own, but a fancy 'white city chicken' that we bought at the market yesterday to celebrate our success. The meat was more tender and cooked faster. Sizwe said they weren't as good for us but there were never any complaints as he ate them. We were ready for them; pap, Mama's delicious chicken stew, and my potato salad. It was a meal guaranteed to be a hit. It was a meal to sweeten Baba up.

Luckily, he was already in a good mood. It was clear that they had enjoyed their trip away.

While Mama got her detailed version of the case from my father, I got mine from Sizwe. He seemed to have swelled since he left as if all those men had thrown some shavings of their own manhood in his direction and he had caught them all. He spoke with a still foreign, but definite authority that I hadn't recognized before. I zoned out of listening to him to focus on looking at him, I don't think I had ever really *looked* at my brother. I guess he really was entering manhood now.

"In the end, they decided to give the cattle back to the chief's brother with the understanding that they were clearly his. But for his trouble, and because nobody could find fault with anything he did, the chief's brother was instructed to compensate the farmer for his 'loss'. He would receive either three goats or a single cow from the chief, all within a week of the ruling, and the issue was put to rest."

"Do you think they did the right thing?"

"I think it's as fair as they could manage. I would have just given the cows back to whom they belong and called it a day, but I understand why they are being so generous to the farmer."

"Because they have to stand by their own laws. Even if they make no sense."

"Exactly."

As I lay down to sleep that night, keeping a sharp ear for sounds of fighting coming from Mama's flat, I thought about how much more I liked my brother today. Maybe that's what happened when they got older. I strained myself listening to them, but at best all I could make out were some murmurs. Maybe Mama had decided against telling him tonight? I hoped not, better to just get it over with, then we could deal with it in the morning. That's when I remembered school, the only thing I would be dealing with in the morning. It felt like such a distant place after my three day weekend, a distant place I'd given no thought to, and thinking about it now helped to take me to sleep. I fell asleep thinking I would have to catch up on what I missed.

...

On our next Saturday together, I finally caught up with Mama's secret life. She had in fact told Baba and as expected he wasn't thrilled, especially about it being done behind his back. When she told him how much we made, he asked to see the money. Not to take it, but because he thought she had misquoted or counted it wrong. She gave it to him, half of it, and he was astonished to find that she had been telling the truth. The astonishment wore off and left in its place the conversation Mama had been dreading.

"So, what do you want to use this money for?"

"Well, it's for us, for the family," I pictured Mama fidgeting and looking at the floor as she answered him, "we can use it to pay for food and everyone is saying that we should have electricity by this time next year, so we can use it to buy that once we have the box setup. And whatever else you think we need. I was also thinking that we could save it for the children, for their schooling. Maybe even university." I pictured her soft voice getting even softer as she spoke so that the last word came out as a whisper.

"What school? Sizwe is finished with school and he doesn't need university, he's already training with me. Even Makhosi, isn't she doing good at her school now?"

"Yes Baba, you're right, you are really helping Sizwe. I was just thinking about Makhosi, for after she finishes high school."

"So you are the provider now, MaBiyela, in this family? Hmmm?"

The inevitable.

"Cha, Baba. *No, Baba.* I just wanted to help. I thought we could do it together, so that you don't have to work so hard."

"I see."

"I thought maybe that you should hold most of the money, because you are better at it than me. I could have just enough so I don't have to bother you for every little thing."

I looked up. I hadn't thought of that as an option, of Mama saying that, but maybe it was just the thing? It allowed for Baba to still feel in charge and for her to continue her work, all while secretly saving half of all our earnings. It seemed a small price to pay and I could tell Mama felt the same way, there was more excitement than anger or regret in her voice. As we worked I let myself dream about what we would do with our new wealth. Perhaps she would take us on a trip to the town to go eat at a restaurant, just the two of us. Then on our way home, we would find the two best dresses and buy them, one for each of us. Before returning home we would buy all the groceries we wanted, not having to choose between what was a luxury and what was a necessity. We would come home to cook the best meal imaginable, enjoying the string of compliments from Sizwe and my father. It was my perfect day.

Baba took his time to take Mama up on her offer to carry the money. We were hopeful in thinking that this meant he wouldn't, that he would let her decide for herself what to do with what she earned. It was a few weeks before Baba crushed our fantasy. He was coy in his demanding, a very subtle game I was learning my parents played very well. "MaBiyela, I'll be going into town tomorrow, I might need some change." It was a statement, easy and simple, that Mama was expected to interpret and fulfill. He did not *ask* her to give him the money, nor would he, and yet the request was made. Mama understood and handed it over instantly. Of the R2, 875 that Mama placed in his hand, he left her with the R875. Admittedly, it was more than what either of us thought he would leave her with and for that we were grateful.

What he did with the money remained some-what of a mystery. He came back with all the things he bought every month, along with three extra grocery bags of treats we were not used to. Some of the things were the same, just bet-ter brands. He even bought Mama a new mop and some new good quality dishcloths and wash rags, three bars of really nice smelling soap and the long green sunlight bar that we were used to. It was a slice of luxury, thick enough to enjoy but thin enough to disappear quickly so we didn't get too big for our boots. Yet, even with all these add-itions and upgrades, I couldn't imagine that Baba had spent more than R300 on top of what he normally did. So the bulk of the money he took from Mama remained unaccounted for and yet he never gave it back to her. She would never ask for it.

Mama proved to be a maestro with money. Even the crumbs that Baba left her with, she was able to save most of. For the entire month she kept only R300 floating to cover anything that we might need and since Baba had already done the shopping, we didn't need much. I started get-ting an allowance, R2 every school day, and tak-ing a page out of Mama's book, I saved most of it. Sizwe refused Mama's offer of R5 a day, "If I need anything I'll ask, Mama, but thank you." Where I had been thrilled before, his response made me feel like a child.

For the first few months, Mama and I sold

only once a month. With our system perfected, we upped that to twice a month. We traveled to further regions with different grant days than us which allowed us to sell more. Baba obviously knew that we were now making double the money and Mama and I held our breath every weekend, wondering when he'd start taking double. But he didn't. In fact, by the end of the first month, he had only ever asked for it once. It led Mama and me to hope this would be the cycle. We wouldn't mind handing over half of one weekend's sales if we could keep all the rest, it was almost even fair, like a tariff for independence. Hopeful though we were, it was too early to know for sure.

By the third month we knew we had a system. Baba had remained consistent in taking only R2000 a month and we were free to save the rest. Sizwe helped us where he could, carrying more pots on a third wheelbarrow and returning in the afternoon to help us pack up and carry back what was left. He never stayed to help us sell and I was grateful. This was *my* special thing with Mama. We were becoming something close to local celebrities. Wherever we went, Mama's station was the best. It was becoming fashionable to have one of her pots.

Things were going well. Despite everything I was keeping up with school- the only condition Mama set for allowing me to continue helping her. Weekdays were for school and for Mama they were for chores, for being a wife. Some-times I'd come home from school and after my homework and chores, I'd paint the pots that had dried. But we still did most of the work on week-ends. Two of them a month were for making and decorating the pots and the other two for selling. I had not heard my parents fight in a long time and I took that as a sign of peace. It seemed that a new source of income had really changed our lives for the better.

CHAPTER 4

I remember the moment our happiness shattered. It was late afternoon and Mama asked me to fetch my twenty-litre bucket and accompany her to the water pump. It wasn't far but we had picked a bad time and it wasn't empty. There was a group of women there clearly enjoying an animated conversation. They were younger than Mama but, I thought, old enough to be married. I had seen two of them before, the other two I didn't recognize but I knew none of them were Mama's friends. She had very few friends left. I remember women coming to visit for tea when I was younger, but they had thinned over the years. Now she mostly exchanged pleasantries about the weather and the progress of their children.

"*San'bona*," Mama greeted them as soon as they were in earshot. They grew quiet and the air around them was dense, heavy with an alertness that wasn't quite right. Two of them responded to our *"San'bona"* softly in unison, while the other two looked at us as if though we were something foul. One of them finally gave a feeble, forced *"Yebo."* I may have imagined it, but I thought I saw one of them snicker at Mama before looking down and occupying herself again with the water pump. She was the last to fill up and the other three were clearly waiting for her to finish so they could be on their way. The entire time they waited not one of them spoke. Not a single word. When she finished they all expertly put the buckets of water on their heads and were on their way.

Mama and I didn't address what just happened but it must have bothered her as much as it did me. I didn't even fully understand it. What exactly had just happened? I had seen such behavior amongst my peers, of course, but never amongst grown-ups. I had never seen grown-ups be anything but nice to each other, sometimes they were even too nice. Yet those women had displayed a blatant unkindness and it shook me. Did they hear something bad about Mama? Was somebody spreading lies about her? About me? "Mama?"I wanted to ask her what happened or console her in some way but I had no words. "Mama?" I repeated to no avail. What did I want her to say? What did *I* want to say? Mama didn't answer me. Nor did she look at me, but I could see the slump in her shoulders and that was enough. We filled up our buckets in silence and mounted them on our heads. As Mama did hers I stole a glance at her face and the hurt I registered made me hate those women.

Whatever Mama felt or thought, she channeled through her work. She dove into her pots even more than before. That's when she was happiest. When she was working she was once again strong and in control. She talked more then too, giving me glimpses of the woman I knew. As we worked I felt that maybe she was past that awful event and I was glad.

...

One morning before school I noticed the water was running low and knew we'd have to get more when I got home. I came home to find all the buckets full. "Why didn't you wait for me, Mama?" I asked, confused. She'd given herself twice the work. "Oh it's nothing, nana, I had the time." On Saturday morning she didn't call me to fetch my bucket like I was expecting, we fetched the water first thing in the morning on weekends, instead starting on the dishes. Dishes were one of *my* chores that I always did *after* we fetched water. It made no sense why she was changing our schedule but neither did asking questions. I picked up the broom and started sweeping. She called for the buckets straight after lunch and the shock must have shown on my face, "Mama? *Now*?" Ignoring my tone, she nodded and got up, "Asambe." *Let's go.* I could tell from her tone that it wasn't a suggestion and I knew arguing was futile but I couldn't stop. "Mama, *in this heat*? Can we not wait until sundown?" Mama flashed me a look that dared me to say one more thing. Still in shock, I picked up my bucket and followed her. This was as bizarre as Baba bringing his own dishes to the kitchen, and then washing them. As we walked in the uncomfortable heat, I struck me that Mama was purposefully going to the pump only at the times she knew it would be empty. My heart ached and I hated those women even more.

CHAPTER 5

March 2011

Mama knocked on my door after I had already lay down to sleep, shattering the rhythmic mundaneness of our lives, shocking me out of my oblivion. I stood to open the door for her, lit a candle and we sat down. We had an electricity box now, but only the kitchen and my parent's flat was connected and Sizwe and I still used candles. It was unusual for my mother to seek me out so I knew that something was wrong. I also knew she wasn't the kind of person to be prompted so I waited for her to decide she was ready to speak.

"Tomorrow we are going to see your Aunt Sli in the township. We're going to visit her and her family." I was beyond confused. 'Tomorrow' as she referred to it was a school day, Thursday. I knew Mama valued few things the way she did my education so for her to disrupt my week made no sense. It scared me. "Mama, what's happened?" I was studying her now, she didn't seem hurt. Not physically and I couldn't see the signs I'd come to recognize when she was hurt in other ways. She was talking calmly, very matter-of-factly, giving nothing away. "Shhh, don't worry. I'll wake you up, the first bus to town leaves at five o'clock and we must be ready. Leave out enough clothes for a few days and I'll put them in my suitcase in the morning. We'll come back on Sunday. It's alright, nana." That last part was thrown in there, an obvious afterthought. *'It's alright.'* I knew it wasn't.

I have never not wanted to go somewhere, ever. Yet now as Mama presented that opportunity to me, what I felt most was fear. Why did we have to leave? She left me and I couldn't sleep. I spent the night pleading for morning to come and dreading it just as much. When morning came Mama was a wind, in and out, silent. We were ready, fed and packed in record time and I still had no idea what was going on. I hadn't been up this early in a long time. I kept expecting Baba to come and say something, goodbye perhaps or even to start a fight- anything to signify a semblance of normal. Not a single thing stirred outside of us and we were out the gate to the bus stop without a sound.

The bus stop wasn't far, less than ten minutes if you were walking slowly, which we weren't. When we were about halfway, I decided to initiate a conversation, careful not to ask any direct questions because I knew that wouldn't work. "Does Aunty Sli know we're coming, Ma?" Mama looked at me, amused at my attempt at cunning. She took my hand and said simply, "hush."

I had only taken the ride into town twice and it was always an adventure. The first time was when I had chickenpox and the second was for Mama's elder brother's funeral. I remember the excitement of going somewhere new, too young to comprehend the reason. I was excited again and this time my excitement felt appropriate. I was going to see my aunt and uncle and where they lived.

I hadn't seen them since they came as a family to visit us a few years ago. After their parents left, Zandi and Zinzi had stayed behind, spending half of their ten-day school holiday with us. I remember playing from morning to night breaking only for my chores, which they insisted on helping me with, and food. It was nice to have sisters, even if they were only borrowed for a short time. We'd promised to do it again, but it only happened that once. It seemed so long ago that I wasn't sure if we had as much fun as I remembered. If we did, then why didn't they come back? It had easily been five years since I saw them last, maybe more. The thought made me more nervous, what if they didn't like me and didn't want me to come? My anxiety was made worse because I was almost certain they didn't know we were coming in the first place.

I forced myself to focus on the road, to focus on the adventure and all the things that were new. I focused too, on my mother. I stole glances at her but didn't get much, at least she seemed relaxed. She sat with her face slightly tilted away from me like she was listening to some faint, distant music. I stopped looking at her to look outside, taking advantage of my window seat. I watched all the sights I knew so well whizz past me.

The ride to town lasted between an hour and a half to two hours depending on the driver, the weather, or if the animals respected the road that day. Most of the scenery was the same for two-thirds of it: gravel road; thatched roof huts inter-laced with brick flats, outhouses; dirty children with happy faces playing in the dust; women congregating at water pumps, their faces and gestures animated. There were almost as many animals; cows, goats, donkeys, chickens, and dogs, as there were people. Every once in a while, there was another vehicle on the street. Every person we passed, without fail, stopped to wave at the bus with the people on their way to do interesting things in town. I waved back to all of them.

In the last thirty minutes as we neared the town, the scenery got more interesting, more modern and more condensed. There were hardly any more huts, in their place stood the square-shaped houses made up of multiple rooms connected by a passage. It looked crowded to my eyes which were used to large homesteads with vast plots between them. Space. As you left those settlements behind and drove the final fifteen minutes to town, it was difficult not to know that you were now in a different place. A single detail made all the difference. Tar. After being on a gravel road for over an hour, the transition onto a tar road is almost a shock to your system. It feels like gliding on air, gliding on air fast. We glided past the prison, the unofficial start of town, and some of the men waved to us in their bright orange uniforms. We had entered the town of Empangeni.

As we neared the heart of the town and the bus made its way to the bus rank where they all parked, signs of life began to spring up. You could see people walking, and talking. Some carried things on their heads, presumably having walked from one of the surrounding settlements to sell in the town. You could see men facing away to pee onto walls as they shouted to each other loudly. There were more cars than you could count, and even more taxis full of people who didn't own cars yet. We pulled into the rank and the bus got loud with everybody getting ready to disembark. Mothers readying their kids, young men trying to squeeze past the large, older women who they knew would take long. I was in no rush, it was all such a feast for my senses.

We were seated somewhere in the middle of the bus, and we waited patiently as the people before us and those that had been standing milled out. I carried the plastic bag full of vegetables from Mama's garden. 'You don't go into someone's house empty-handed,' I could almost hear her say it now. She carried the suitcase with our clothes.

On the ground, there were stalls and more stalls. Men and women selling everything you could imagine, from ointment for sore joints and a miracle medicine promising to cure all things, to flip flops and insecticides. The women who made their living by selling had white faces from the calamine lotion that they wore to combat the sun. There were also mobile sellers that walked around announcing what they were carrying; cell phone chargers, bath towels, sweets, cool drinks, peanuts. I followed the smell to find the boy selling roasted chicken gizzards, R5 for a skewer of five. It was a wonder to me that anybody made the trip past the bus rank to shop at the big stores, I was sure that if they tried hard enough, they could find everything they needed right here.

Mama wasn't having as much fun as I was simply observing the people at the rank, she pulled my hand rather forcefully and I knew she was annoyed. Had I made her wait? Had she called me while I was lost in my head and failed to hear? I followed, making a concerted effort to keep up. We walked past the vendors and stopped to cross at the *'robot'*. Traffic lights were a symbol of sophistication, we didn't have any in my village. Even in the townships, there were none. Stop signs, yes, but definitely no traffic lights. We waited for the little green man to show up, and we crossed with the large crowd that had been waiting with us. We were taking no detours, I knew we were going straight to the taxi rank. We funneled through a small shopping complex and came out on the other side to the taxi rank. Even though the walk between them wasn't even five minutes, the two ranks were worlds apart. The people they transported were from different worlds.

We stood out on this side of town. We were rural, and they were not. The township people didn't like sharing *their* town with us. Nobody ever said it, but we knew. I knew and I didn't care. Even the people that had themselves come from the same villages weren't overly welcoming. Even less so were the younger people that had been born in the townships so their lifestyle was all they knew, they just couldn't find understanding or patience for our 'backwardness'. I ignored the looks passed my way at my outdated clothing or the plastic bag I used as a bag. I tried to be like Mama and pay them no mind. Undeterred, she asked the taxi conductor for the correct taxi and we got on. The place we were going to was called 'Mshayazafe', which directly translated to 'beat him till he's dead'. It made me shiver because places and people were always named purposefully, with meaning.

We waited fifteen minutes for the taxi to get full- the drivers would not leave without a full taxi- and we were on our way. The townships were so densely populated that all you had to do was wait long enough and the taxi would fill up. Taxis were not at all like busses. Busses were entire worlds, too large and too noisy to focus on details. Taxis offered me the proximity and quiet to effectively spy on the other passengers. We sat again in the middle, with Mama by the window this time and me next to her. This position gave me great access to most of the people beside and in front of me. I would have to give up on the people behind me because looking at them would be glaringly obvious.

The driver was middle-aged, and he spent most of the trip on his phone shouting happily at whoever was on the receiving end. His shouting reminded me of old people who yell into cell-phones because the person they are talking to is far. Next to him was a young woman with her braids tied up in a ponytail. She was trying her hardest to reject the advances of the man wearing a leather bucket hat next to her. "Aw'fake inumber yakho phela." *Why don't you put your number on here.* He pushed his phone in front of her face and she turned to look out the window, waiting for it to be over. Behind them was a woman older than Mama and she seemed to be traveling with her daughter and granddaughter. The little girl, clad head to toe in pink, fidgeted on her mother's lap. Next to them was a young woman who would on occasion smile at the little girl, but mostly looked quietly out the window. Then it was our row, made up of myself, Mama, and a woman who had clearly just done her monthly grocery shopping. Her plastic bags took up her foot room as well as mine, but I didn't mind. She was on her phone, struggling to load airtime. Next to me, Mama was smiling. Not at me, I don't think at anything at all, I'm not even sure she knew she was doing it. Still, I smiled back.

She had no trouble identifying our stop, we were amongst the last three people to get off. I stepped outside and the excitement hit me all at once. I took in how different everything looked. Not just the houses and structures that people put up, but even the natural environment. I recognized the plant Mama had told me about instantly, the reddish/ maroon shrub that grew everywhere. It was so common here, and yet so distinct. I had started to see it around the town, but I could see it even more now. We walked through the small passage where the taxi dropped us to came out on a side street. As we walked down the road and I played a game with myself to see if maybe by some miracle I could point out their house. The quick walk was down-hill on a beautifully tarred road. I wanted to walk on it without noticing, without being excited but I couldn't. I couldn't wait to take off my shoes and stand on it, barefoot, just to remember what it felt like under my feet.

We passed a cathedral and I had to stop to take it all in; the high white walls, the arches, the stained glass. Mama had to gently nudge me to start moving again. And then, two houses down on the opposite side of the road, I saw it. I shouldn't take credit actually, I would have walked right past their house if I hadn't seen *her*. She stood outside with a little boy on her hip, talking to a neighbor through the mesh fence. I stopped because it felt like looking at Mama, only younger and plumper. Mama stopped too, for her own reasons. We stood there, the pair of us unable to move or think of what to say. It was Aunt Sli who, having sensed our presence, turned around and for a second joined us in our frozen staring -and then there was sound and movement all at once. She put her son down and ran to us, while shouting simply and repeatedly, "Londi? Nguwe loyo?". *Londi, Is that you?*

I watched my mother become a child. I don't think I've ever seen her so purely happy. They hugged, talking at the same time. It amazed me how they seemed to be having a functional conversation because it seemed like nobody was listening. My mother broke away to pick up the little boy, who had finally made his way over to his mother. I shifted uncomfortably on my feet, wondering when my mother would remember my existence, but also enjoying her blissful oblivion. It was my aunt who reached out her hand to me, and I gave mine in response. "You've grown so much, you're practically a woman now." I gave my aunt a polite smile as I remembered just how badly I'd failed at being a woman in Mama's absence.

There we all were, happily caught in a beautiful moment. Aunty Sli ushered us in and I held my breath, expecting at any moment to see my cousins and accept my fate. They failed to appear as we made our way into the cream-painted, five-room house and I remembered it was a school day. Her husband, a teacher at one of the local high schools, wouldn't be home either. It would be just the three of us for most of the day. As soon as we sat down and she'd put Mama's suitcase away, Aunty Sli turned on the kettle. Tea. Of course. "Thank you, my loves, you have no idea how much I miss *imfino*," she pulled her hand out of the plastic bag I'd been carrying. "The closest I can get to it here is spinach, can you imagine? It's too wet for it here, the climate is too mild." Mama's face matched my own horror. I felt sorry for my aunt, spinach was no substitute.

...

It was a hot day, and the best thing you could

do on a hot day was go outside. We spent the day under a mango tree on a big grass mat lined with a light blanket. Aunty Sli stuffed us full of Oros juice and shortbread biscuits and I wanted nothing more. I listened as they exchanged stories, old and new. I watched them laugh to the point of tears as they clapped their hands together the way women always did when their stories reached the climax. They were in their own world, and while I enjoyed watching them, my presence felt like an intrusion. Every so often, Aunt Sli would direct a question at me and I would answer it, both of us being polite.

Mostly, I played with my little cousin, Musa. He welcomed my attention and I was grateful. But even as I played with him, I was engrossed in their stories, playing them out as movies in my head. "Uyay'khumbula leya nkukhu oway'gxoba ngephutha, yafa, way'fihla emvakwendlu?" *Remember that chicken you accidentally stepped on, that died and you hid it behind the house?* I chuckled as Aunty Sli recollected how when their mother discovered the chicken, Mama had gotten the beating of her life. I still couldn't imagine my mother being in trouble, but I was grateful for these slices into her youth. I continued to listen when the tone of their conversation changed. "Why didn't you tell me, Londi?" Aunty Sli asked, her voice almost breaking. Instead of answering Mama looked at me, "Nana, aw'yestolo uyos'thengel' isinkwa." *Baby, won't you go to the store and buy us bread.*

CHAPTER 6

I could sense the tightness between them when I walked into the kitchen. Gone was the free flow of warmth that I had left behind and I wondered about the conversation that had just taken place, the conversation I had been sent away for. They were preparing to start dinner, the rest of the family would be on their way home now. Still, at only four o'clock, it seemed rather early to be making dinner. Mama was chopping onions and Aunt Sli was rinsing the rice. "Make yourself a sandwich if you're hungry," Aunty Sli said as I put the bread away. "I'm okay, thank you, Aunty. Can I help with dinner?" She shook her head, "no need my darling. I'll put your mother to work."

I took Musa outside and watched him play. I took a deep breath in and it felt like the first I'd had in a while, the kitchen had become an airless vacuum. I stayed outside until the girls got back from school in the white van that served as the staff car. Uncle Muzi sat in the front with the driver and a woman sat between them. I assumed that they were all teachers because everybody who sat in the back was in uniform. The three of them filed out of the van and made their way towards us, obviously surprised to see me.

"Makhosi?" I heard the question in Uncle Muzi's voice just before the girls screamed my name and ran over to me. I was showered with hugs ending only when Uncle Muzi reached us. He smiled and reached out his hand to me. "Well this is a lovely surprise, did you come with your parents?"

"Yes, Malume, with Mama, she's in the house."
Uncle

The women had heard all the commotion, Aunt Sli pushed the door open and released her husband of his bag. Soon we were all in the house, and I was struck suddenly by the intense magnitude of our invasion. We had barged into someone else's life and now they were forced to reconstruct everything to accommodate us. We were certainly welcome, but we were still in the way of their routines. I wondered if Mama felt the same way. As soon as the girls got home, Aunty Sli was officially off the clock. She picked up Musa and she and Mama made their way to the dining room. Uncle Muzi changed out of his work clothes and joined them. "Please get their tea started," Zandi asked me as she and Zinzi went to change their own clothes. I turned on the stove happily, grateful for something to do. After that I squeezed myself anywhere I found gaps, helping where I could.. Zandi served them the tea and with our duties fulfilled, we were free to feed ourselves. I still wasn't hungry but I didn't want to be left out. We took our plate of sandwiches outside to enjoy in the shade and out of earshot of the grown-ups.

I learned that Zandi was a year older than me and a grade above me, so she was now in matric. Now in grade ten, Zinzi, while two years younger than me, was only a grade below me. She had skipped a grade in primary school. She also went to a different school than her father and older sister. As we ate I filled them in on everything I could think of that might interest them. The stories of Mama and her pots and how she would let me sell them with her was my biggest hit. I was proud to be involved in something that even my sophisticated city cousins thought was cool. They asked if Sizwe was still mean- he had mostly avoided and ignored us when they came to visit. I told them he had gotten slightly better. "What do you want to do after school, mzala?" *cousin*

Zandi's question threw me off guard, it wasn't really something that I had given much thought to. "I'm still not sure, what about you?"

"But you're in grade eleven now, you're almost

done with high school. You should really think about it, soon you'll have to apply to a university or a technikon."

"I don't know..."

"Why not? You should talk to my father, he knows so many people at the schools and the universities. Mama said you were smart so you could even get a bursary, or a grant maybe."

I was stunned. I was enjoying this conversation so much yet I could contribute nothing. I couldn't even think of questions to ask because I was so confused. Luckily, Zandi was a natural talker, I was starting to remember this from when they'd come to visit. All she needed was an audience, she could talk circles around Zinzi and me.

"I'm still a little confused about what I want to do. I want to be a teacher like my father because I think I would be good at it. Other times I want to be a reporter and work for a newspaper. I like that because I would be getting the news and reporting it to everyone. I don't know, Baba says I still have time and should take my time deciding so I'm not too worried."

She stood up, we had been done eating for a while now. I was happy for the somewhat abrupt end to this session.

"We should go make dinner. Zinzi did you finish all your homework?"

"Yeah, at school. Do you need me to help you with anything?"

"No, it's okay. Makhosi and I can handle dinner tonight. You can go see 'Sno if you want." Zinzi's smile lit up the entire yard, she practically ran with the plate back to the kitchen, washed it, and was gone. Sno was her best friend who lived three houses down. I worked out that they didn't get to hang out too much during the week so this was a treat for her. Zandi and I set out to continue where our mothers left off with dinner. I made the rice that Aunty Sli had rinsed and a side dish of butternut, while Zandi made the chicken stew. Conversation with her was easy and comfortable, like catching up with an old friend.

We all ate dinner together in the dining room, which felt too small for all of us, while we watched the news. When we finished, I washed while Zandi rinsed and dried and Zinzi packed. Normally, I hated doing the dishes, but with them it was fun. We made a last pot of tea for the adults and then the girls took me to their room to set up for the night. There were two single beds in there and to accommodate us they would share the one, while Mama and I shared the other. I helped them put fresh bedding on mine and Mama's bed. Normally, they all took a bath before bed, but with so many people in the house now it would take forever. Instead, we put water in the tub and the three of us splashed about, washing our feet. I couldn't help thinking about how different everything would be if I had them instead of Sizwe.

We sat in the room, in silence. Zandi at the desk, for her nightly study session, Zinzi reading a book and me just thinking over the events of the day. It had been a really good one. We only moved when it was time to pray, something they did together every night. Aunts Sli started the chorus and the rest of us joined in. Uncle Muzi then read the verse of the day and spoke briefly on it, before they all turned to get on their knees where they sat. I caught Mama's eye and she nodded, so I copied my cousins. I watched from the corner of my eye as Mama turned her own body, before lowering to the ground. It was so strange for me but Mama did it so naturally that it made me think she prayed in private much more than I imagined. Everyone prayed, each their own prayer out loud. I listened to their prayers, following whichever voice broke out of the murmur of the group, feeling intimately connected to everyone in the room. As each person finished, they kept quiet and waited for whoever was still praying until only Uncle Muzi could still be heard.

"...guard us and bless us God, in our woken moments and in our sleep. May we wake better people than we lay down, ready to serve you better in all we do. In your son's name we pray. Amen."

"Amen." It was the chorus that ended the night's prayers. As I finally lay down to sleep that day, it was the warmth of Mama's arms around me that gently coaxed me to close my eyes. I felt her love in all its force, a sense of belonging that lulled me to sleep. I felt an ease in her too, like she felt the same peace I was feeling, that she would enjoy this sleep as much as me.

...

The second day was as pleasant as the first. After helping Uncle Muzi and the girls get ready for school, we had our breakfast. It wasn't as leisurely as I would have thought, because Friday's were one of Aunty's garden days. The township municipality tried to encourage farming by allocating the residents plots where they could plant crops if they so wished. I was surprised at how big the plots were, and how fertile. A gentle stream ran through it and served all watering needs. My job for the day was mostly going up and down to fetch water and bringing it to Mama and Aunty wherever they were. Mama tilled the soil and Aunty picked whatever was ripe and then they would switch. Their schedule seemed irregular and made no sense to me, but they looked perfectly content.

We got back to the house just before noon. We guzzled juice and then, our thirst quenched, settled down to enjoy sandwiches and biscuits. It was nice to be still after all that work. A little after two in the afternoon when we were done bathing, Aunty Sli started preparing dinner. I didn't quite understand until I saw what she was preparing. Sugar beans, they took about two hours of boiling just to soften. After which you then fried them in oil with onions, adding spices to taste. The *pap* and side dish we would make later and I looked forward to that kitchen session with Zandi.

That afternoon as we sat shielded from the afternoon sun, Aunty braided Mama's hair. She had lovely hair, thick, coarse, and long. It was also always covered up, wrapped tightly under her *doek.* She didn't have much time for it, so apart from keeping it clean, styling it mostly took the form of thick, chunky braids. I was quickly learning that Aunty Sli was an excellent hairdresser. She was braiding Mama's hair into a wavy pattern of thin braids that eventually made their way to the back of her head. It looked like little, wiggly snakes in a dance on Mama's head, it was beautiful. I had also noticed just how healthy and neat Zandi and Zinzi's hair was, township schools allowed girls to grow their hair and I envied them. Mine was cut short, as per my school's regulations.

After prayers, the girls and I played cards and I helped Zinzi undo her hair. She would keep a style for three weeks before it started to look old and she needed to have it redone. Zandi did the same, but she would be undoing hers next weekend. This way their mother was never stuck having to do two heads in one weekend because it took so long. While we played cards, I saw Mama and Aunty Sli go into the bedroom she shared with Uncle Muzi. A few seconds later he joined them and closed the door. I looked at my cousins and could tell they found it strange too. We could make out their voices, but no words. Whatever it was they were discussing, they didn't want us to know about. We continued our game of crazy eight, no longer out of enjoyment, but necessity. The game gave us something to focus on, allowing us to pretend that we didn't know that they were in there, that closing themselves in a room wasn't strange. We just continued playing until they finally came out and I felt myself breathe easy again. They stayed in the lounge a while longer, enjoying a last cup of tea. That night I held Mama and wished that that gesture did for her what it did for me.

...

There is something magical about Saturday. It seemed more so there. Just waking up and knowing that Zandi and Zinzi would be there all day made me so happy. I helped do all the chores with a gladness I was not used to. It was as if washing dishes and mopping floors was magical as long as it wasn't at our house. The women made breakfast, which smelled like heaven. They fried eggs and sausages and toasted the bread. Aunty also made oats, Uncle Muzi's breakfast of choice. He would eat the eggs too, but only after his oats. His pre-breakfast chore was watering the yard and all the plants, before raking the leaves. We did all the cleaning, the deep weekend cleaning. Aunty Sli and Mama would do the washing after breakfast.

The girls and I had our breakfast outside, sitting on the steps in front of the door. I'd never eaten anything so delicious in my life. We washed the dishes and then we spent the rest of the morning chatting away in the shade. Aunty Sli and Mama were happy to soak, wash and rinse the clothing, but we would hang it out to dry. An easy enough task, the sun was glaring and it was the perfect day for it. I was wringing the water out of Zinzi's skirt when I heard Mama's sharp intake of breath. I followed her gaze to find a face I had happily put out of my mind for as long as we had been here. There Baba stood, furious. He had silent thunder rumbling under the skin on his face. My heart stopped. He looked directly at Mama, only at her, and when he spoke his words were low and thick. I shuddered with each syllable. "Let's go." It was all he said. It was enough.

"Makhosi, go pack your things." It was the shell of Mama's voice. She still hadn't moved, seemingly rooted to the spot. I think she was waiting to see what Baba would do first. I looked at everyone and all I could register on the girls' faces was an awkward discomfort. But not from Aunty Sli and Mama, on their faces I found fear. I was sure I wore it too. We all seemed to be stuck in limbo, nobody moving until Uncle Muzi came over to where we were. Baba had clearly walked right past him to get to us, which was both disrespectful and rude. Although his face was perfectly composed, beneath it I sensed anger. He rid himself of the rake he was still carrying, leaning it against the side of the house. He then moved closer to where Baba was and reached out his hand to him.

"Mthethwa, welcome. I'm sure you didn't see me when you came in. What a surprise, you must be tired. Let's get you a drink." He looked at his wife as he said that last part, who nodded acknowledgment, before he continued his rather one-sided conversation with Baba, as he ushered him into the house. I knew they would sit in the lounge and that was about the extent of the things that I knew. I didn't know if I should still go and pack my things, I didn't know if I should help with making the refreshments, because he was *my* father. Mama moved and I turned to look at her. I watched her breathe out like she had been holding her breath for ages, before wiping her wet hands on the front of her pinafore. She said something to Aunt Sli who responded by taking her by the hand and leading her to the kitchen. As she walked Mama made the motion with her head for me to follow them. We could hear the men talking, both sounding much calmer now. The two women hugged and then Mama took my hand and lead me to the bedroom. I was grateful for the smallness of the house as I stole a glance in the lounge as we moved through the passage. It did me no good, I only managed to see the side of Baba's face and caught my uncle's eye before the second was over. We left Aunty Sli to set a tray of refreshments for Baba.

"We have to go home, that's all. Everything will be alright." She spoke as she folded clothing back into the suitcase and her hands shook as she did it. I tried to help by folding them before handing them to her so all she had to do was place them in the suitcase. Every question I asked Mama brushed off and it was driving me insane. That, coupled with the fact that we dared not speak above whispers, because Baba was *right there just a few steps from* us and I was ready to lose my mind. I wanted to know what was going on. I knew we had left without telling Baba. I knew that he had found us. I knew that he would be taking us back home. I knew that what I knew wasn't enough and the only person who could talk to me about it wasn't doing it. I was scared for Mama and I was scared for myself. If I knew what was going on then maybe I could help. I felt the hot frustrated tears fall down my face as I tried to stifle all sound. It helped absolutely nothing when Mama started crying too. We just sat there on the bed in silent tears not knowing what to do. I was upset with my father, not fully knowing why and not caring. I hated that just his presence was enough to make us feel trapped, to make Mama feel trapped, to make us cry and force us to do it without sound. I was dying to have her tell me exactly why he had come here, but with every second I dreaded the moment when she actually would. Aunty Sli came in and I could tell she had been crying too, seeing us as we were was all she needed to get started up again. We sat there for a few minutes, leaning on each other and wiping each other's tears. Finally, Aunty took the lead holding Mama's hand and gently wiping my cheek.

"You have to go, Londi, he won't let you stay, but Muzi will tell him what we discussed last night." A look passed between them and I felt awkward. "We're going to help you, *sisi*, okay? It's going to be fine, but you two must pull yourselves together now. You can't come out looking like this otherwise he'll never believe it any of it. I'm sure he won't believe it anyway. I've heated up water so you two can bath. Okay, now it's time to put some smiles on those faces."

It was the shock of it that was effective. She dug deep into both mine and Mama's sides and tickled, I squealed and burst out laughing. Mama was laughing too, her legs involuntarily going up in an effort to protect herself. We rode the wave of that laughter, stimulus no longer needed after the ignition. We laughed and laughed until we again had tears in our eyes. We left the bedroom to bath, Mama and I together. As we dressed, we could actually hear the two men sharing a laugh. We looked at each other but said nothing. There was a lightness in the air again, having finally dealt with all that tension. We were dressed and ready and listening to Uncle Muzi's quick departure prayer before I even knew it. "...Lord, guard them on the travels, protecting them from all the forms of evil that exist around us. Keep your loving eye on them until they get home and may we see them again soon. Amen"

"Amen."

...

Nobody said a single word the entire trip home. Where possible, Baba separated himself from us, but not completely. He walked ahead of us and would turn every so often to make sure we were keeping up, or maybe to make sure that we were still there. In both the taxi and the bus, he sat in a different section. I didn't mind at all. I knew there would be a lot to be dealt with soon, but there was still a distance between us and soon, and I was so grateful.

Soon came sooner than I hoped. I was making my bed for the night, layering my blankets on my mattress so I would be more comfortable- when I heard the shouting that I had been dreading. The fact that Baba had managed to bottle inside all the rage that I had seen on his face for the entire journey meant that he had just been waiting for the moment when he could explode. At home, Mama would have no option but to take it. I knew it would mean fighting, I knew it would mean threads of their conversation finding their way to my window when they forgot to be quiet. It would be easier to hear Baba's booming voice over Mama's soft one. Earlier, Sizwe and I had met in the kitchen. He asked me why we hadn't said anything about leaving and I told him I didn't know. He asked why we hadn't brought back nice food from town and I told him it hadn't been that kind of trip. That was about an hour ago and I had left him reading in the kitchen. I felt the sudden need to go back and find him, to be around him so I wasn't alone.

He was still in the kitchen, although he wasn't reading anymore. He sat on the veranda with the door open and was looking up at the sky. I sat next to him, tentatively. There was no wonder in the sky I wished to explore. My eyes were fixated straight ahead to Mama and Baba's flat. I think that's what Sizwe was doing too and the stars were his way of trying to distract himself. I felt him looking at me and when I turned to meet his gaze I saw that he was very upset. I was shocked. I don't think I'd ever seen him show any real emotion before. Perhaps we'd never spent enough time around each other for that to happen.

"But seriously Makhosi, how could you guys just leave like that? Without saying a word. To her husband? I'd be angry too."

"I didn't know." My voice sounded foreign, even to me. It sounded weak, but I really didn't know. Maybe I just didn't want to. I wished we were still at Aunty's home preparing dinner, or praying, or playing cards.

"It's not right and you know how Baba is. He's not going to let this go easily. He's going to-"

It was a shout that stopped my brother mid-sentence. It was Baba's voice and it was a little hard to make out exact words at first, just tone. He was angry and the more he shouted the angrier he got. Before long he was screaming and it became easier to make out exact words. As his words drifted down to us, they stung me with such venom that I couldn't imagine what they did to Mama.

"...kind of a wife just leaves her husband to go to another man's house? What is Muzi to you? And then you drag *my* daughter into this! What kind of a mother would teach her daughter to behave like that? You want her to just follow men and be loose? Is that what you want? What do you think-"

I heard Mama's voice, I heard something in it break as it built. She was shouting too and as I listened with my heart pounding I heard her scream too.

"...taken everything from you. Everything! But don't you ever think you can disrespect me by questioning-"

I heard it. Whatever that blow was, I *heard* it. The sound of skin touching skin with great force. The silence was deafening. My head reeled and my limbs were no longer in my control. I was instantly on my feet and I was about to bolt to get to Mama when Sizwe grabbed me and kept me firmly in place. I struggled against him, hot angry tears flowing freely now. I wanted to save Mama, I wanted to burst in there and get her out of that room and the two of us would run through the night to safety. Back to Aunty's place or to somewhere new where Baba wouldn't know to look for us. I struggled against my brother with all my might and he held me back with all of his. It seemed like a very long moment, an excruciatingly long moment, but it passed. As I calmed down, through my panting I could hear him say, "What did you think was going to happen? Now look what's happened. She shouldn't have done that, Khosi.." It was my brother's turn to sound weak. He sounded like someone saying what he believed he should, without the conviction of actually believing it.

"Makhosi, please just promise me you won't go there tonight. It's the best thing you can do for Mama, okay?" He waited for my nod, releasing me slowly as he did. It felt weird to be able to move my arms again. I nodded. He got up and said he was heading to bed. I wondered if, like me, he wasn't going to sleep anytime soon. I sat down, suddenly ready to contemplate the stars. To get completely lost in their splendor and vastness and forget everything.

CHAPTER 7

I woke up early the next morning with all the weight of the night before still on me. I longed to see Mama and dreaded it at the same time. I found myself avoiding her for the first time. I made my bed extra slowly and swept the floor. There just wasn't enough to do before I was forced to go outside and face reality. I think Mama was avoiding me as well, I think she was avoiding everyone. She wasn't in the kitchen when I went to make my tea, but the water was boiled so I knew she had been there. She must have woken up much earlier than usual to do all her chores before any of us woke up. That meant she would have served Baba already. I felt my blood boil and sat down to calm myself, but it was no use. I was still angry.

After everything he had done and said to her last night, she would still wake up and serve him like nothing happened. I'm sure he drank the tea and ate the sandwich with no guilt. I made my tea and managed to get through the entire meal without anybody wandering into the kitchen, which was strange. Maybe even my brother was avoiding everybody. I finished my breakfast then went back to my hut to read over my schoolwork. If this was the game we were all playing then it wasn't fair for me to hog the shared spaces. That, and I was ashamed to see my mother. I was ashamed at how I had done nothing for her when she needed me most. I was afraid that if I saw her today I would see the mark on her face, or wherever it was on her body and I would be reminded of my weakness. So I stayed in my hut.

I was hit hardest by the emptiness of the next day, Sundays were *our* day. It was the day for our pots. She would sculpt and I would paint, but not today. I felt vindicated in that I hardly saw her. She wanted to be left alone. I hadn't seen Baba all day either, learning from my brother that he had left early in the morning. Sizwe wasn't exactly sure where, the court maybe. I was sure he just wanted to get away from the fog that had been created last night and that still remained in the air. It was still close enough that we could all choke on it if we weren't careful. I wanted to leave too, but I didn't know where to go. By the afternoon Sizwe was finally driven to do just that. I saw him slip out of the gate, heading west along the road and I envied his freedom. This meant it was just Mama and me now, the perfect time to talk to her but I still couldn't. I knew she was in their room, she had been there for hours.

The guilt and the shame finally forced me to go see if she was alright, if I could help. I took a deep breath in and knocked on the door gently, before pushing it open. I heard no resistance so I went in. Mama was in the bedroom, laying on her back, looking at the ceiling. As I walked into her space she made eye contact with me, briefly, before looking back at the ceiling. I walked through the lounge area before getting to the bedroom, deciding that her not telling me to get out meant I could come in. I sat at the foot of their bed, awkwardly. Desperate for the right thing to say and it eluding me completely.

The mark *was* on her face. So that's where he had struck her. He had used an open hand, I could tell. He had used great force, that too, I could tell. The left side of her face carried the symbol of my father's strength and his weakness simultaneously and I marveled at the irony. I looked at my mother and knew that was why he wasn't there. He couldn't bear to look at her after what he'd done. I couldn't bear to look at her either, but I wanted to. I forced myself to look at her long enough to commit her swollen face to memory. She didn't flinch, didn't move. I thought looking at her would embarrass her, as it did me, but she was unmoved. When I finished, I got up to lay down beside her and we stared at the ceiling.

I felt uncomfortably inadequate being next to her. I wished Aunty Sli was here, she would know what to do. All I could offer her was my presence, so I just stayed there and waited. After what seemed to me like an eternity, Mama sat up and shimmied over to the edge of the bed. She gave me a look that told me I was to do the same. My heart rate picked up as she fixed her face to say something. When she spoke her voice was normal, soft. I had heard her sound like so many variations of herself in the last day that this was comforting. "Are you alright, my love?" She asked me with such tenderness, that I knew she was really worried about me. After everything that happened, she was worried about *me*.

The guilt of what a horrible daughter I was resurfaced. I had been avoiding her, too ashamed to face her and see the hurt she had endured, and her first concern was me. I couldn't have stopped the guilty tears if I tried, and I didn't have the strength to try. She smiled and wiped them away, waiting patiently for my reply. I nodded. I still hadn't found my tongue, so I swallowed nothing and waited. "It's alright, don't worry. Everything is going to be fine." She smiled at me, and I couldn't hide my shock. What was there to smile about? I wanted to ask more questions and I wanted to get real answers. But I knew better than to push. I smiled back at her, trusting, hoping that in time she would reveal more. "I don't want you to think about what happened, or to worry about me. I'll be just fine. I need you to just focus on school, alright?" But it wasn't alright. "I mean it, nana, it will be alright."

"Yes, Mama."

...

That incident became a standout point after which there was no return. I felt that everything had been building up to that point and after the eruption, nothing could ever be done to make things as they were. Mama withdrew further into herself, something I hadn't known was possible until I saw it happen. It shocked me, the ability my father had to make my mother disappear. She sucked herself into herself and re-created her world around the one thing that still made her happy, her pots. They were the only thing that she enjoyed enough to get lost in, and during that time they were the only thing that existed. Baba didn't exist, the women in the village didn't exist and at times, I felt that even I didn't exist. Where they had once been a hobby and an outlet, those pots became her life. When she made them she was alive.

She still did her duties, moving us all along from day to day. On the surface not much had changed, but everything was different. We all took up our roles like robots each day, just to get us through. We knew them so well from years of careful practice that we continued to run smoothly, but beneath the surface, and not even that far beneath it, we were crumbling. Our family was falling apart and I don't believe any of us knew how to fix it, I didn't think any of us could. I convinced myself that everything was alright and as more scream-less nights passed, my conviction grew stronger. Mama and Baba just had a fight, and every family had fights.

Whatever else it did, the biggest impact of Baba's hand across her face was that it made her stop pretending. The full scale of her sadness washed over her and it was so heavy that you could see it. It was so deeply set within her that after it was exposed she couldn't reel it back in, not fully. We were slowly learning what lay at Mama's core. Slowly, she let us see the pieces of her entirety. And slowly, we tried to hide from each piece. She wasn't repulsive in a way you could clean up quickly, like vomit from a sick child. Her repulsiveness had depth. It was the knowledge that the Mama we knew was vanishing in front of our very eyes. We were repulsed at the idea that perhaps we were responsible. She moved around the same and if you didn't care you could have missed it, but we cared, so we saw. The light I sometimes saw in her eyes was gone. There was something in her emptiness that physically drove us away.

We dove deeper into the pretense. We treated it like an art. I could feel it, we all could but nobody said it. Mama's pretending to be alright was so vital to the survival of my family that when she stopped we had to start. I wanted to be better than my father and my brother, I wanted to stare down her sad cloud and stand my ground. I wanted to be her refuge. I wanted to not be repulsed by her, but I couldn't. So I joined my father and brother and we pretended. We pretended everything was alright, and that Mama was just going through something that she would get past. We pretended that we didn't know she had been carrying our entire universe for so long that it finally broke her.

The tension at home started to build like a real physical weight that I could feel. I carried it with me everywhere, but I felt it most when I was at home. I felt it most when I was with Mama. With that weight between us, we continued to make our pots. The weight of her failing marriage, the weight of our failing family, the weight of things not spoken about. Perhaps most heavily, the weight of her sadness, which seemed to grow daily. I knew she needed me and I wanted to meet that need. I swallowed the instinct to run away and gave myself to her in the only way I still knew how. I convinced myself in those moments as we made our pots, that we were sharing her burdens. I dedicated hours after homework, I dedicated sparable moments between chores. I dedicated Saturdays and Sundays. Mama dedicated her entire self.

I watched as the events of that night affected all of us. That dark fog had finally sucked all the oxygen out of my family and we all choked. Differently, but equally. My brother's reaction was to avoid it as much as he could. I hardly saw him, sometimes I'd hear him walk across the yard after I'd gone to bed and when I saw the kitchen light go on I'd find joy in the knowledge that at least he was eating. My father started staying out longer too, he always had work to do. A case here, a case there, his council needed him more and more. It became monotonous and even though I started to expect to not see him until after dark after we'd eaten, I still waited up for him too. I'd watch from the kitchen as his figure disappeared into their flat. I'd listen to their door open and close and watch Mama carry his food out to him. So that night when he still wasn't home even after I'd finished my first post-dinner cup of tea, I noticed. As I finished my second cup and he was still not home, I grew nervous. Mama had put his food aside so it would be ready when he finally came home like she had started to do now, so I knew she was expecting him back. When it was nearing 8 o'clock, ridiculously late by all accounts, I searched her face for something. There was nothing, not concern, not anger, as she carried on ironing his shirt for the next day.

I allowed myself to feel worried about Baba, because I refused to believe that he simply wouldn't come home. Whatever was happening between them, whatever he or Mama had done, that was simply not what we did. He had to be in trouble and that was the only reason he hadn't come home. He would come in the morning and explain everything to Mama and everything would be alright. In fact, that might not even be necessary, because he could be on one of the late busses right now. He had missed his bus home and had to wait for a later one. When I woke up he would still be in bed, tired from having traveled so late. I tossed and turned that night, my entire sleep unsettled. Baba was still not home when I woke up.

That morning, Mama's face was still an emotionless mask I could not read, but her movements were loud. As she washed the dishes I saw anger, fury as she swept the floor. I saw hurt as she rinsed the dishes and irritation as she tended the fire. As she insisted on drying the dishes, I saw defeat. I wished she would let me do something, anything. I saw anger again as she did the washing. It was Saturday, once my favorite day. Mama stirred the beef curry as Sizwe made his way to Baba's hut. It was around the time the two of them would leave for their manly adventures, leaving Mama and me to our pots. When he realized Baba was not home, he walked over to us, dumbfounded.

"Ma, where is Baba?" he spoke to my mother, but I knew he could feel me glaring at him. I don't know why, but I felt the need to make sure he saw how upset I was. How upset *we* were. I wanted him to know that there was now a clear divide between us and them, and his partner had broken a rule and we were upset. We would not stand for it and there would be consequences. I wanted him to feel the hurt that Mama felt and that I felt for her. I wanted him to feel it, because I knew we would never be bold enough to make Baba feel it, to even bring it up. Sizwe was my consolation prize and I hoped the daggers I was throwing at him with my eyes hurt.

"Angazi." *I don't know.* She offered him nothing more. She didn't even look up from the curry she was stirring. Sizwe looked from Mama to me and I knew this was my chance. As he held my gaze, I showed him all the pain. I was transitioning to full-blown anger when he finally looked away, but I got my satisfaction before he did. He looked ashamed. I thought that maybe, like me, he was starting to really see how bad a person our father could be. He nodded acknowledgment at Mama, that he had heard her before slowly turning and walking back to his flat. He didn't look at me. A few minutes later I saw him walk out the gate to God knows where.

CHAPTER 8

Baba arrived at a quarter after five, around the same time he would arrive on Saturdays if he had gone to the courts with Sizwe. Except he arrived alone, Sizwe had been back for an hour. It was earlier than normal for him, but I knew he wanted to be there when Baba arrived. I was the first to see my father making his way to the gate. I was outside with a jug, fetching water to soak the potatoes. I saw him through the small squares of the fence. My stomach clenched, and I rushed inside to tell Mama. No, I rushed inside to warn her. We had just started dinner, having washed up from our pots. I was peeling potatoes when I realized there wasn't enough water in the kitchen, and I didn't want them to turn brown. I half walked, half ran back into the kitchen and I was practically still outside the door when I hissed to Mama, "He's here. Baba, he's at the gate."

Mama looked up at me quickly, the animated nature of my actions obviously startling her. When she had heard my one sentence, she sighed. She held out her hand for me to give her the jug of water like she didn't trust me to hold it anymore. She nodded, more to herself I think because that motion did nothing for me. She poured the water into the kettle and removed the onions she had been frying from the fire so she could boil the water. Baba would want his tea. She gave me back the jug so I could re-fetch the water for my potatoes. I walked out as she was setting the tray with his special cup and saucer. She did it all so easily, so calmly. Where was all that anger now? I was fuming on my own. She put two slices of the sweet cornbread she'd made yesterday, and waited for the kettle to boil. Its whistle indicated it was showtime, she would go and face my father. She placed a slice of lemon in his tea and then stood holding the tray, before handing it to me. "Go serve your father."

My feet were lead as I walked the short stretch to Baba and Mama's flat. With each step I was angered that I had to serve him and I was almost angry at Mama for making me do it until I thought about how difficult it would have been for her. I knew I was being used as a pawn, but I also felt like I was helping my mother. It wouldn't be right for Baba to not be greeted with his tea in his own home, so this way Mama could still be respectful without having to face him just yet. I was helping Mama and this was my secret mission, to gather as much information as possible for her. I took a deep breath outside the door, balancing the tray on my left knee and securing it with my left hand while I knocked with my right.

Baba opened the door for me. He had just changed into his home clothes, a pair of faded khaki shorts and worn-out t-shirt that had once read IFP on the front. The big elephant logo of the political party had long since faded, although I could still make out parts of the trunk and the outline of an ear. I walked in and placed the tray on the table."Unjani, Baba?" As I asked him how he was, I studied his face to see if I could find out on my own. He looked tired. His eyes were red, but in a way that made me suspect they had been even redder before. I wasn't sure, but I thought I could smell fire on him. Faint smoke. That was all I could gather as he told me he was fine and thanked me for the tea. I walked out as he was reaching for the tray. Sizwe was standing outside his door, now fully aware that Baba was home. He watched me as I walked back to the kitchen, and then disappeared into his flat again. I guess he wasn't going to speak to Baba just yet.

Nothing happened. Mama and I carried on with dinner, and when I told her what information I had gathered she nodded in a way that suggested she really didn't care and carried on with dinner. It was as if nothing had happened.

She served him his dinner and the entire time my heart was in my chest. She came back about fifteen minutes later and I knew they had talked. I was dying to know where he was last night. Where he had slept. Why he hadn't come home. Mama saw the questions on my face, I know she did, but quietly carried on with her chores. For the first time, I was frustrated and angry at *her*. She was an impossible teammate. Why couldn't she share with me like I shared with her? I swallowed my rage, it was futile to try and push my mother. I washed the dishes and went to bed. There were no sounds coming from their flat as I fell asleep.

On Sunday, as we all continued to pretend like nothing had happened, Mama finally told me the explanation Baba had given her. We were working on the pots and Sizwe and Baba were gone. As she concentrated on creating a perfect rim on the neck of the vase she was making, Mama relayed the story to me. Baba had gone to the court and when they were done, some of the other men said that they were going to the ceremony held across the dam at the Mkhize household. The eldest daughter was being recognized as a woman, and a huge feast was being held for her coming out ceremony. Baba went with them, to pay his respect and celebrate with the family. It ran long and so Bab' Mkhize insisted Baba and Bab' Dludla stay the night as they lived the furthest away. In the morning Bab' Mkhize insisted they stay at least until lunch, and that was why Baba only made it home in the afternoon. I studied Mama's face the entire time and she was so serene. I knew she hadn't questioned a single thing he said, just accepted it and moved on with her life. I wanted to ask if she believed him, but I didn't. I knew there was a lot more she wasn't saying. I didn't say anything. It was about an hour of silent working before she spoke to me again. This time she actually stopped what she was doing, so I knew what she was about to say was important. So I stopped what I was doing too.

"What is the most important thing to you, Ma?" her voice was soft, calm. I hadn't been expecting a question, but especially not that one. I looked at her confused for a while and when she continued to quietly stare at me I realized I would have to answer.

"Uhm, I don't know. Our family, I think." I wanted to say "You," but I was afraid that she wouldn't like that answer.

She smiled at my response. "Our family," she repeated. "Yes, family is very important." I noted how she didn't say 'Our family is very important,' but I didn't say anything. She was looking at me in a funny way and I felt that for the first time in a long while, she was really *looking* at me. She could see me and she was happy with what she saw. My stomach fluttered. Whether I read that right or wrong, I tucked that moment away and kept it safe. "To me, you are the most important thing." There was a grave seriousness to her just then, that added a chill to her warm words, but only to the tips, so the moment was still mostly warm. "And the next important thing after that, is your future life. I want you to have everything that you can dream of and nobody to be able to hold you back. So I want you to do something for me, okay?" She was still so calm, with smiles in her eyes. I looked at her with questioning eyes, I would do anything. "I want you to change the thing that's most important to you, from our family to your independence." She took my hand gently, "When you achieve that and you are a big, important person, then you can change your most important thing back to your family." She smiled at me. Confused as I was, I couldn't help smiling back.

"Will you do that for me, Ma?"

"Yes Mama."

"Ngiyabonga, sthandwa sami." Thank you, *my love.* "Now all we have to do is make sure that you get your independence."

I wasn't sure what that meant, but I had found the spark in Mama's eye again and I would do whatever she wanted to keep it there. We had a goal and that goal gave her purpose. She had a reason to wake up and keep going again. We started making even more pots, Mama's new goal was to sell three weekends per month, one of them being in town. When she said that my mouth went dry. Town. Did she mean the *town*

town? Where we had gone some weeks ago in order to get to Aunty Sli's home? *That* town? She did mean that town. I was beside myself with excitement and then, almost instantly, fear. Baba wasn't going to like this. He didn't like us selling as it was, what more if we decided to go all the way to town to do it, and selling almost every weekend. Surely Mama had thought about all this, she knew the risks. Probably better than I did, and yet she was still calm, seemingly reading my mind.

"Don't worry about your father, it's fine."

I wasn't sold, but I accepted what she said. Our entire lives became engulfed by the pots. We lived and breathed them. Mama worked all week between chores and I gave any spare time I had to them. The only thing that took precedence was my schoolwork, but after my homework and study were done, I painted the pots. On weekends we capitalized on the time we had and for the first two we didn't sell. We built our inventory. The third weekend was grant weekend, an opportunity we never missed. For everything else that was happening, we still found joy in selling our pots. Mama was happy, coming alive with every transaction. We were selling three weeks out four, traveling to different districts with different grant days. I wondered where Mama kept all the money, there must have been a mountain of it by now. Wherever it was, I hoped it was out of my father's reach.

CHAPTER 9

My parents seemed to be living in different worlds that they no longer tried to connect. I never saw them together, I never heard them talking. I never heard anything. The only person I really spoke to was Mama. My brother and I also seemed to live in non-connected worlds. Sometimes, when we were absolutely pressed to communicate, we grunted things at each other, but mostly we ignored each other. He and Baba seemed to have worked out their differences and were back to their weekly disappearing acts, and for that I was grateful.

...

Mama and I made our first trip to town a month and a half later. Two days earlier, we'd made the 1.5 kilometers walk to 'the container'. It was an actual container, like those you see on cargo ships, with telephones inside. For 50 cents a minute, you could make your call. Mama called Aunty Sli, dialing the number from a piece of paper she pulled out of her pocket. I could only hear what Mama was saying on her side, and it wasn't enough to piece together their entire conversation. As always, Mama was frugal with her words. I did gather that this was something they had discussed before because Mama was able to refer to it simply as 'that thing' without having to explain further. I also learned that Aunty Sli would be meeting us in town from Mama's parting "Alright, see you then *sisi.*" On the silent walk back home I fought the urge to ask if Zandi and Zinzi would also be there.

When we got to town, they were waiting for us at the rank; Aunty Sli, Uncle Muzi, Zandi, Zinzi, and little Musa. I spotted them from inside the bus and their faces made me so happy. I didn't think they would *all* be there, but with all our parcels we needed all the hands we could get. It wasn't until we actually stepped out of the bus that they saw us. I was quick with greeting my aunt and uncle so I could focus on the girls, it was great to catch up with the girls as we packed one of the two wheelbarrows Uncle Muzi had brought to help us transport the pots. "Ma got you guys a great spot to sell, over by the taxi rank, you're going to love it." I was surprised by Zinzi's revelation, had Mama known? "Yeah there's so many people there just looking for something to buy, I'm sure we'll make a killing," Zandi added enthusiastically.

When we set up, Uncle Muzi spoke briefly with his wife before saying goodbye to us. I waved, offering a smile, he was nice. Aunty Sli and Mama got comfortable on the lawn chairs that my aunt had packed. As the two women sat and chatted amongst themselves, I watched them for a little bit. I watched Mama, struck by how beautiful she was when she laughed. When she was happy. They touched each other a lot. Aunty Sli would brush the dirt off of Mama's skirt or gently pat her back. When they laughed they automatically reached out their hands, the crescendo of their laughter materializing only when they made contact. I was struck by how easily they touched, how much they loved each other. I couldn't picture my parents touching. I moved away then, suddenly aware of what felt like an intrusion.

When they heard our prices, Zandi and Zinzi insisted we add a markup to everything, a sentiment shared by Aunty Sli. Although Mama protested at first, in the end we increased all our prices by R30. "Londi, you made a beautiful product available to them and you should be compensated for it. Not to mention the selling time you're losing by having to travel here," Aunty Sli was difficult to argue with. The girls introduced me to another effective way of improving our sales- advertising. They each grabbed a pot, pushing one into my hands, and before long we were showing them to people all over the rank and pointing to where they could go and get theirs. Zandi was the best at this, she would walk up to a lady and present the pot and say casually, "Isn't it beautiful?". Most of the women would stop long enough to admire it and then she would say, "it's not even that expensive. You can get this one for R50, there are some cheaper ones too. Over there." At which point she would point to our stall and more often than not, the woman would go to take a look. Zinzi's approach had been more of just shouting, "come and get this beautiful pot," more to the wind than anybody in particular, but she switched tactics after witnessing her sister's success.

It took me the longest to find my voice, I was fine to sit at a stall and talk to those who came up to us, but this fishing for customers was very different. People scared me. They all seemed busy, like they had something important to do and I wasn't comfortable demanding their time. I tried psyching myself up to say something to someone, but the words never left my throat. I must have looked like I wanted to say something because a lot of the women I approached looked at me expectantly before that turned to a funny look as I failed to deliver. It took one kind, perhaps more patient than kind, woman to cure me of my chronic shyness. She looked at me expectantly, when I fixed my face to talk to her and she continued to do so after I failed to actually say anything. Then she smiled at me with laughing eyes and simply said, "Yes?". Her warmth put me at ease and soon I was babbling on about how my Mama made that very pot and I painted it. That was my first sale.

...

Baba was home when we go there, and he walked out of his candlelit room and stood at the door to greet us. Mama greeted him back, but I couldn't find the words to. I realized I was holding my breath, waiting for something to happen. Something to shatter this moment, a scream from him, maybe a bang of the door. He turned and sat down, getting back to his newspaper. Mama gently pushed me into action, "go get tea started, Ma." She gave me the instruction and followed Baba into the room.

As I changed into my home clothes I wondered what they had discussed about the pots. Mama had said nothing, but clearly Baba knew we had gone to sell in town. Probably even that we planned to do so again. He hadn't thrown a tantrum when we got home and had most likely sent my brother to walk us home. What did it all mean? Had he warmed to the idea of Mama working? Had he realized how awful he had been to stay away from home? Was this his way of making up for it all, finally? I let the idea hold me as I brought the fire back to life. The idea that perhaps we were a family again. We made and served dinner wrapped again in our comfortable silence. I slept easily, tired from the day. I dreamt of my parents touching each other and laughing.

CHAPTER 10

That week we got the news that MaSibisi had died in her sleep. She was the wife to Bab' Biyela, a well-known man who served on the small court with Baba. She had been ill, a fact everyone repeated easily. Nobody discussed what she had been ill with. They lived across the little dam that was mostly used for watering cattle, a dam right next to the road so you passed it on the bus ride to town. It wasn't far, about twenty minutes if you were walking comfortably. The funeral would be held that following Saturday and it would be expected that both Mama and Baba attend. They would travel separately, Baba with a group of men and Mama with the women. I was shocked when Mama asked me to go with her, she had never done so before. I quickly nodded my response before she changed her mind. I had hardly known MaSibisi so I wasn't going to fulfill a deep desire to pay my last respects, I was going for Mama. She was never one for social activities or meaningless banter and after the incident at the water pump, I knew it was getting more difficult for her to be amongst her peers. I would be her buffer and her wall.

When Mama mentioned to Baba that she would be taking me with her, he was mostly unmoved bar for asking what Sizwe would eat with everyone gone. He then solved the problem by saying, "No matter, I'll just take him with me then." Great. When Saturday came, my family set out in as much black as we could manage for the funeral next to the dam. MaSibisi would be buried in their backyard, in the secluded part they kept just for that purpose. As we cried and sang sad songs to mourn the death, I would picture all the family members that had died before her celebrating and dancing as they welcomed her home. It made the death almost beautiful. I remember my confusion and panic the first time I saw a cemetery, all those people lost in the middle of the city, buried next to complete strangers.

Mama and I were late, so we missed the group of women as they made the walk, collecting each other along the way. They sang sad funeral hymns as they walked. Baba and Sizwe had left earlier to volunteer themselves to help dig the grave if need be. Though, family members and close neighbors would most likely take care of that, it was still a polite and respectful gesture. Mama and I left, following the faint music of the mourning women, content not to catch up. As we walked I contemplated how similar weddings were to funerals. The men and women sat separately, in distinct age groups. Neighbors came to help cook and brew beer in the days leading up to the event. There was a perpetual chorus of song and countless children running around. The only difference I could see was the clothing, weddings brought color and funerals only black. The second difference was the sound that filled every silent space. At weddings, it was ululating and today it would be wailing.

After the burial, everybody separated into their respective groupings where they would take their food. It was easy to tell who belonged to the family because they were running around trying to get everything for everyone. I defied the rules and went to sit with Mama as she joined the other married women. The women sat arranged in two rows that followed the circular shape of the room. There was a clear path only from the door to the center of the hut, which is where the food would be placed. We were amongst the last to walk in so we ended up in the back, behind a group of women we didn't know. All the women I recognized as our neighbors were mostly sitting across from us, MaSibiya called loudly to Mama as we sat down. Mama smiled and greeted her back gently, making the older woman sound even louder. We were seated in the middle of what seemed like a friendship circle, judging by how easily and happily the women spoke to each other. Periodically, one of the women would start a song and everyone would join in. They sang church songs, songs Mama remembered and had missed singing. I couldn't hear her, because the choir drowned her out, but I knew she was singing with all her might. When they quietened down, the chorus was replaced by the murmur of countless conversations.

I was looking at the lady in front of us. She was beautiful even from the one side of her face that I could study. She was talking to her friend, who sat next to her and just from their faces I knew they were talking about something secret. Their faces were like those of schoolgirls passing notes with bad words about the teacher, eyes shining with the thrill of potentially getting caught. The food came, *uphuthu* and *imfino*, delicious enough on its own, but it was accompanied by the leg of the cow, cut into bite-size pieces and cooked to perfection directly over hot coals for the women, by the young men. It was the part of the animal traditionally reserved for women. I felt like I was cheating, but I couldn't wait to tell the girls at school that I had been able to eat it. Mama and I ate in silence and I couldn't help listening to the women in front of me. "What are you talking about? You know you don't have the same problems as the rest of us."

"And what do you know about my problems?"

The other woman finished putting a piece of meat into her mouth and clapped her hands together mockingly. "Your poor husband, if he were still alive…"

"Well, if he were then I wouldn't be in this mess now would I?"

I was shocked, the ball of *phuthu* and meat in my hand stopped halfway to my mouth. How could the beautiful woman be a widow? She was so young, so beautiful! Mama nudged me, bringing back my awareness. She was glaring at me with a look that said, *'Stop eavesdropping! It's not polite.'* I stopped, at least I tried to. In the end I settled for eavesdropping secretly. My face down and my movements quiet, I continued to eat casually while I listened. I looked sideways at Mama, and there was something so calculated in her own casual eating that I realized she was doing it too! She smiled without looking up, and I knew she could feel my eyes on her. We were a tag team yet again, this time listening in on the secret lives of the young and beautiful.

"Well your new man sure takes care of all your needs now doesn't he?"

"Shh! Mgnani, aw'kahle! *Friend, stop it!*"

"Oh stop, nobody can hear me. *Eish*, but you have guts, my friend. I'm scared of you. That poor woman, she probably doesn't even know. Remind me never to leave you alone with my husband."

"I don't want your husband," she said it laughing as her friend gave her a mock hurt face, before laughing too.

I couldn't hear them anymore, my heart was pounding and I found myself afraid. What had I just heard? I didn't want to hear more. I looked over at Mama, and she sat frozen. I knew she didn't want to hear anymore either. My heart pounded as I failed to control my thoughts. I saw the woman without a husband. I saw her meeting with a man who had a wife. I heard him tell her she was beautiful. I saw the man not come home to his wife. I saw Baba. I was as powerless to the tears as I was to my thoughts. I let them fall silently, as I tried to reason with myself. I had no right to think what I was thinking. I had no proof. I felt Mama's hand on my mine and I turned to look at her face. She was crying too and suddenly I had my proof. I looked up at the woman again, oblivious to our existence and I studied her face once more. She was no longer beautiful.

The rest of that day was a blur, but the exchange between my parents that night was crystal clear. It was after dinner and we all assumed our positions, Sizwe and I in our rooms, our parents in theirs. I sat quietly in my room. I was calm on the surface, but I was seething on the inside. I kept seeing their faces, *her* face. Mama had said nothing of it, but I heard her anyway. As we walked home, I could sense her own pain and anger. Pain at the humiliation that she was a joke to those women. I'd watched her look around, trying to figure out if every face she saw knew and was also laughing at her behind her back. She had not confronted the woman, but I knew there would be a confrontation. Her anger demanded it. She too was seething.

I heard their door close and then I heard my mother screaming at my father. Not in response after he had finally pushed her too far, not as a defense, but as an attack. It made me sit bolt upright after I had started to lay down, it made my heart pound as I tried to imagine the scene. Mama was not only screaming at Baba, she was doing so loudly. I think for the first time she just gave in to her anger, without a thought about trying to shield us from their fights. She was in that moment, drenched in anger, but alive. Fully alive. I could make out everything she was saying without straining which, for the most soft-spoken woman I knew, was a testament to just how angry she was. The only times I wouldn't hear her was when the panic in my own body made its way to my ears. The fear of what Baba would do when the shock of seeing Mama like this finally wore off. Just then her screams would find me again and jolt me into action. First to sit up, then to stand until finally, I found myself outside my door, looking towards where my parents were. I was so transfixed that it took me a long time to realize that Sizwe was outside his own door, doing the same thing. We locked eyes only briefly, the only witnesses to the growing turbulence of our home.

"Do you know how humiliating it is? Do you know how those women were looking at me? And for what?! For what?! For that young girl? You'll shame me and our home, for what?!"

She was getting calmer now, her voice falling from a scream to a shout. For the first time, I couldn't hear Baba. It was as if their roles had been reversed and it was strange. She was quiet for a while, Mama, but then I heard her again. "Is that all you can say to me?" It was a shout, but it rose again, "What if you get her pregnant? You swine! What if you get her pregnant?" It fell again, as though she were really considering the option for the first time. I certainly was. I had been angry and anger grips you and holds you in the current moment and sometimes it lets you look into the past for more ammunition. But the future? I had given no thought to that, I had not considered that actions have consequences and that if Baba and that lady did what we thought, there could be a baby. I looked at my brother and he was staring at me. I could tell that this was all information he didn't know. His face was warped in a manner than suggested anger, shock, confusion and perhaps more, but I didn't care. I looked back at my parent's room, Mama was all I cared about. I was waiting for Baba to leave. I just knew that eventually, he would.

"Stop! You're making a scene. The kids can hear dammit, is that what you want?!" So my father was getting angry too. I knew there would be no good end, but at least there would be an end.

"I want you to stop this thing with this woman! Stop it right now or I swear-"

"You swear what?! You'll leave me? What will you do? Tell me!" It seemed Baba no longer cared if we heard them either.

"I will. I'd rather die alone than be with such a weak man. You're weak, Mthethwa!"

It was the last thing she'd say to him that night. I didn't have to see it to envision the strike. I heard their door open and saw the light from their room spill out. I walked over to their door as Baba was leaving, pulling his jacket over his shoulders. He turned to look at me and I recognized the thunder in his eyes. I froze in my tracks. He finished wearing his jacket, looked back at Mama then turned and left. After a few steps, I heard him spit and curse. Only when I heard the gate and had assurance he would not be back, did my feet find their function again. I looked over at Sizwe just in time to see him close his door.

CHAPTER 11

I found her on the floor. It didn't look like Baba had pushed her there, it looked like she had voluntarily slid, trusting the wall behind her to safely direct her all the way down. She was crying now, not the dignified cries of ladies that remained pretty throughout. Not the silent cries I had always seen her do. The sound came from her core, loud and painful, interlaced with muffled words. As I moved gingerly into the room, I started to make out what she was saying. Her words were choked up by the sticky, bubbly mixture of mucus and tears in her throat but I still listened. Mucus and tears were mixing on the surface of her face too, and I pulled a wet face cloth from behind the door. I turned to take the three steps it would take to get to her but stopped cold on the second. I could finally make out what she was saying. "Go to her..go to that dirty whore."

I had never heard Mama say anything so vile, the word was wrong in her mouth. *Whore*. That's when I knew that Baba had broken more than her face, that he'd broken something much deeper. I turned around and closed the door. Nobody but me would see her like this. I sank down to meet her on the floor, gently brushing away the hands she put up in weak protest. I cleaned her face. There was a half-empty glass of water that I had gotten earlier for Baba, I reached over and gave it to Mama. She drank slowly, washing down the mess in her throat. We sat like that and after a while, she slid down further and lay her head on my lap. I hummed her one of the songs from earlier that day, the one she had sung from her heart. I didn't quite know the words but I could remember the melody. I hummed softly until I heard her childlike hiccups turn into deep, slow breathing.

We sat like that for close to two hours before Mama came to. I didn't realize it but I had fallen asleep too. It was her waking up from underneath me that woke me up. As we uncoiled ourselves, it all came back to me. It all came back to her too, I could see from her face. She looked tired. "Let's make some tea, Ma." I thought she would have told me to go to bed, but tea was a much better idea. We made our way to the kitchen in the dark. I made the fire, reviving the coals that were still hot under the ash. Mama fetched the water before making us jam sandwiches. When the tea boiled we poured our cups and carried our sandwiches to her room. It was so absurdly wonderful, a sort of a sleepover. It felt like we were breaking a rule and we didn't care. The clock on the wall confirmed that it was a quarter to eleven, I had never been up with Mama this late before. We didn't speak as we ate, but I would look up at her periodically, she was lost in her thoughts. I was quiet too because I feared that if I spoke, then she would remember I was still there and our sleepover would end.

That was the night that she told me what she had done with our money, all the money that she had kept secret from Baba. We were perched up on their bed, me still with a jam sandwich in my hand and Mama with her cup of tea. She drank it even though it was long cold, something I could never understand. "It's like tea juice," she would say. As she drank her tea juice she told me about the account that Aunty Sli and Uncle Muzi had opened for her. With my mind racing I tried to keep up with all the details. They opened it under my name because I was a minor and could have it done by a third party. Uncle Muzi had a friend at the bank who helped them do it. Then came the part that changed my life. She put down her cold tea and looked at me like she meant to. When she spoke it was in a whisper, even though we were alone in the room with the door closed and Sizwe had long since put out his candle. "Ma, this account is for us. I am going to leave your father."

My world stopped. My ears rang and my heart

pounded. Was I scared, or was I excited? Could I be both? I knew now why she had whispered it, it was a dream so delicate that it could be destroyed simply by being heard by the wrong ears. Mama took my hands in hers, the jam sandwich fell to the bed and neither of us cared. Unable to create sound, I willed her to go on with my eyes. Her whisper was even softer now, forcing me to physically lean into her. "When we have enough to start a new life, we will go to Sli and she will help us get to Durban where our older cousin can help us get set up. We're going to have a different life, Makhosi. You're going to have a different life." I still couldn't make a sound. Mama was quiet too for a while as if saying all that out loud had changed something for her. It had for me.

All of a sudden I wasn't just wishing for Mama to run away from this life and take me with her. Now we had a *plan*. We had money and we had a plan and we had friends. There was Aunty Sli and her husband who were the best people alive and there was an aunt in Durban who, although I had never met her, was also the best person alive. We could do it, we could run away and never look back and Mama would be safe. We didn't talk after that. Mama didn't remind me to not tell anyone or explain that we would have to work so much harder to make and sell more pots. It didn't need to be said. She pulled the blanket over us, indicating that it was time for bed and that I could stay. As I pulled the blanket over my head, I recognized the scent of my father.

...

I woke up sweating from an awful dream. Interwoven in it had been everything swimming around in my head that night. I saw Mama dressed in fancy town clothes but in the dream, they were her regular clothes because she lived in a town. I saw the beautiful woman sitting in front of me, but when she turned she had a twisted face. She took a step toward me and I could smell my father. She started chasing me and I woke up in a panic. It took a few seconds of troubled panting to recognize where I was, and then remember why I had slept in my parent's bed. Mama was gone, I knew she would be preparing tea for our breakfast. I got up and made the bed, embarrassed to have been left sleeping by her. She always woke up before me, but somehow it was different knowing we had woken up from the same bed. I went to my own hut to make the bed I had abandoned last night and sweep before I joined her in the kitchen.

"Morning Mama, has Sizwe had his tea?" Mama nodded. So my brother was avoiding common spaces again. It didn't surprise me, if I was him I would too. I knew he would leave to see some friend soon enough, anything to get him away from home. The thought made me sad for the first time, but I brushed it off. I had other things to think about.

Mama set the pot of beans on the fire. She had already sifted them, removing the small stones that always found their way in there. I loved beans, especially the way Mama made them, but they did not love me. My brother once joked that I was a farting grenade after eating beans and we all laughed together. Him, Mama, and I. I could see the memory of it in my head, but it seemed so distant now. I pulled my painting kit out and started to mix the colors I would use that day. My theme was warm, like a fiery sunset. Reds, oranges and yellows, it was my favorite. I saw Mama get settled into her own spot, and soon the two of us were working away, each lost in our own thoughts. I imagined she was thinking about how much money we needed to get away, where in Durban we would live or maybe what shape of pot to make next. I looked at her face and started to think differently. Maybe she was thinking about how Baba had spent his night. I felt the grip of anger try to get me and I quickly shook it off. I would not think about that. I focused instead on the hairstyles I would try when I went to a fancy town school. I imagined water coming out of a tap in Mama's own home. I imagined her smiling and being happy all the time.

...

Schools would be closing for the short September break in a week and it would be the perfect time to sell in town. We could sell all ten days and to say I was excited was an understatement. This week leading up was all the time we had to make sure we had enough stock for an entire week of sales. We were machines, we worked so hard. My fingers grew numb and it meant nothing to me. Mama and I were in our own world. I stopped going to school from the Wednesday before closing onwards. The teachers had to have all their numbers in by Wednesday so that the Principal could go through them and sign off on all the reports. Years of government schooling had taught me that the last three days before schools closed were an educationless period, where students roamed and teachers didn't care. Where this had once made them some of my favorite days, I was now grateful that it meant I could be absent with absolute peace of mind. Mama and I needed every day we could get.

She got up every so often to check on the beans, and sometimes she sent me to do it, but everything was secondary to our pots. She cooked the beans in one large pot, indicating that we would be having the same thing for dinner. It reminded me of the time that I had been left to look after Baba and Sizwe alone while Mama was gone. It indicated a new level of her no longer caring about the duties of a 'good' wife, standards broken finally by my father's inadequacies. I watched her add water to the clay, face fixed with focus and I wished she could see herself as I saw her. She didn't stop being a good wife, she merely stopped being a slave to her marriage. She was now focused on something important that was her own.

Baba came home after sundown. Mama and I were still working, making use of the last few hours of daylight. Sizwe had come home about two hours ago when hunger finally prevailed. He ate alone in the kitchen before making his way under the shade of the big tree next to his hut, where he stayed for the rest of the afternoon. He'd asked if we needed help and Mama had smiled in a way that made me smile too. She told him he could add more logs to the fire in the kiln which he did, before returning to his tree.

That small action, that tiny gesture had shifted things. He had taken a step towards our side, closing, ever so slightly, the gap between us and him. I knew my brother felt bad, because what Baba did was wrong and I think this was his way letting Mama know that he thought so. Still, I wasn't ready to accept Sizwe just yet. He was my father's child, like I was my mother's. When Baba came home it was like a game of chess, but it was unclear whose move it was. So nobody moved. The three of us carried on with what we were doing as though nothing had happened. I thought about how ordinarily Mama would get up as soon as she spotted him through the fence to start getting his 'welcome home' tea ready. I watched as she smoothed the opening of the pot she was currently working on.

Baba was out of his element. It was uncomfortable to see someone who was so used to being the center of the universe suddenly be treated like he was of no significance. I made an effort to appear calm and unbothered on the surface, although I felt wrong on the inside. I wanted to join Mama in this act of defiance, I wanted to not care about the consequences. So I fixed my eyes on the pot in my hand and proceeded to draw the same line, over and over. I looked calm, but inside I was terrified and ashamed. I was terrified because I had been witness to Baba's temper enough times to know that he didn't take kindly to Mama not treating him like a king and I was ashamed because I couldn't meet his eye. I didn't want him to see me disrespect him.

Even after everything I still wanted him to be pleased with me. If I didn't look at him then maybe he would think that I just hadn't seen him instead of knowing that I was being rude. I was ashamed because I lacked the bravery that Mama had, even though I knew that she would be the one to face whatever consequences it brought. I was ashamed because I was weak and my defiance was fake. Baba stood by the door of their flat. He was looking at us, taking it all in. I sensed motion coming from Mama and involuntarily turned to look at her. She had stopped working on her pot and was now looking directly at my father. Stunned, I couldn't help but look at him then, at them, engaged in a staredown. Brief, because after a few seconds Mama broke off to continue work on her pot, but gravely intense. I saw my brother get up and walk into his flat. It gave me a weak joy to know I wasn't the only one who couldn't handle it. Baba walked into the flat. Nobody said a word.

It was about five minutes later, five minutes that felt like an eternity later, that Mama spoke. "Go make tea for your father. Dish up for him too." She was calm, the instruction delivered in the same tone she would tell me to go get the washing. I did as I was told, swallowing the nothingness in my throat as I made my way to Baba. I opened the door to find him changed and on the floor, legs spread with a newspaper between them. I placed the food on the table and unsure what to do, I did what I thought was correct. *"Saw'bona, Baba,"* I croaked the greeting in a voice I couldn't recognize. He didn't respond. He didn't look up to to see me, or to say thank you for the food as he normally did. He turned the page in his newspaper and I realized that despite my weak efforts, he had declared me as an enemy anyway. As I left I regretted only that I had cared about his approval. I sat back down with Mama to finish up the last of the pots before it was too dark to continue. This time I offered her no report back on how my father looked. I knew she didn't care.

He slept at home that night, and I wondered what would happen between them after we all went to bed and they were alone with each other. I washed the dishes after Sizwe, Mama and I ate in silence. Mama declared she was tired and was off to bed. She made her bedtime tea and when Sizwe and I both said we didn't want anything, she locked up the kitchen. I insisted on carrying her tea for her, desperate to walk her to their room and make sure that it was alright. It was silly, because the single-cup was all she had to carry, but she let me do it. We reached the door and I stood there, feeling stupid. The room was back to being theirs now that Baba was in it, once again, it felt foreign and respectable. Gone was the warmth I had felt the night before. Mama opened the door and I could hear Baba snoring. That sound gave me such comfort. I heard Mama's exhale as she turned and took her tea from me, nodding slowly as if to say, 'See, I'll be fine.'

...

I spent my last two days of school working on the pots when I got home and thinking about working on them when I was at school. By the time Wednesday came and I was *officially* on holiday, it wasn't a day too soon. I would miss getting my report for the term, but I already knew all my marks. I was still doing really well, coming first in most subjects. Mama and I used the rest of the week to make and paint more pots. On Saturday we would transport half of our stock to town to sell, there was no way we would sell that many pots in one day so Aunty Sli would take what was leftover home to store. On Sunday we would do the same thing, thus moving all our stock to Aunty Sli's home, but we would also go home with her. Mama and I would spend the entire week with Aunty Sli and her family again. This way we wouldn't spend four hours a day just in transit, giving ourselves more time to actually sell. "Do they know we're coming this time?" I asked softly, wanting it to be cute, light, and funny but I was too serious. Mama nodded, she was serious too. I remembered a time when I would have worried over what Baba would say or do and it seemed so long ago.

We worked like ants over the next few days; quietly, swiftly and joyfully. I have always imagined that ants like working, and that is why they are so good at it. Sizwe had adopted the role of kiln master, silently tending to the fire that now burned all day long, which meant he was home all day long. We still hardly spoke to each other, directly anyway. Still, something was happening between us, with every kind look he gave Mama and every kind word I heard him say. Every joke he made in an attempt to hear her laugh, I kept a tally of it all. It was all adding up to something, but I had no idea what. All I knew was that didn't mind him so much anymore and it was okay that he existed, sometimes it was almost nice. I think he felt the same about me. For those few days, Baba was mostly gone throughout the day but he would come home after sundown.

The rift between him and Sizwe was evident, but it was also obvious that neither of them had done anything to address it. I knew that Sizwe staying home with us was taken as a slight by my father, a sign that my brother had switched sides. I want to believe that my brother *had* actually switched sides, that he saw my father for all his flaws and was appalled by it- and maybe he did, but I couldn't help seeing how much he also missed my father. How if Baba just sat him down and explained his actions, Sizwe would find a way to understand them. But Baba was not one for explaining, so instead the screeching silence of it all created a sinkhole that sucked in everything between them. I realized my brother was a scared child, hurt at being abandoned by one parent and retaliating by redirecting his affection. Still, I was grateful because I knew Mama needed all the affection she could get. Ironically, I finally felt connected to him. I was a scared child too.

...

Saturday morning Mama and I were dressed and ready for the eight o'clock bus. Sizwe helped us to make the seemingly countless trips back and forth with the wheelbarrows to get the pots to the bus stop. By the time he had helped us get into the bus and securely fastened the large plastic bags that held them, Mama had to pay for the entire row of seats we sat on, and they were piled as high as possible. It would be a long ride and Mama and I would have to stay awake so we could keep our hands on them for added security. Last night as we ate, Mama asked Sizwe if he wanted to come to town with us, saying we could use the extra hands. I had studied my brother's face, understanding maybe too well all the emotions that danced across it: happy that Mama had accepted him in, but not yet ready to completely let Baba go, and if he came with us there would be no turning back.

He didn't want to hurt Mama, but he didn't want to hurt Baba either. I felt sorry for him for the first time in my life. He was sheepish in his answer, it made me sad to hear him say it. "No Mama, I think I'll stay home, take care of things here. I know you two will be fine." Our eyes met and not knowing what else to do I offered him a slight almost-smile, it was meant to be sympathetic. He looked away and left the kitchen. I remembered that as I waved goodbye to him through the bus window. He nodded, too cool to wave, but he waited until we were out of sight before he turned to go home. I know, because I watched him until he was out of sight.

CHAPTER 12

Uncle Muzi, a true lifesaver, was there to meet us with an empty van when we got to town. It was the same staff car that picked them up every morning, so I guessed that the owner was a friend. I didn't know that he could drive, because he didn't have a car, but I wasn't surprised. Knowing how to do things suited him. The back was empty, the benches taken out so that we could have more space for the pots. After what felt like forever, we finally managed to get all the pots out of the bus and packed into the van. Even though we were being crafty with placement, the van was still packed to the brim. I was instructed to ride at the back and hold everything and Mama would stay and man the station where we had set up. She had no choice but to keep all the pots that couldn't fit in the car, resulting in the largest display of pots we had ever set up.

There was no way we would sell that much and whereas before that had worried me, I now saw its benefits. The display was so grand that it commanded attention, people naturally found their way to it. It was also just as well because the girls wouldn't be joining us this weekend. They were at a church camp from Friday to Sunday night, so we'd see them on Monday morning. I waved to Mama from the little window on the back door of the van as Uncle Muzi and I carefully made our way through town.

Aunty Sli was at home cooking an early dinner so we wouldn't have to do it later. She had already packed our lunch in a large lunchbox and there was a plate of food covered on the kitchen table, for when Uncle Muzi got hungry. As he and I unpacked the pots into the shed that mostly housed their garden tools, Aunty Sli was putting the finishing touches on dinner, a fish curry from the smell of it. I was already looking forward to supper. We weren't there long, she put on her hat and grabbed a light jersey for later. She then picked up Musa and he took his rightful place on her hip while she scooped up her bag with her free hand. Uncle Musa put back one of the benches in the back, so we would have a place to sit. Instead of sitting in front with her husband as I had expected, it appeared she would be sitting with me. I climbed in first and then she handed Musa to me, followed by her bag. Then she got on and only after she was seated comfortably did the car move. I loved all the little ways that Uncle Muzi was kind to her. I wished I didn't notice them, I wished they weren't so strange.

We got to Mama and the women hugged, Mama's face and mood instantly lifting. "Unjan' sisi?" Aunty Sli asked Mama with genuine concern, still holding her close. I let them be, and they seemed grateful. Every time I looked back at them, they were in deep discussion. The day passed and we watched as our stock dwindled. We sold about a third of what we had set up, which was plenty. Uncle Muzi arrived at half-past four, giving us enough time to pack everything into the van and also enough time for Mama and me to make it to the rank for the five o'clock bus. We said our goodbyes, and there was great comfort in knowing we would see them all again tomorrow. On the bus, Mama and I both fell asleep.

Sizwe was waiting for us at the bus stop, ready to carry Mama's bag and the few plastic bags we had. He nodded at me and greeted Mama. It was good to see him. "I warmed up the food and dished up for Baba, I ate too," he reported back to her. As Mama and I ate our supper I found myself thinking about him. Had he always been a nice person?

We woke up the next day ready to do it all again. Mama had woken up to cook a large pot of curry that would be enough to last Baba and

Sizwe two days. After that Sizwe would either have to cook or they could live on bread. We had bought plenty of that as well as food Mama and I thought was easy enough that he could make it. "We'll be fine, Mama," he'd insisted as he helped us to the bus stop one more time, although he didn't sound sure. The bus driver seemed slightly annoyed and Mama had to assure him this was the last time she would occupy an entire row. We recreated the previous day, only we worked later, knowing we didn't have to rush for the bus. Uncle Muzi came back to fetch us at six o'clock and the two of us packed away most of the pots that were left, as Mama and Aunty Sli carried on chatting, slowly rousing their bodies from the sitting position they had held for so long. We couldn't have left a moment too soon, a second later and I would have died of starvation.

As we prayed that evening I found my brain traveling to our home. I prayed for Baba and Sizwe, I didn't know exactly what to say as I prayed for them, so all I said was, "I pray for Baba and Sizwe," hoping it was enough. I saw them in my mind's eye, Sizwe heating up the stew Mama had made and serving it to Baba. I pictured him not knowing that he had to fetch the tray and the dishes sleeping in Baba's room as a result. I brought my mind back to the present moment. They would just have to be okay and survive without us until we got back. I wondered what Mama prayed for, I couldn't hear her because, like

THE POTS

me, she prayed on the inside. I focused on the one person I could hear clearly, Uncle Muzi. He always prayed with his outside voice, leading us through the exercise. Right now he was praying for Zandi and Zinzi, that God may keep them safe where they are and that they may come back tomorrow filled to the brim with a deeper understanding of His love and wisdom. He prayed for Mama and me, thanking God for bringing us to them once again. I focused on the warmth that hearing him say that brought.

...

The girls arrived as we were having breakfast, I could hear Uncle Muzi thank the driver that dropped them off. The man hooted as he left and I ran out to greet my cousins, barely giving them a chance to straighten out before making my request. "You guys must be tired, but do you think you could help us sell tomorrow?" In response, they looked at me like I was ridiculous. "Of course, silly," Zinzi spoke. Zandi chimed in, "If we could stay up all night for praise and worship the entire weekend then we can definitely go and sell pots for a few hours. Besides, we have a lot to talk about." She gave me a look that held genuine concern, so I looked down. I knew she would ask, I wondered how much they had heard already. I wondered if Mama had told Aunty Sli *everything* that happened, and I wondered if I was allowed to. We reached the kitchen door and I was happy to have successfully avoided that for now. They went over to greet Mama, telling her how happy they were to have us back again.

"Girls, do you want to lay down for a bit? You can start tomorrow, you know. We'll all understand if you're tired.'

"No please Mama, we're fine. We're young!" Zinzi shook her hips to demonstrate just how young they were. Aunty Sli mock slapped her thigh and we all laughed, "Alright then young ones. We're leaving as soon as everyone is ready so be quick. At least you two are done," she said looking at Zandi and Zinzi. I finished the last of my porridge as I waited for the kettle to boil so I had hot water to bathe in. Because Uncle Muzi was a teacher, he was on holiday too. His friend would drop the car off as soon as he was done with his errands, and after he used it Uncle Muzi would drive it back to him. Whoever that friend was, he was a good one and I was grateful for him.

Selling that day was like it had been that first Saturday altogether. I was so happy the girls were back and as we worked we spoke. I wasn't going to talk about Baba not sleeping at home. I didn't want to see the look on their faces as I said those words. I didn't want to say those words. If Mama wanted to share that then she would do it herself. I told them that my parents had a fight, and Baba had hit Mama. So we thought it best that we should move somewhere else for a while.

It sounded shady, even to me. I didn't want to tell them that he hit her. I wanted to stop after 'they had a fight', but people don't move after a fight, so I had to make it more serious. "I know you want to move to Durban, Mama said Aunt Simphiwe will help you." I looked up as Zandi offered her thoughts carelessly, freely. I didn't know that we *wanted* to move anywhere, really and truly, but maybe we did. Talking about the move with my cousins made it very real. It was a thing that we were doing. When Mama had spoken about it, that had also made it real, but this was different. They were asking me practical questions, like what would we leave with? Would we have to buy everything new in Durban? Did we have enough money?

I loved that we called it 'the move' and not 'running away'. Running away was more honest, but calling it that it would give rise to all the questions I didn't want to answer. The questions I stayed up asking myself; Would we really run away? Would we really get to Durban? Could we do it before Baba figured it out? And, if we did, how long until he figured it out? And, when he did, what would he do? It was obvious to me that he would come here first and Aunty Sli and Uncle Muzi would try to protect us, but what did that all mean? Would they lie to Baba and say they didn't know where we were? And then finally the question that had been developing in my mind ever so gradually. Could we really run away and leave Sizwe behind? At first, I thought nothing of it because it was just an idea and Sizwe was Baba's child anyway. But now he was becoming Mama's child too and he was becoming my brother. Could she leave her child? Could I leave my brother? I thought of him watching our bus until he couldn't see it anymore and I remembered watching him back in return. I tucked the memory away and went back to selling. The girls were now talking about something else, and I was grateful.

The week went like that, slow and fast at the same time. Every day was the same as the one before, but we found new ways to laugh and enjoy each other. There was no more mention of 'the move' unless it was about its happy connotations. Like the braid styles Zandi thought I should try first when I could finally have hair extensions or what words I should never use because they would instantly identify me as rural. "Uyabo, uma seniseThekwini, ngeke nisathi 'ubhontshisi', sek'mele nithi 'amabeans'," Zinzi offered unsolicited 'how to hide your ruralness in the big city' advice in her best Durbanite accent and I laughed so hard I almost choked. Why couldn't Mama and I move here instead? On weekends we could go back home to check on Sizwe and Baba, and Sizwe could come and visit us whenever he wanted. I found myself in these daydreams more than I liked, but I couldn't help it.

The girls and I cooked most nights and it was my favorite part of the day, when I felt I belonged the most. Conversation often turned to the pots and how we could sell more. Zandi, half crying from chopping onions, tried to share her latest idea. "I think we should have two stalls, *sniff*, because then that way we could get seen by even more, *sniff*, people. Especially if we, *sniff*, put the other stall in a good spot where most people who aren't, *sniff*, going to the rank can, *sniff*, see it. We could be selling, *sniff*, twice as much. We definitely have enough people and more importantly, sniff, enough pots. *Sniff*."

As difficult as she was to take seriously with that delivery, she had a very good point. We decided the best place was by the traffic light right next to the steps that led to the mall. It was easy enough to convince the adults, as long as we were completely in charge of it. They would float by every so often, but it was completely our responsibility. One of us had to still recruit customers for the first stall. It was doable, it just meant a lot of moving around for the three of us.

We started selling at two stalls on Tuesday and it went so well that we did it for the rest of the week. Without telling Aunty Sli or Mama, we added a R10 markup to all the small pieces and a R20 markup to all the big ones. Our stock sold out, so when they finally caught on they had no issue with it. At the end of each day, we handed all the money to Mama or Aunty Sli. Mama tried to pay Zandi and Zinzi again for their work but Aunty Sli stopped her.

"Don't be ridiculous now, what are you going to do? Pay them every day?"

There was a sadness growing between all of us as the week progressed. It was the knowledge that soon we would no longer be together. We tried to live out every day the best we could, to really make it count but every day we could feel it get heavier. On Thursday morning after we finished setting up, Uncle Muzi asked me to get back in the car with him. I looked at Mama and she smiled and nodded. He opened the front door for me and I hesitated before going in. I was suddenly very aware of my nervousness, my overwhelming ineptness at being this close to him. I sat in the passenger seat, as far away from him as I could manage and stared dead forward, not wanting to do anything wrong, not knowing how to behave. I had never spent time alone with a man except for my father, and even then it was brief moments when I was serving him, when I had a clear task to perform. I didn't need to serve Uncle Muzi anything, I didn't have anything to serve.

I reminded myself to breathe and the breath came out too loudly.

"Are you alright, Makhosi?" I nodded, still looking forward. I didn't know anything about talking to men, but I did know that looking them in the eyes was a sign of disrespect. "Hey," his voice was gentle and he said the 'hey' in a way that asked me to look at him. I panicked as I tried to figure out the right thing to do; if he wanted me to look at him then I should, but, obviously, not in the eye. I turned and looked directly at the collar of his t-shirt. I heard him smile. I had never *heard* someone smile before. I didn't know you could. He continued to speak in his calm, soft way and I was glad because that meant I had done the right thing.

"I'm sure your mother told you about the account. I was able to open it for you but there are some things you need to do in person, like sign for it and choose a pin number. My friend is in today so he will help you. Alright?" I nodded, my eyes moving up and down along his shirt.

We went into the FNB bank and it was clean and cool inside. He told a lady who we were there to see and she flashed him a ready smile and told us to take a seat, his friend was busy. We sat quietly and although I really liked and respected him, I was glad he didn't speak to me. I picked up the *House & Home* magazine in front of me and flipped through it, trying my best not to outwardly react to the homes I saw. The lady, still smiling, was back to call us fifteen minutes later. I followed Uncle Muzi, who followed her. I watched as he reached over the desk with a computer and shook the man's hand, both of them smiling.

"Unjani mf'wethu?" *How are you, brother?* I

played with my thumbs as they exchanged greetings and remarks about the soccer game from last night. Finally, the man turned to me and said, "So this is the girl?" Uncle Muzi pulled out a chair for me as he responded, "She's the one." He then turned to me and in his calm and soft way said, "S'fundo here is going to help you with everything. Take your time, I'll be waiting for you back where we were sitting."

In the forty-five minutes that he had me, S'fundo explained how the account worked, described what a good pin was, and had me create and repeat mine correctly twice before showing me how to use the ATM machine, all with the patience of a saint.

"Your pin is your secret. Don't share it with anybody," he said as he asked me to sign the papers pertaining to my account. He eased my instant panic by saying it was okay if I just printed my name. And with that, I had a bank account. Still giddy, I accepted the envelope he handed me with all of my things: my bank card, my STOP card, and countless pamphlets. When I waved goodbye to him, it felt like I was doing so to a friend.

As we walked out Uncle Muzi turned left and walked away from the car and, not sure what else to do, I followed. When I figured out where we were going I beamed.

"Finally," he said, laughing. We walked out of the KFC with two ice cream cones. As I slapped my tongue against the cold creaminess on the ride back, I felt a pang of guilt. He must have read my mind because he said simply, "Ongekho akekho nesisu sakhe." *Whoever is not here, is not here with his/her stomach.* I smiled as I enjoyed the last of my once again guilt-free ice cream.

...

We left on Saturday morning. Aunty Sli and Mama had gone to the garden early in the morning to get Mama and I parting gifts. There was so much produce I thought the two of them had gotten slightly carried away. We prayed together for the last time with our bags packed and by the door. It was still amazing to me that we had sold everything, except for the three big pots we didn't try to sell. They were a parting gift from us to them. The last pot, A huge and beautiful one painted with sunset colors, Mama asked Aunty Sli to give to the potter's widow next door. "Tell her I figured it out and please tell her 'Thank you'." I don't know why Mama didn't walk over to thank her herself and I didn't ask.

She and Uncle Muzi had taken the ride to the bank yesterday to deposit all the money we made that week into the account, she was the only other person who knew our pin. They had gone just before three o'clock when banks closed, so whatever we made between three o'clock and half-past five was what we would be taking home with us. I was happy that our money was protected. We finished praying and I couldn't stop the tears from stinging the back of my eyes. I saw Aunty Sli wipe hers and that made me feel better. Hugs were long and warm and I committed them all to memory before Uncle Muzi took Mama and me to the bus rank. He made a detour via KFC and got three ice cream cones for all of us. It was a last kindness, and I was grateful. I was grateful he was such a kind man.

Mama left me to guard our things while she went to the huge Boxer Superstore at the rank. She emerged with armfuls of plastic bags, filled with food and supplies for home. We would board the ten o'clock bus, which would put us home at midday, in time to start preparing lunch. Home. I fell asleep thinking about what awaited us at home. Would Baba be home? Would Sizwe? I fell asleep to the violent jerkings of the bus as I dreamt about home.

Mama and I made the short walk from the bus stop, saying goodbye to the freedom we had enjoyed all week with each step. Yet, somehow I found myself not feeling sad. As the kitchen came into view through the gate, I felt myself get excited. I would never have predicted it, but I was actually happy to be home. I looked at Mama and she seemed at peace. Sizwe saw us and came to the gate to help with the plastics bags.

"*San'bona.*" It was a formal greeting from my brother directed at us both, the first indication of how long we'd been gone. "If you'd told me you would come back on this bus I would have been waiting for you at the bus stop," he sounded slightly upset. "I know, my boy" Mama responded, gently soothing his upset away. Baba was not home. Nobody mentioned it. We fell back into our life with lightning speed. Mama and I changed our clothes and got started on lunch. She was making chicken curry, and I could tell that Sizwe couldn't wait.

"Stop looking at me like a man starving, the food will be ready soon. *Hau, kanti* what have you been eating all week?" Mama's soft laugh warmed the kitchen. I looked over at my brother knowing that he would have a playful laugh on his face from Mama's gentle mocking. I was wrong. Where he had been happy just a second ago, as soon as Mama said that I saw his face pull tight. He looked at the floor as his jaw clenched. Something was wrong. Mama was hunched over the fire, making it bigger so everything would cook faster. She hadn't seen his face, so she didn't know that he was hiding something. I coughed suddenly and his reflexes forced him to look up at me. His eyes met mine and the questioning look in mine made his turn away. That, or something else. I would have to talk to my brother when Mama wasn't around.

"Hhe, boy?" Mama brought us back to the present. She had clearly been waiting for a response and was looking at him now, eyes soft.

"No Ma, it's just that nobody cooks like you, I've been missing your meals." Mama beamed at him and at least this time he smiled back.

CHAPTER 13

Finding time to talk to my brother proved difficult. Not so much because I couldn't find the time, but rather because I had no idea how to talk to him. How was it that I could speak at length with the girls and boys from school about things neither of us cared about, but I had no idea how to talk to my own brother about things that really mattered? I was also afraid that whatever I managed to get from him, if anything, would be bad. If so, I'd have the responsibility of telling Mama and I didn't want to tell her anything hurtful. So I had to find a time when she couldn't see us, and that was difficult because I was always in my mother's sight. But difficult wasn't impossible, and I was desperate to know what my brother knew. I didn't like that look on his face. Whatever burden he was carrying that caused it, I wanted to know. Our parents, our burdens.

Baba arrived before dinner, dressed as though he had been to court. He seemed alright, normal. I was watching everything, searching for clues. Mama took his food to him and stayed for a while. She came back about an hour later to make their bedtime tea. It was much earlier than usual, but I knew she was tired. I was tired too, perched on my bed, I only stayed up to see if she would be okay. I watched her walk back past my hut with the tray of tea. She was okay. I now worried less about them when they were alone. They didn't fight as much anymore. I still waited before I went to bed, to see if I heard anything that would require me to run to their room and look after Mama, I just did it with less anxiety.

As I sat in my room, I thought about how this might be the time to go and talk to Sizwe. His light was still on and my mother was with my father. I imagined they would have many things to talk about, which would give us time. But, as I looked over to my brother's hut, I dreaded the conversation and a sudden tiredness came over me. An actual weight on my shoulders that I allowed to push me down into the covers. Tomorrow was another day.

The next day was the Sunday before schools reopened. Mama and I knew we had to get as much done, because as soon as school started up again, my schedule would be very different. I dreaded going back to the mundaneness of school, but I also longed for it. For the first time,

I would have a story to share when people asked me what I did over the holidays. We fetched wood very early in the morning so that by the time Sizwe woke up we were coming back. I was impressed that he started the fire in our absence.

We had our tea, and after I served Baba his, Mama and I went to fetch water. Our supplies had almost been completely depleted, so we would be making three trips each. As we walked to the pump, I was feeling chatty.

"It's funny how different 'work' can be, Mama?"

"Hmmm?" she turned, encouraging me to go on.

"Well, at Aunty Sli's we woke up every day and went to work, and right now we're just doing our chores- the basic things we need to do for us to live comfortably every day. And yet, the work felt like playing and the chores feel like work."

"Hmmm…" I could tell I wouldn't get any more from Mama. We were quick at the pump, it was empty. Thankfully.

As we approached the pump on our second trip we saw that other people had gotten the same idea. It wasn't surprising, Sunday was the day most people tried to squeeze as much out of the weekend as possible. I knew Mama wished we'd come back later, but it was too late to turn back now. I studied the group as we approached, there were two girls a few years younger than me and they looked like they came together. One had filled up and the other was waiting for a woman older than Mama to fill up first, out of respect. There were two other women, younger, that were also waiting to fill up. Once done the older woman stood by her bucket, it seemed she needed to gather the energy to start up again. I heard one of the young girls offer to carry her water for her, but she got shooed away.

"These old bones still work my dear, they just need a little patience, but thank you. God bless you." We reached the pump as the girls were leaving. I recognized one of them, her name was Mbali and she lived a few houses past the bus stop. She was nice

We greeted everyone as one of the younger women started to fill up her container. The two of them were chatting quietly between themselves about the one woman's toddler. I eavesdropped joyfully. Apparently the little girl had the flu and the mother was asking the other woman if it had made its way to her son yet. As they spoke I created images in my head, to accompany their stories. I imagined what their children looked like as they played with each other, tiny hands and dirty feet. A smile formed on my face as the cute image danced around my head. I looked up to see if the women were paying any mind to me, and breathed a sigh of relief when I saw that they weren't. I was about to look back down but my eye was captured by something further past the women. I felt the seconds pass as my brain tried to recognize what my eyes were seeing. It seemed so familiar and just at the tip of my fingertips, like the space between seeing a face you know and finally remembering where you've seen it before. As it came closer, my mind became clearer. It was one of Mama's pots.

For a long time I saw only the pot, becoming more distinct and beautiful as it came closer. It was medium-sized, painted in hues of green and blue and could carry perhaps about half the amount of water that an average bucket could. But the woman carrying it would also have to account for its weight, which the plastic buckets didn't have. I had never pictured anybody using our pots for actually fetching water. They were beautiful and delicate, and while they were absolutely functional I still saw them as mostly ornamental. My eyes then moved down to answer the question in my brain. Who would choose to carry their water in such a beautiful pot? As soon as my eyes dropped I wished they never had. I felt my blood boil as my gaze fell on her beautiful face. Why was she here? How could she be here? I watched her walk the last few steps that stood between her and the pump, she must have only been five steps from Mama and me. I could see the mother and child cooking over a fire that I painted on that pot. Everything seemed to be moving in slow motion. Everything except my pounding heart, that was at full speed.

She greeted, a loud general greeting meant for

everyone. The women responded but I couldn't. I cringed as one of the women made a comment on how beautiful her pot was. *Cut*. The only other person who said nothing was Mama. Mama. I had not thought of her. I had been so angry on her behalf that I had forgotten even to look over at her. If I was so upset, then what was she going through? I turned to look at her face and I found on it a look I knew well. Hurt. She was hurt, but behind that hurt I saw a flicker of anger. She was looking at the woman from the funeral, directly at her and the woman was looking back. I saw hurt and anger give way to pity as Mama held her gaze. I saw pity soften her eyes as she slowly shook her head and broke away, returning her gaze once again to the ground.

The confrontation was over, Mama would say nothing to the woman. Not with her words. *Cut*. I looked back at her, the beautiful woman I had dreamt of with a twisted face. The other woman, the one with the son I had imagined earlier looked at Mama and suddenly her face lit up with recognition. "*Hhawe*, isn't this one of the pots that you made, MaBiyela? You must make me one!" *CUT*. I wanted to hate that woman just then too, but I knew she meant no harm. And yet her innocence made it worse. I continued to look at the beautiful woman. Her face *was* twisted, but not in the way I had dreamt it. It was her mouth, twisted in a smirk that said she had won. It was an evil, hurtful smile. Subtle, calculated to inflict the most pain. *Cut*. She flashed her eyes at me and in the moment our eyes connected I lost it all. The blood boiling in my veins had reached its peak, my body could no longer contain what was inside me and I had to get it out all at once. *All her cuts finally made me bleed*. I had to make *her* hurt, I had to make *her* angry. I had to make *her* feel all the things she had made Mama feel, all the things I was feeling right now.

"Shame on you! Your husband must be turning in his grave to see his wife being the village whore!" I hissed at her. I didn't know I could conjure up that much vile, that I could look at someone older than me and feel no respect. I didn't know that I could spit venom or sharpen my tongue but I was glad because I wanted to *cut* her. I didn't know that I had my finger pointed at her until I felt Mama gently push it down. I didn't know I was crying until I felt the hot, angry tears wash over me. I wasn't even really sure I was there until I was brought back to the moment by the old woman.

"Enough!" Her voice cracked like a whip and everything stood still. "Enough. This is not how women conduct themselves. MaDlamini, I hope you know what you are doing, my dear." Her voice was soft now, knowing she had all of our attention.

She was quiet and thoughtful for a while like her mind had taken her somewhere far away, the way old people are sometimes. And then as quickly as she had gone, she was back. "Because my girl, so sure as the world is round, what goes around comes back around. Every time." She stood then, seemingly she had rested enough. But then she stood still and pointed to the pump, "MaBiyela, fill up and go home, dear." Mama and I did as we were told. The other two women left, and I could tell they weren't quite sure what they had just witnessed. I was grateful to the old woman. I thought about what I had just done and the only thing I wanted was to fill up and go home.

I had still not heard Mama's voice by the time we got home, and it would be a while before I did. For the first time, I was glad of this. Mama wasn't the person I wanted to talk to right now. The person I wanted, no, *needed* to talk to now was my brother. The conversation I had dreaded so much just the day before was now the only one I wanted. I didn't care how he tried to cover it up, I would make him tell me. I felt my blood start to boil again as I lowered my bucket to the ground. I felt it with every step I took to his hut and even with every bang on his door. I knew Mama could see me, but I had stopped caring about that too. There was no longer an 'if' now, I knew whatever Sizwe revealed would be awful, and I would tell Mama, regardless of what it was. I turned to look at their bedroom and I felt fresh anger. I was happy Baba was not home, because in my current mood and my new found disregard for adults, there was no telling what I would have said to him. I banged even louder on Sizwe's door, stopping only when I heard him making his way to it.

His face was covered in fresh annoyance. That and the drunkenness of sleep, I had obviously woken him up from a nap. I felt bad about that, but nowhere near as angry as I felt over everything else. "What do you want?" His face, aside from the annoyance, was blank. I was struck now by how ill-prepared I was. I hadn't actually thought any of this through. I could tell my brother was getting more annoyed with me and that I would have to get something out quickly.

"Can I come in?" I could tell he wasn't expecting that. He remained where he was, with his body blocking the door. He was thinking about it. I could tell the idea of me being in his room gave him discomfort, but he didn't have a good reason to say no. It gave me discomfort too, I couldn't remember the last time I had been in my brother's room- and I had certainly never *asked* to be in there. But desperate times called for desperate measures. I needed to talk to him and I wanted to do it privately.

"Just make this quick, okay?" He said it as he turned and walked back into the room, leaving me to follow. I nodded. I had no desire to be in there any longer than I had to be. I left the door open just a crack, I think in an effort to make the moment less serious than it was getting. It was strange being in his room and for a while, all I could do was just take it in. His bed was made but disheveled, I could see the soft dent where he had been sleeping. The curtain and window were both open, but it wasn't a very well ventilated room. I could smell him, all over. A soft musky scent that I knew only as my brother. It was neat, even the desk where he kept his books was carefully arranged.

On the wall right next to his bed there was a mixed matched collection of 'art'. The biggest image was a poster from a magazine of Michael Jackson. Next to it was a smaller image, the size of a page, of a pretty woman with long black hair and a short white dress. I didn't know who she was, I wondered if he did. The rest of the wall was decorated with pencil sketches that he had done over time. His subjects were far-ranging, from animals and nature to extravagant houses. He was a really good artist. I had often seen him sketching outside, but I hadn't realized he was this good. I was looking now at a drawing of a lioness, her eyes so lifelike I felt like we were having a real staredown. Sizwe coughed and the sound pulled me back. His face told me he did it deliberately for that purpose.

"Sizwe, what happened while we were gone?" He sighed, long and hard. I could tell he had been waiting for this question and dreading this exchange. Like me.

"Khosi, just let it go."

"No."

"Khosi.."

"Please just tell me. You know I won't leave you alone until you do. You don't know what happened today. You don't know what it did to Mama. Please, I just need to know, okay?"

"What happened today?" It was the way he asked, with that look of real concern that now entered his face whenever Mama was mentioned. It made me sit down on the edge of his bed and tell him everything. About the beautiful lady and the funeral, about her ugly heart and hateful smirk. About how it seemed a bit too convenient that she would suddenly start using our pump when she never had before. About the nerve she had to actually come and fetch water with one of Mama's pots. How I thought that Mama's spirit had taken such a beating now that I feared she might just choose to stay down. I wiped the tears that had crept silently down my face. I didn't want to cry in front of my brother. Yet, what I felt most wasn't embarrassment, it was relief. I felt understood and in a world full of people I knew he was the only one who could make me feel that way. He was the only other person who cared, who *could* care as much as I did about what happened between my parents.

I felt him sit down next me, both of us facing forward. I felt the truce, declared silently between us. He breathed out, bracing himself, I knew. I knew he would tell me the truth. I made a vow not to interrupt him until he was done. When he finally spoke, his voice was flat. Deflated. The voice of someone telling you something they wished they weren't. "MaDlamini. Yeah, that's who that lady is. I didn't know anything about it until last week, Khosi. I swear. I saw her at the funeral. She was talking to Baba but it was brief and I thought nothing of it. Then last week when you and Mama were gone, she..." He paused and I turned to look at him. This was not the time to stop.

"She what, Sizwe? Just say it."

"She came over. She came over to cook for us on two of the nights. She never stayed over, she just cooked and then..." My hands were on my face covering my mouth. The shock was painful and I had to hold myself not to scream, so I wrapped my arms around my sides, keeping myself together. Her face flashed in my mind. I could feel the tears prickling the back of my eye sockets again. I looked at my brother and begged him in my mind's voice to just say it all. Get it out quickly. His mind must have heard mine. "They ate together, I don't know...they closed the door and I don't know. She came twice and the second time Baba must have given her the pot because she left carrying it."

His voice was softer now, almost a whisper. "I didn't want to be here, Khosi, but Baba asked me.

He said I should make her feel welcome. He asked me. I didn't know what to do. I don't know...I'm sorry." He was crying too now. We sat there, silent and crying. Knowledge clung to me like dead weight, and I regretted ever wanting to know. But as I listened to my brother's choked sobs, taking turns with my own, I was at least happy to share that load. I tried to imagine what it was like to physically be there when this was happening and just the thought made me sick to my stomach. We sat there for a while.

Coming out of my brother's room was like coming out of a cave. It had been dark and somewhat uncomfortable in there but at least we had been safe from the outside world. Now, the light hit me with the full force of reality. I was starting to feel less and less sympathetic towards my brother, yes he had had to tell me, but now I had to tell Mama. I *had* to. There was no choice in it, not to would be to disrespect her, it would be unkind. I wanted to prolong it for as long as possible, the reality in which she didn't know what had happened in the week that we were gone, but I couldn't. There was no telling how many people knew, how many sneered at her in secret. While I couldn't stop that, I could at least let her in on the secret. She was sitting under a tree with a cup of tea in her hand and a vacant look in her eyes.

Just do it, just do it. I chanted in my head over and over as I walked over to her. *Just say it.* I sank down to my knees on the grass mat in front of her, lowering my bum to my heels so we were on the same level. Before my mouth even opened I was crying. I had to wipe away the tears and slowly breathe myself back to control. *Just say it.* I will never know how I managed to tell my mother what my brother had told me. I will never forget the look on her face after I did. I blurted it out, staring at the floor the whole time, knowing that if I looked at her I would break down. When I was done I allowed myself to look at her face and I have never seen emptier eyes in my life. She looked at me with a complete blank-ness. No anger, no pain, no sadness, no regret, no hatred. Nothing.

She simply nodded and then stared off at the distance. I felt distinctly unwanted by her at that moment, so I got up and left. I didn't want to be there either. I didn't want to be in the presence of her shell. She stayed there under the tree for hours. I prepared lunch, and after that dinner. She ate neither. Sizwe served Baba that day and again that night. I think he knew he was the only one left who could somehow still stomach being around my father. That night as I went to bed, I was grateful that the morning brought school and I could again escape home for most of the day.

The week was a blur. It was a collection of seeing and not seeing my family. Mama worked herself silly, and she hardly spoke. Not that any of us really gave her the chance. We all avoided her. We all avoided each other. Even Sizwe and I fell back to not speaking, understanding, but not speaking. I never heard my parents fight now, I never even heard them talk. Even Mama and I barely communicated. School became my refuge, I stayed there even long after the bell had rung and everybody else had rushed home. I told my teacher I prefered to finish all my homework and readings while everything was still fresh and hoped they believed me.

I didn't want to walk through the gate to find Mama busy with a pot. Where it used to make me happy before, now it either made me sad or angry. She looked like a ghost at work and I didn't know what to do. Seeing her make her pots no longer made me happy because it no longer made her happy. Sometimes the anger would well up in me and I wanted to shout at her. I wanted her to scream, at Baba and tell him she didn't need him, or even at me, for being so cowardly. I would have been happy if she just screamed, at nothing, at everything. She deserved to scream at everything. She should have wanted to scream at everything, and yet she didn't. Instead, she began to disappear again into her own silence. A silence that seemed stronger this time.

I still painted all the pots that she made. When they were dried and cooled and ready for painting, she would put them in my room. I knew Sizwe still attended the kiln fire, but we all operated from a distance. I painted after school, between chores and whenever sleep decided to leave me high and dry. Mama was getting thin. She hardly ate, replacing most of her meals with tea. Sometimes I would hang around her at meal-time, because I knew if somebody was around she at least made an effort to touch her food. It wasn't much, but it was something.

I stopped drawing families and in their place now most of the pots had a single sad woman on them. Sometimes she would be sitting staring into the distance, sadness on her face. Other times she would be leaning on a wall, sadness on her face. It didn't matter what I did with the surroundings, I couldn't remove the sadness from her face. It was as if my brush had a mind of its own and no matter what my brain willed it to do, it only obeyed my heart. I knew Mama would see the images and a small part of me hoped that she would see that sad woman and want to stop being her. One day I tried to draw myself into the picture. I had finished drawing Mama, she was sitting with a cup of tea, looking into the distance. You couldn't see her face, but her body was sad. I spent an hour not knowing where to put myself in the picture and in the end, I gave up. I no longer knew where I fit in Mama's life.

I started serving Baba again. Not because I wanted to, but because I wanted to give my brother a break from it, and because I didn't want to see my mother do it. I would go in, greet, put the food down and leave. My greeting no longer asked how he was, it was just a salutation. A formality that if skipped, it would be awkward. More awkward. He didn't respond to my greetings, which I appreciated. He was getting thin too. I would collect plates of half-eaten meals and wonder if in some way he was suffering like Mama was. Like we all were. I hoped he was suffering. I made sure to make him more tea to compensate for the food he wasn't eating, like I did with Mama. He came home every night now. Sometimes he'd be gone for long, only arriving long after we'd eaten supper, but he slept at home. Sizwe spent less time at home too. He always came home, but Mama and I started covering his dinner and he would find it on the kitchen table when he finally did come back. Unlike Baba the latest he came home was eight o'clock, two hours after we ate. I knew because I would wait to hear his door open when he got home. I didn't know why, but I couldn't sleep until I knew he was home.

We slowly developed a system, the three of us. Mama's role was one of letting go and so Sizwe and I counterbalanced by picking up those roles. I fetched all our water and sometimes I would walk in on my brother washing the dishes. I cooked most days, but he started to help by making rice or *uphuthu* while I was still at school, that way I only had to make the curry for supper time. Mama still cooked the lunch meal and for that I was grateful. It meant I wouldn't have to first cook when I got back from school. Her letting go wasn't uniform, sometimes she would complete a full day of chores and it would be like everything was normal again and then the very next day she wouldn't even sweep. It made it difficult to plan around, so I always prepared to do everything. If she surprised me then I took it as a day off, but I stopped expecting it.

The only thing she did, consistently and without fail, was her pots. I wanted to be happy that she was starting to find the joy in that again, sometimes as she worked I'd see a smile on her face. Brief and tentative, but it was there. But I was still angry, I wished that she would help me carry the load of our family. Help Sizwe and me, because although we never admitted it, not even to each other, we were struggling. He was home more now, but instead of giving me peace it filled me with a deep sadness. He was home, because he couldn't afford not to be. There was so much to do and I just simply couldn't do it on my own and still keep up with school, so he stepped in. I saw the bags under his eyes and I saw the slight stoop in his shoulders. I saw the bags underneath my own. I really wanted to be happy for Mama, I wanted her to get better and be happy again. I wanted to not resent her, because everything Sizwe and I were doing together, was what she would have done alone. She had done it for so long, that surely it was okay for her to take a break, just for a little while. I repeated that to myself when I felt the resentment grow inside of me, I told myself it was only for a while.

I resented my father too, I resented everything about him. I wished he would just leave of his own volition. Silently in the night. I was convinced that was the only way that we could survive, if the source of Mama's pain was gone then she wouldn't be sad anymore. Then this phase would really be for a while and the three of us would slowly fix our family. We could all go to Durban, or we could all stay here. If Baba would just leave, he could even marry the beautiful woman, because she had no husband. I didn't care what people would say, I didn't care about the humiliation it would bring. They already looked at us like filth anyway. I felt it everywhere I went, the stares and the stories they shared with their eyes. I felt it at school too, with each friend who suddenly grew distant. I even saw it in the teachers' eyes, judgement or pity, sometimes both. I think Sizwe also started to stay home more so he could avoid people's judgemental eyes. I only went to the pump early in the morning before school, getting up an hour earlier to avoid people. Most times, I was already up anyway.

CHAPTER 14

Late Thursday night, I looked over to see Mama attacking a piece of chicken. I couldn't think back to anything that had made me as happy in a long time. I'd cooked the curry with onions and potatoes, adding some chilli peppers, salt and the stock cubes. It was different to how Mama made her chicken, but I was extremely proud of it. It was delicious. It actually inspired a compliment from her, "Ma, this is delicious. You're better than me now." Her words were so scarce now that each of them was precious. We sat there and I let myself get warm inside, feeling like the old times. Baba was not back yet, but it was early for him. Sizwe came back for seconds. He didn't say anything, but that was the greatest compliment he could give. Now he was sitting outside his room, slouched and enjoying the night air with his eyes closed. I was happy, I think we were all happy.

I heard him first, "Nx!" His voice coming through the fence. I could hear his footsteps as he passed close to us to get to the gate, it sounded like he had stepped on something and was cursing at it. I got up to fix him a plate, I was actually glad he was home. My curry was so good I wanted as many people to taste it, even Baba. I could see him through the kitchen door as he made the walk from the gate to their room. I stopped, because something was wrong. He was walking like the men I'd seen at social gatherings who had had too much *umqombothi.* He was staggering as though walking straight was just too much of a task for him. He was drunk. All I could do was stare. I wasn't ashamed, I wasn't angry, I was astonished. Dumbfounded. Alcohol had never been an issue in my household, nobody did it. At weddings I had seen my father take a sip as the calabash made its way around, as was customary, and he always swallowed with the face of someone who didn't enjoy the taste. Beer, he never touched. I heard him say once that it was poison that stole men from themselves. So to see him drunk was enough to put a stop to my world. Unfrozen, I ran to him, unable to stop myself. Something must have happened. My father didn't drink.

I opened the door and was slapped by the smell of him. He reeked. Worse still, he reeked of beer. He was slouched over on the old sofa, legs spread. I could see the ashy skin in the no man's land between his socks and the edge of his trousers. I walked in gingerly, because I was still unsure about what to do and because I still thought that something was wrong- that he had an explanation and he wasn't just drunk. Poking him got me a grunt and a slow opening of the eyes. Red eyes. "Amanzi". *Water*. I was close enough to smell his beer breath and my stomach turned. I studied the lump in front of me. His eyes had closed again. "Are you hungry, Baba?" He nodded but his eyes remained closed. I was glad he could eat, I'd heard that spicy food helped with drunkenness. I doubted he would even taste my curry.

In the kitchen Mama had not moved, but she had finished her chicken. I didn't say anything. I had nothing to say. From where she was sitting she had seen him stagger in too. What was there to say? I poured the glass of water and placed it next to his food on the tray. Mama was looking at me, her expression unreadable. I took Baba's food to him. I had to poke him again, harder this time to get him to get up. He reached for the water and drank like a man possessed. His eyes pleaded for more, so I took the glass from him and handed him his food. Then I handed him the spoon.

My brother had woken up and on my way back to the kitchen I was met with the questions on his face. I shrugged. What was there to say? I was going to fill up the glass but when I walked into the kitchen Mama handed me a jug instead.

She still had not moved. I filled the jug and took it and the empty glass back to Baba. The food was almost gone from his plate. He must have been starving because I had not been gone for that long. I poured the water into the glass and handed the glass to him. Again, he drank thirstily. I refilled the glass again and this time he drank three sips before putting it on the tray next to his food. He would be okay now, I could leave. I turned to go back to my room, closing the door behind me. He coughed and I stopped, turning to see what he needed. "Baba?" I heard a kindness in my own voice that had been missing for a while.

"This is delicious," he said. I closed the door gently behind me.

Sizwe walked in as Mama was tending the fire under the kettle. We sat there, the three of us, silently drinking our tea. I had school the next day and I should have been getting ready for bed. Instead I poured a second cup of tea, as did my brother and as did Mama.

"Baba is a drunk." I said it to nobody in particular, and nobody in particular responded to me. Was he a drunk? Or was he just drunk? How many times must a person be drunk before they are definitely a drunk? Was it possible to go from never drinking to being a drunk in a single instance? "Baba is drunk, tonight." Again I said it to nobody in particular, but just in case somebody was listening, I wanted them to know that I had been wrong the first time. He was simply drunk. He was not a drunk, because we all knew he hated alcohol.

I looked at Sizwe and I saw the devil in his face. His jaw was clenched, his entire body was clenched. Something black was seeping out of him, I could feel it. It was past anger. Anger felt red and he had reached the level black. There were no words in me to share with him, nothing I could say to calm him, nothing I wanted to say to calm him down. I wasn't frightened by his aura, in fact it excited me. He had enough of it within him to project what I knew we were all feeling. I left them alone then, my brother to seethe in peace and my mother to watch him.

I knew I wouldn't sleep, not until it was almost morning, but at least I was alone. I didn't want to think about it, any of it and at least when I was alone I had more of a chance of succeeding at that. When I looked at Sizwe, or my mother I saw the story of our lives on their faces. The lines on Mama's face and the bags under Sizwe's eyes. Each of them told a story I didn't want to hear anymore. I could only imagine what I looked like. When I looked at myself now it was only to make sure there was nothing on my face. I heard feet coming towards my hut, Mama's feet. Nobody else walked that lightly. She knocked and I opened. She was carrying a mattress, a sheet and a blanket. I understood and I helped her make her bed. I wouldn't be alone, but at least she wouldn't be with him. As Mama lay down and I blew out the candle I thought of our sleepovers at Aunty Sli's house. How different that had been, playing the memories in my mind felt like spying on the lives of people we didn't really know. They certainly weren't us. At some point we fell asleep, together, but apart.

I didn't go to school the next day. I was up on time, earlier in fact because Mama naturally got up before sunrise, and her movements woke me. I still had an hour before I had to get up for school, but my body wouldn't fall asleep again. So I got up and went to the kitchen where I knew I'd find her. She was making the first fire of the day. "Good morning, Mama" she looked up and gave me a real smile and my face reacted by smiling back. That was when I decided on not going to school. That smile we shared before the sun came up gave me the feeling that this would be a good day and we hadn't had one of those in a while. I wasn't going to waste it at school. I went outside to go fetch the water Mama would use to make tea. I set the jug on the table, smelling the ash as Mama revived some old coals that were still hot from last night. Her fingers were a mix of black from the dead coals and white from the ash. All the buckets were full and the dishes were all clean, because I had washed them after dinner. If, like today, we had enough water, then early morning was my favorite time of the day because it was one of the few times when there was nothing that I needed to do. I spent my morning watching the sunrise.

I stood leaned against the wall of Sizwe's room, looking as far away as I could see. It was nice to watch the sunrise, to be reminded of the great beauty of something I saw so often that I stopped seeing it. I had forgotten how gradually and dramatically the sky changed, how spectacular the light show was. That short window where the sky isn't any one distinct colour, but is all of them all at once, distinctly. I saw black give way to red and amber, orange and yellow and then slowly into the clear white of morning. I found myself smiling into the distance, once again cementing the knowledge that I was definitely not going to school today. I felt as though the sky was smiling back at me. That was two smiles in one morning, that was a clear sign.

I turned to go back to the kitchen, it was time for tea. I walked in to find the water already boiled, and Mama sitting on a chair with her steaming cup. She had laid out a cup for me and placed her used tea bag inside. We had always used one tea bag twice so that the tea would last longer and over time I had developed the taste for weak tea. With Mama's pots we didn't have to worry about sharing tea bags anymore, but my tastes were already ruined. If I was forced to use a fresh tea bag then I would seep it for only a short time, so the tea would still be weak. While this gave me the taste I like, it always felt like I was being wasteful. So where I could I would wait to make my tea last, reusing a bag. Mama was the only one who had caught on to me and where she could she always stored her used tea bag for me. "Thank you, Mama," I beamed at her, grateful for the little things.

It was time for me to be getting ready for school and I couldn't keep my plan to myself anymore. I set my tea down and looked at her.

"I'm not going to school today, Mama." She looked back at me, "Hmmm?" was her only response. But it wasn't a sharp 'Hmmm' like she would give if she meant, "What?!", it was soft and questioning as though she was saying, "And why is that, Ma?" With my calculations of Mama's tone done in my head, I proceeded.

"I would just like to stay home today. I feel very tired." Tired. That was not even on the planet of excuses that Mama would have accepted for missing school before. She had consistently stressed the importance of school to me and unless I was dying and physically unable to move, then I was going to school. Being tired was not an excuse for anything. I don't even think I was *allowed* to be tired, ever. But that was before...everything. I had a feeling that being tired had a new meaning and depth for all of us now. That being tired went past physical fatigue into something more dangerous. I had a feeling that Mama was tired too and she would let me be tired at home. She took a deep breath and let it out loudly and then she shrugged her shoulders.

"Okay, but you're going to catch up on everything this weekend and you're going back to school on Monday. And no more missing school after that."

It was about two hours before Sizwe walked into the kitchen to make his tea. He gave me a funny look that screamed, 'You shouldn't be here,' but all he said was "good morning" directed at both Mama and me. It was weird being at home when I should have been at school but it was also nice. Nothing exciting was happening but all the normal things felt like they were new. Like making jam sandwiches to go with our tea. We stayed there, enjoying the morning and each other's company. We were all carefully situated in our bubble, fully aware and perfectly content. We didn't bring it up. It wasn't until he walked outside and we all saw him that we felt the bubble deflate. The image of my father was the thorn that popped it. He had changed into home clothes, the faded khaki shorts, and a faded white t-shirt. He was standing just outside his door, facing forward so that all we saw was his side. He had a glass of water in his hand and he would bring it to his lips every so often. I remembered the smell of beer on his breath from last night. I wondered if that water was the same one that I poured. He was standing there a long time, and in that long time he didn't turn his head toward us once. He walked past the door, then, turned the other way and disappeared from sight. I saw the toothbrush that had been hidden from view before, he was going to brush his teeth behind the house.

I looked around me, trying to study the faces. Mama looked distant, she was looking at where Baba had been standing and then she slowly turned and sipped her tea. Sizwe had that clench in his jaw again and something else. It wasn't the black seething that I had seen last night, it was something less vile, less sharp. He looked annoyed. Our eyes met and I wondered what I looked like. The issue of Baba's tea was now being silently discussed. I could not remember a time when either myself or Mama had not woken Baba up with his tea. Often times he would still be in bed, awake, but still in bed and he would instruct me to leave it on the table and I knew he would get up after I left. Other times he would already be awake, sitting with a newspaper between his legs.

The one constant thing was that his tea was always brought to him before he ever thought to venture outside. It was something so standard, so ingrained, that it was never discussed. It just was. So to see him walk outside before this happened indicated a shift. It was an action so small that those who didn't know the inner working of our family would have never picked up on it. But, we knew the inner workings of our family and Baba's kingly position had just taken a subtle fall. That he had gone outside before he had been served, meant that he had at least for a second been unsure about whether or not we would do it. I think he went outside to make sure we saw him, in an effort to remind us of his position. He went outside to make sure we saw him and were reminded of all the ways we were expected to show him our love and servitude. Something we had always given him freely without questioning.

We watched as Baba walked back into his room. He had played his card and now he would wait. It was our move. Mama shoved a small log into the fire, sending sparks flying. I watched as she then picked out a small splinter and began to clean her nails. So Mama was out. That was a message as clear as day that she could not be bothered about Baba, or his tea. If someone was going to serve him, it would not be her. So I turned my attention to my brother, perhaps he would do it in an attempt to stabilise things and restore balance. He was looking at me, I knew he was playing the same game in his head. He got up and poured the boiling water into his half-full cup. He then added a new tea bag, sugar and milk. He sat down slowly and sipped his tea. He looked at me as he sipped, his message clear. He had no intention of serving Baba either. It was up to me. Mama didn't make eye contact, I think it was her way of telling me that what I decided to do was my decision. Even my brother had chosen a spot outside to focus on. It was my turn to decide if I was on this side or that, if I would detach myself from Baba as well.

All of my movements felt like an out of body experience. As I set the tray down and began to prepare his breakfast I felt the weight of the room. I felt their eyes on my back. I felt what they wouldn't say, that I was weak for not taking this stand with them. I agreed with them too, Baba did not deserve to be served like royalty. He didn't deserve my kindness and I wanted to stand with my mother and brother in solidarity. But, I couldn't. I was as angry and as disappointed in him as they were, but the truest part of me wouldn't allow me to do what they did. He was still my father and even if he didn't deserve it, I was too ill versed in disrespecting him that it felt physically impossible to start now.

I wanted justice for Mama, but depriving him of breakfast felt grossly inadequate. As I moved through making his breakfast, I realized something else. Sizwe and Mama were not mad at me. I think deep down that my action was what bound us even tighter. I think they hadn't done it because they knew that I would have felt I had to. I wasn't ready for everything to be completely smashed. We were failing as a family, we all knew it, but if I joined in with Mama and Sizwe then it would be all too obvious. It would be all too definite. I made Baba his tea to try and preserve us somehow. I think deep down Sizwe and Mama were glad I served Baba his tea because they wanted to preserve us too. The tray was heavy as I walked out of the kitchen.

I put the tea on the table and then stood there, looking at him. He was on the sofa, the same one I had left him on last night. He sat with his eyes glued to the newspaper in his hand. I looked at him for so long he pulled it down to look at me. I would have never stared at my father before, staring was rude. But I was overcome by an intense need to look at the man, to *see* him. Who was he, really? All the things I knew about my father revolved around a schedule of some kind, a schedule set up around serving him. I knew when he woke up because that was when I served his breakfast. I knew what foods he didn't like because I'd see them still on the plate when I fetched his dishes. I knew when to start cooking certain foods because meals were set around when we anticipated him home. He liked his food hot, and we didn't have a microwave. I thought of all the millions of tiny ways that Mama served him every single day and the millions of ways she had taught me to do the same, but who were we serving? I looked at him so long I knew I was making him uncomfortable. I think before he would have shouted at me, I couldn't even be sure, because I would have never done this before. I searched his eyes for answers, but I got nothing back. It felt like he was looking through me. I had seen that look on Mama before. I left him then, I didn't want to be there anymore.

I left the room with the dishes from last night and then fetched him his water so he could bathe. That was it, until lunchtime when I would serve him his food again and return later to fetch those dishes. Sizwe had left the kitchen and Mama was getting ready to make *uphuthu*. I made myself another cup of tea. I watched my mother as she moved around, and I let those movements lull me into a daydream. "Hmmm." The way she said it made me look up. It was amused with the slightest hint of a threat to it. I followed her gaze and then I understood. Looking through the window I saw Baba walking to the gate. I saw him walk through it and I watched him until I couldn't see him anymore. He was dressed the way he always was when he went to the court meetings, so I told myself he was going to work. I looked through the window again to see my brother. He was standing in front of his door, staring at the gate. Staring after my father. Sizwe turned back around and disappeared into his room, closing the door behind him.

We went about our day like that, in a state of pleasant cohabitation. After the initial anger that his leaving brought that is, because regardless of what we told ourselves, none of us believed he was going to work. And he might've been, but some things can never be overlooked once you've done them. Now whenever he left home, we would question where he was going.

Him leaving home would always bring up feelings of anger tied to the disrespect he had shown our family. Although, after that initial anger wore off and this happened quicker than I thought it would, we were free to bask in the ease that only existed when he wasn't there. We hated to see him leave but loved it when he was gone. I was falling in love with the world that was starting to exist between the three of us. There was something almost joyful in our silent spaces. I felt safe in them, a wonderful feeling when you haven't felt safe in a while.

Mama cooked *imfino* to complement her mealie meal. This was my absolute favorite meal, it was the same leafy vegetable that Aunty Sli said she couldn't find where she lived and had to substitute with spinach. I wondered how they were, I knew they didn't know anything of what was happening in our lives because Mama hadn't phoned Aunty Sli in ages. I wondered how much Mama would have shared if she had. I hoped their life was as happy as I remembered. Sizwe loved this meal too and I looked up in time to see him cleaning the last of it off his plate. Mama looked pleased, at ease.

After lunch, she stretched out and took a nap. I had seen her do this before, but always after everything was packed away and dishes were done and she had completed some task or another. It always seemed like she napped as a reward for herself when she felt like she had earned it. Her sleeping like this straight after lunch struck me as odd, because it wasn't *earned*. She had just taken it because she wanted it. I was inspired at once and without thinking about it too long I pulled up close to her and took my sleep too. I heard Sizwe pile all the dirty dishes in the container we washed them in before he walked out. I knew he was going to lay down as well. It was something he always did, a part of a routine, but for Mama and me it was so much more.

We got up after the hottest part of the day, me first. I left Mama to further enjoy her nap as I started on the dishes. Sizwe came in a while later and seemed to have read my mind when he revived the fire. It was tea time. As we sat down to enjoy our steaming cups of tea, I tried to think of things to say to my brother that he might find clever. I wanted to talk to him, the way I imagined brothers and sisters did. Not when they were forced to do it, like we had been by life. Not to discuss the pressing issues of our family dynamic, but just simply to talk. Like you would to a friend, about things that they enjoyed talking about and that you enjoyed talking about too. I flipped through the things I could ask him about, like his drawings. I could ask about the lioness and what he had been thinking when he drew it, or maybe even about the posters that he had stuck up. I could ask who the girl with the long black hair and short white dress was. The idea made me flush and I thought better of it. It must have shown on my face, because just then he looked at me. "What?" he asked me in his cool, calm voice. I shook my head. I was not bringing that up.

It turned out that he had been wanting to talk to me too. "Khosi, why didn't you go to school?" I was confused for a second. Not because I didn't understand the question, but more because it was now so late in the day that I had naturally assumed we were all past this.

"I was just really tired." He was quiet for a while, but he was looking at me. When he spoke he had the tone of someone who had wanted to say so much more, but decided to say something else instead. Something easier to digest.

"Just please don't miss any more days, okay?" He looked at me long enough to make it clear that he expected an answer. I nodded. I knew he was serious and I meant it. Sizwe had completed matric two years ago, but his marks hadn't been too great. I had never asked him what he wanted to do after school, or with his life in general. He had just sort of fell into going to 'work' with Baba, because he had the time and Baba enjoyed teaching him everything he knew.

I had assumed he would do what Baba did when he knew enough. His involvement had started off slowly, with him only dedicating certain weekends to it, but gradually he had gotten more and more involved with the courts, this year especially. I knew his grooming was getting more serious when he and Baba went away for the cow case. When Mama and I sold our pots for the first time. I smiled at the memory. Sizwe had come back more grown up and he had continue to grow up before my very eyes. His relationship with Baba had really been under strain since then, I couldn't remember the last time that I saw him dressed in his good pants and white shirt. I felt a pang of guilt as I thought about the future he may have been forced to jeopardise.

Baba came home as we were eating dinner. Sizwe heard him first, hissing things under his breath as his voice neared us. I dropped my fork. I could actually hear from where I sat that he was drunk. Just like that, my appetite vanished. Perhaps because Baba had come home drunk last night, this should have been less shocking. And yet, because he had done it yesterday was precisely why it was so shocking. Yesterday he had been drunk, but by all accounts tonight he was a drunk. I couldn't believe it. Was this really happening? He didn't even like the taste. Was this all to prove a point? But what point was that? That he could hurt us? Was this punishment for this morning? If so, it still didn't explain last night. I mulled it all over as Baba was getting closer, until he was in the yard making his way to their bedroom. He wrestled with the doorknob, which was never locked and staggered in, finally having figured it out.

The silence between the three of us in the kitchen had changed. It was no longer comfortable, it was heavy. Laden with my father's drunkenness. The calm faces I'd seen earlier, the faces that were able to ignore Baba and his actions were gone. In their place were faces that were very much affected by his every action. Mama's hand had flown to her mouth when she first heard his drunken grunts and it stayed there. The look of utter disbelief. Sizwe's expression was similar, but his disbelief was heavily interwoven with pure anger. I was in shock, staring from their faces down to my fork. I think we were all shocked for the same reason. Baba had called our bluff.

In a twisted game of silent dynamics, he had come out victorious. He was excluded from the bubble of our love, a bubble created to keep him out and celebrate life liberated from him. But it's mere existence was his victory. We were, all of us, so afraid of him to truly do anything to let him know just how upset we were. We cowered together and pretended it made us brave, but that drunk man was still controlling our lives. His actions were still the most important thing and we existed only to react to him. He was the culprit and yet we were the ones shamed, we were the ones who avoided the outside world while he engaged with it to the point of drunkenness. I think in that moment we finally woke up. We opened our eyes to see the blatant stare of his uncaring, his remorselessness. It boiled within us, and we felt the hurt. Fresh and anew, deeper than before.

We were still engulfed in the silence, each of us with our own thoughts. There was so much swimming around in my head, but there was one thing that would come back again and again. One thing I was sure of. I would not serve that man. He could starve for all I cared. Mama stood up and left the kitchen. I don't know why, but she walked straight to where he was. I think she needed to see him, to see for herself. As she left a look crossed between Sizwe and me, a look that didn't need words. Something bad was going to happen and we needed to protect Mama. He nodded. *I've got it.* He was standing in the door, something we were never allowed to do because it was rude, and he was looking at Mama. I was standing by the window, also looking at Mama. She was outside the door looking in, so we could see her, but not Baba. She didn't talk, she didn't say a thing. She just cried. A soft weeping that was periodically interrupted by sharp intakes of breath. I didn't know what to do, so I cried too. I could feel Sizwe watching me, but he didn't move. I have no clue how long we stood like that, crying and looking. I wondered what Baba was doing, was he looking at Mama? Was he conscious?

I only stopped crying when Mama stopped. She wiped her face on her faded green pinafore and walked back towards us. She didn't come back to the kitchen where Sizwe and I were standing like soldiers, instead she went directly to my room. She was sleeping with me again tonight. I saw the lamp go on, and I knew she was making her bed. Sizwe threw a log in the fire and I prepared the cup. Mama needed tea. I watched him pour the entire jug of water into the kettle and he was right to. We needed tea too. I decided to retire early, as soon as the water boiled I would make our tea and then Mama and I would beg for sleep. Maybe she would want to talk to me, and if she did then I would be there. She probably wouldn't, but still I would be there.

The kettle whistling brought me back and I stood to pour the tea. Sizwe had prepared his cup too, a white one with a guitar on it. I had no idea where he had gotten it, but it had always been his cup. As I poured the boiling water into the cup I saw him move from the corner of my eye. "Aaah!'. 'Aaaaaaaaaah!" I returned my attention to the boiling water I was pouring and watched it hit my foot in slow motion. I had looked up at my brother, distracted by his sudden movement and now my three smallest toes were burning. I put the kettle down, instantly searching for cold water to pour over them. My brother didn't even offer any help, he didn't say anything and as I was about to curse him out for making me pour his stupid tea, I realized he wasn't even in the room. Had nobody seen me burn?

I hobbled to the door, the throbbing in my foot getting so intense I was sure I could *hear* it. There he was, standing with his back to me. I was about to say something to get his attention, but something about his stance made me stop. That's when I heard Baba and saw him too. He was about half way between his flat and my hut, blocked from most of my view by Sizwe's body. I shifted so I could see him clearly, his white shirt unbuttoned all the way down. His belt was unbuckled but still on, the way he did when he sat down on the floor. Normally he opened his top button too, but not this time. Sizwe stood between the kitchen and my hut, he and Baba facing each other. I think my brother hoped that the threat of his body would send Baba away. I think I hoped so too.

I could barely make out the things that he was trying to say, but his hand kept on gesturing for Sizwe to go away. He edged closer to my hut, one gingerly step at a time. I don't believe he was at all afraid, just straining under the load of his drunk body. My heart raced, and soon it even drowned out the throbbing in my foot. Baba was so close I could hear him now.

"Where is my wife?" The slur in all his words sounded vile to me and I wanted him to shut up. He persisted, repeating himself over and over in the way that only drunk people can.

Mama opened the door and my feet developed their own brain. I was outside, right next to my brother who had moved even closer to my hut. He stretched out his hand without looking at me, blocking me from moving. *I've got this*. His eyes were fixed on Baba. Baba saw Mama and I think his feet developed their own brain too. He ran forward, and it seemed lighting fast for a man who had been taking one painful step at a time just seconds before. Everything happened so fast after that. He got to Mama before Sizwe did, and I saw her wince as his hand gripped her arm.

"Ngiyeke!" *Leave me*. I saw Mama's shoulders shaking as she tried to get free of him and I saw Baba stagger slightly backwards. He wasn't sure on his feet, the alcohol having robbed him of balance.

"You are my wife!" He slurred loudly as he regained his footing. "I am your husband!" He said it, but not necessarily to her. I think he was telling all of us. "Woza!" *Come*. He grabbed her with even more force and Mama's body lunged forward. I jumped forward, as far as I could manage with my foot. I was determined to push past my brother, if he wasn't going to do anything then I would. Then Sizwe moved. With the might of an army, or perhaps with just their anger. My father was still slightly taller than Sizwe, but only by a fraction. I forgot that as I watched my brother tower above my father. First he pushed him away and my father fell back, letting go of Mama as he did so. I ran to her, wanting to be close. My father was struggling to get up so my brother dragged him up.

"Wenzani?" *What are you doing*? It was my brother, holding my father up by the collar, dangerously close to him. *Wenzani*? He asked him again. I could tell that he was angry, getting angrier still with every passing second. I saw the black that I had seen seeping out of him return to him. I clung to Mama as he asked Baba once again, '*Wenzani*?' said so low it was barely above a whisper. I averted my eyes, my entire body knowing what was coming next. I should have closed my ears too, because I will never forget the sound of my brother's fists on my father's jaw.

My eyes flew open and even though I didn't want to watch, I was transfixed. I couldn't look away. I saw my brother turn into an animal, pounding my father's flesh like it could feel no pain. I heard my father's muffled cries, his arms and legs trying desperately to get him free. But my brother had him pinned to a wall, pinned against my hut, and he was not letting go. I saw my brothers dark skin make dents on my father's slightly lighter skin. His fists landed where they willed, on Baba's face, his stomach, his sides. I saw the shirt that used to be white, turn red, soiled with blood and dirt. We were in that moment for an eternity. It was a moment we all shared, all of us as a family.

Sizwe continued until he didn't, the rest of us knowing he was the only one who could stop himself. In the end he was panting, Baba's face still close to his and I heard him say it one more time. '*Wenzani*?' His face was streaming tears and his eyes were so vacant I didn't know if he knew he was still saying it. I didn't know if he knew he was still holding Baba, I didn't know if he was *there*. Mama pulled herself gently off me, and walked over to her son. She grabbed him gently and lowered his head to her chest, and he cried. Something deep, long and loud. I knew he was back then, back from wherever his mind had taken him as he beat Baba to a pulp and he was free to cry for everything. For what he had kept inside, for all that he had done, for all that he had not done. I think he cried for Baba too and for me and Mama. I looked at Baba's face. I could hardly recognise it, but I saw the tears that flowed from his almost completely shut eyes and down his cheeks.

Mama held Sizwe until he stopped crying and after that until he stopped shaking. She walked him to bed and lay him down. She wiped clean his tear-stained face and bloody hands. She covered him with a blanket and put out the lamp in his room. She returned and did the same for Baba. I stood transfixed at the door of my hut until she came back. She walked past me to the kitchen and I followed. I should have known she would be making tea. She looked at my foot, rubbed a white cream on it and wrapped it in a piece of cloth. We didn't talk. After tea we went to bed in my hut. Instead of climbing into my own bed, I went into hers. She scooted over and although we slept silently, she held me close.

...

The next day was Saturday and I was glad. I would have been forced to break my promise to Sizwe if it was a school day. I didn't see Baba at all that day, not once. Mama went in to check on him from time to time and she had resumed the role of serving him his meals. She was light. Her movements were easy and the air around her floated. It was so refreshing after the heaviness I had gotten used to seeing her carry. She checked in on Sizwe too, another one who kept himself confined to his room the entire day. I went in with her the one time, but I sensed he didn't want me around. Mama was okay, but not me. Not yet. I wondered how long it would take before they said a word to each other. Flashbacks of the night before had been playing in my head all day and I knew it was the same for all of us.

Mama and I got all our chores done quickly, all while looking after them. It was easier to take care of them when they were confined. We were left to our own devices so long as we provided food and drink; and water to bathe. I wondered how long they would keep this up. They had to face each other, that was the only way to get past this, and nobody could facilitate on their behalves, it had to be them. I thought of Sizwe's fists on Baba's face and I shuddered. Everything changed last night and I wasn't sure any of us truly knew the extent to which it had. That morning when he had walked outside before he was served his breakfast, something had shifted subtly. Last night, something had also shifted and nothing about it had been subtle. But, what did it all mean? What would happen when my father, sober of alcohol saw my brother, sober of anger? What was he saying to my mother as she nursed his face and body, cleaning the marks left on him by his only son? Was he embarrassed? Was he angry? There wasn't a second that my mind wasn't plagued by these thoughts. Thoughts that only gave rise to other thoughts, so that by the time I went to bed I collapsed on my bed, exhausted.

Sizwe came out the next day. He came at breakfast and outside of greeting us both he didn't speak. That was alright. What was there to say? I was happy simply to have him with us again. I'd steal glances of him from time to time, when he wasn't looking. He looked smaller now, like he always was, not like the huge man I saw him turn into last night. His hands looked soft, like those used to make tea and tend to Mama's fire, and not like the giant fists used to beat up our father. I didn't know my brother had that person inside of him, that bigger version of himself that he could transform into when he needed to. It made me feel both scared and safe around him, where before I had not been aware of any feeling. Did *he* feel safe and scared around himself now?

Baba came out in the afternoon, just as the sun was setting. He sat on the small bench on the veranda. As it went down the sun turned his skin golden, and I felt something soft and warm for him. I wanted to make him feel something soft and warm too, something that would make him want to forget all the trouble of the past and want only to stay in its warmth. He pulled the harmonica out of his pocket. I had not seen him do that in what felt like years. I had forgotten that he owned one, that he had ever played. My brother was watching him, with an expression I couldn't quite read. The music travelled, in beautiful waves to us and then around us. Mama, who was outside, stopped when it reached her ears, stopped in mid step. She turned sharply to see where it was coming from and when she saw Baba play she smiled. We shared the moment, in silence and stillness. Transported by Baba's music to a place past where we were. And then the moment ended. Mama put her foot down and continued to the line to fetch the now dry laundry, but as she turned back around she was still smiling and Baba was still playing.

My brother asked to take Baba's dinner to him after Mama had set the tray. I searched his face, my eyes throwing questions at him like daggers but he ignored them all. He gave me a look that was calm and strong. *I've got this.* Mama was also searching his face and he gave her a look that was kind and soft. She handed him the tray and wiped her hands on her apron as he walked out the kitchen, dishes clinking with each step. I watched him too, all up until he disappeared into Baba's open door. He had moved inside, still playing his harmonica. Mama and I shared a look as we heard the music stop abruptly. I got to my feet and Mama motioned for me to sit back down. She sat down too, but I could tell all of her was in that room with them. Sizwe and my father were in there for fifteen minutes that felt like years to us. He walked back into the kitchen, looked at us both and he smiled. He didn't say anything, but he's always been the kind of person you could read like a book. He was lighter, whatever weight he had been carrying he had left at Baba's door. He would never tell us what they spoke about and we would never ask. It was a secret Mama and I were happy to let them keep. We settled down for our night time tea.

CHAPTER 15

May 2012

I went back to school feeling like a new person. The lightness that was making its way around my family finally had finally made its way to me. Not even the side glances I caught could touch me, I didn't care about them anymore. Instead, I thought of my father's face, drunk that first night when I carried his food to him. I thought of it bloody the next night, my brother's shoulder blades sticking out as he held Baba's face in his hands. I thought of his face as I'd seen it this morning before rushing to school. It was still bruised badly, but it was healing. I thought of my brother making me promise to not miss school. I thought of the smile on Mama's face when she heard Baba's music. I thought about all these things as I hobbled through the day, my burnt foot still healing, in absolute bliss.

Mama moved back in with Baba two nights

later. She said nothing about it and neither did I. She was also back to her pots, and I was once again in love with watching her do it. She got back into it with the same vigor as before and I did my best to keep up. It was the start of May, which meant I had a little over a month before I had to really start focusing on my mid-year exams. Mama never let me question even for a second that school came first.

As I focused more on school, she continued to sell and with new vigor. She sold three out of four weekends and used the last one to build up her inventory. Mama used her time like it was running out and it seemed like she never stopped. As school got more intense and teachers called on extra Saturday classes I stopped going to town with her. Uncle Muzi and the girls were also being taken up by school so that only Aunty Sli came to sell with her, which I knew suited her just fine. Sizwe refound his own schedule, spending most of his weekends with Baba again. We would watch them leave, white shirts freshly pressed and I knew Mama felt the same tinge of pride that I did.

June went by in a wink, a blur of study and exams. On that chilly Thursday when I finally put my pen down after my last exam it couldn't have been sooner. I had a month and a half of holidays and I thought I would sleep through all of it. I came home to the smell of Mama's chicken stew welcoming me from the gate.

"Well done, Ma. You did it!" she beamed at me. She always cooked this meal for me when I came back with my report card, as congratulations for great results. In the last few years, she had stopped needing to see my report card, something I was very proud of.

"What if I failed, Ma?" I asked her jokingly.

"Then your chicken would have died for nothing." She laughed, wiping her dry and clean hands on her pinafore.

"Silly girl, woz' odla." *Come and eat.* That's when I told her about my great plan for the holiday. "Mama, please don't wake me up tomorrow. Even if the sun is right over me, and don't wake me up the next day either, I think I'm going to sleep for the entire month." She looked at me cunningly, a smile playing on her lips, "Well I guess I'll have to find somebody else to come sell with me on Saturday then." She knew she had me.

All my fatigue seemed to leave after just one night of solid sleep, and although I wouldn't admit it, by Friday I was dying to do something. Aunty Sli and the rest of them would all be there to meet us tomorrow and I couldn't wait. I was more excited for the sleepover, even though it was only until Sunday. "But Mama, I'm on holiday, why can't we stay a bit longer. Just a week? Please Mama?" I pleaded but she was unmoved, gently and firmly letting me know that was not going to happen. "We'll be back on Sunday Ma,

0

0

0

0

we have so much to do here, don't we?" I didn't know that we did, but I knew to quit while I was ahead.

We were all a flurry of excitement and beaming faces as we hugged our hellos at the bus stop. As the girls and I walked to the taxi rank where we would meet the car carrying our parents and the pots, we chatted animatedly. "Mama did it last week, she should be giving me a new style tomorrow, but I think I'll keep this one for another week." I could see why, I looked at the style Zinzi was talking about, pulling her head closer to me to see it even better. Somehow Aunty Sli had braided her hair into diamond shapes that lay flat all over her head. *Diamonds.* I had never seen anything like it and was failing to figure it out. Zandi came to my aid, finding my shock amusing.

"It's not that hard, I can't do it perfectly yet, but it's really not that hard." We all stopped now as she took over pulling Zinzi's head in a different direction for further public analyzation. "You see," Zandi ran her fingers along the one slanted direction of plaits that ran along her sister's head, "she started by braiding these ones down, but leaving enough hair for the other direction later." The braids looked likes lines and lines of '/'. "And then she went in the opposite direction, using that leftover hair to complete the shape of the boxes you see." Zandi now ran her fingers along the '\' way. When she explained and as I watched her demonstrate it, I could see how it made sense, but I still had no idea how you would actually *do* it. "It's really beautiful. I wish I had hair just for that style."

We sold well, the day going by much faster than I thought possible. We rotated around the stall that Mama and Aunty Sli were positioned at. Our own second stall was smaller than theirs because we had less inventory and our stock was all gone a little after lunchtime. So we made our way back to them, making a competition of seeing who could bring in the most customers. I'd look up from time to time to see Mama and Aunty Sli deep in conversation, worried looks on their faces. Sometimes a sympathetic one on Aunty Sli's and other times a smile on Mama's. I was grateful for the friend that Mama had in Aunty Sli, that they had in each other.

"Why are you leaving so early?" Zandi asked the question, and although I had no answer for it, the dismay on her face made me feel warm.

"I don't know, Mama said. But the holiday is so long, I'm sure we'll be back to visit you guys before it's over. Unless you guys are going somewhere?" I asked, remembering their church camp that last time.

"No, we'll be home. I have holiday classes for basically all my subjects. Maybe it's a good thing you won't be here, I'd be so jealous that Zinzi got to spend time with you all day while I slaved at school." Her gentle laugh was contagious. That made sense, Zandi was in matric and if I was having Saturday classes in grade eleven for my exams I could only imagine what she had.

As we cooked dinner and the grown-ups and Musa enjoyed tea and biscuits, we caught up on even more things. Zandi was wearing a long red skirt. It had big black buttons that ran all the way down the front and it sat comfortably on her waist. I thought it was simply the most beautiful single piece of clothing I had ever seen. I enjoyed how it moved with her as she spoke, and had to remind myself to focus on her face as I interrogated her about the future, "So where have you applied for university?" I had been thinking about my own education more lately. Now that we had been selling so much and had managed to save most of the money, university started to feel like a real option that we could maybe afford. I knew I wanted to go to university and get a degree. However, I still had no real idea about what I wanted to study, and maybe talking to Zandi about it would help. I knew she loved this topic because her face lit up instantly. It was evident too that Zinzi was tired of this topic because she instead rolled her eyes and focused on the butternut she was peeling.

"Well, I've applied to four places; UKZN, DUT, Mangosuthu, and UJ. Baba says the more the better, but he thinks I'll get in everywhere. I applied for scholarships at all of them, so if I'm granted one at any of them then that's where I'll go. I have provisional acceptance to all of them so far, with varying scholarship options for each, so that's good. Baba also applied for three bursaries for me and I'm still waiting to hear back from them. That would really be nice if I got one of them because then I would have also have a job waiting for me after I graduated. We should know by September. I just have to make sure that I maintain my marks when we take the final exams." I saw the worry on her face as she said that last part. I knew she would be fine though. I was impressed, I had no idea she had so many options, that she could have so many options.

"What exactly have you applied for?" Zinzi was done peeling the butternut so she started chopping it.

"I don't know. My mind changes almost every day, but I have narrowed it down to just a few options. At UKZN and Mangosuthu I applied for nursing or teaching. At UJ, I applied for business management and at DUT I applied for television production and the bursaries that Baba applied to for me are all for electrical engineering." I had no idea what to say. I didn't know what half of those professions did for sure, but I did know that they were so far apart it was difficult to think the same person had chosen them. I wanted to ask her what she would do if she got in everywhere, and every place offered her a scholarship or bursary. What would she choose if she was absolutely forced to, but it was clear that she wasn't ready to answer that question so I let it go.

"UJ is in Johannesburg, that is so far. Would Aunty Sli and Uncle Muzi let you go?" She shrugged, "I guess so, Baba knows I've applied there and he hasn't said anything. I think they'd prefer it if I stayed close to home though. I think I would too, I've never been that far away from home and then to go and *live* there. I don't know...but its Jo'burg. Imagine me, living in the big city." She threw her head back with the back of her hand on her forehead in an overly dramatic fashion and I couldn't help laughing. "I think the city would suit you just fine." I turned to assess my rice, "Musa got so big," I said looking at Zinzi. I knew she was dying to talk about something else.

Goodbyes after lunch were short and sweet, but heartfelt. We had been to the early church service and I marveled at all the people who showed up in their Sunday best. The little girls were my favorite, in their white dresses with matching socks and shoes. The day seemed to be filled with good spirits and it was nice to be happy, around happy people. Mama and I rode in the back of the van as Uncle Muzi drove us to town. I thought that was incredibly sweet but unnecessary. He would have had to borrow the car for another day, where Mama and I could have easily taken a taxi to town. We didn't have any pots to carry. Still, it was nice to ride in a car so I kept my evaluation to myself.

We were in the car for five minutes before I knew we weren't going to town, because town was in the other direction to the turn that Uncle Muzi had just made. I looked at Mama to see if she had noticed it too, but she gave me nothing. She was calmly looking out the window. So I looked out the window too, he probably just had to do something first. We drove past houses that were different than the cookie-cutter five-room government houses where they lived. These houses were bigger and with bigger yards, and they didn't all look the same. We drove past a container that served as a public phone booth, like the one we had back home. There were lots more of them here, I'd seen four already just in the 10-minute ride we had taken.

We were nearing a school, I could see the big sports ground through the fence. There was a netball court too, with a concrete base and I could see the markings clearly from here. The white lines that divide it into three sections, the half circles that marked from where you could take a shot. I thought about the netball court in my school. It was the same hard, brown earth that covered the rest of the school, grass failing to survive the non-stop daily tramplings of so many feet. We made the markings ourselves, drawing them every so often during each game because we had stomped them to oblivion. The poles were new though, the government had given every school in the area new poles at the beginning of last year. I wondered if the girls here had as much fun playing on their nice court as we did on ours. I wondered if the concrete drew blood if they fell on it. I wondered who would win if our team played theirs and which court would be fairer? I was thinking this when I felt us stop. Uncle Muzi got out of the car and walked over to us. He opened the back door, both the top one and the bottom one which meant he expected us to get out. This time when I looked at Mama she was smiling. I got the feeling that she had known exactly where we were going the entire time.

Standing next to her outside the car, I read the big sign above the school gate. "Khombindlela High School," this was the school where Uncle Muzi taught. I looked at him and he was looking at me, a faint smile on his lips. I started to feel the strange, uncomfortable feeling you get when you realize you're the only one who doesn't know something. He took a few steps and Mama followed him, so I followed him too. We walked the length of the school on the one side, each of us studying it. Even Uncle Muzi looked fascinated, maybe seeing it fresh through our eyes. I *was* fascinated, everything looked *better*.

The structure was similar to my own school, but it was much bigger. It was built in the traditional 'U' shape, made by three connected class blocks. In the center was the quad where I knew they would have the daily assembly. A little to the left was a big hall and further left of that there were rows of solar panels. There were lights in every class, a big one in the center, and I daydreamed about what that was like. On opposite sides of the school a little way away from the classes was the block of toilets. One side for boys and the other for girls. We finished the tour, which was really just us looking through the fence, but I didn't mind. We went back to the car and I willed my heart to be still. It was no good getting silly ideas into my head. As we rode to town I knew it was too late. I pictured myself in Zandi's uniform with a diamond braided hairstyle on my head.

I barely tasted the ice cream that Uncle Muzi put in my hand, but I enjoyed its coolness on my tongue. We said goodbye when he dropped us at the rank, waving until he was out of sight. We did our groceries and I looked at Mama every chance I got. If our eyes met, she would smile and look away, carrying on with her life. I knew she knew I was desperate for her to tell me what was going on, to tell me anything. I took a deep breath and let it out loudly, looking at her face to see if my act of despair had affected her. She continued studying a bag of rice. I took another deep breath and let it out, this time for myself. She would tell me when she told me, this was Mama after all. We finished shopping and went to board our bus. I fought the urge to stare my mother down and looked out the window instead. I was lulled gently by the slowly changing landscape until I fell asleep.

I was woken up by her gently shaking me. "Ma? Wake up," she said. We were still on the bus as I expected, but we were not where I expected. This wasn't our stop. I looked at her confused and she shook her head, "No we're not home yet, about thirty minutes away. I just wanted to talk to you." So this was the time then? I became alert. She handed me a small packet of chips and I took it while she got one for herself. *Niknaks*. My favorite. She made a point of opening her packet extra slow and taking a single cheesy chip meticulously and placing it in her mouth. I don't think she was really trying to do everything extra slowly, but it seemed that way to me. I ate a chip too, to calm myself and redirect my energy. For no clear reason, I was a nervous mess.

She looked at me and smiled after she swallowed her second chip.

"Did you like the school?" *Heart drum.* I nodded, my throat completely dry. "Good. I want you to go there. What do you think?" What did I think? What *did* I think? I looked at her blankly, I was having a difficult time tapping into my own brain. I had so many questions but the connection between my brain and mouth was temporarily severed. Mama laughed and that restarted the flow within my body. And then I had to say everything all at once like all those delayed questions had bumped into each other and had to come out altogether. "How, Mama?" No that wasn't the question I wanted to ask most, I tried again. "When?" That was still not quite the question I wanted. *Crunch.* Mama's *niknak* brought my attention back to her face. She was looking at me with unconcealed amusement.

"Next year. Your uncle said he would be able to talk to the principal and they should be able to get you a place with the matric class." She took another chip, I think more to give me time to take everything in rather than to satisfy a craving. "I really want you to go to university Ma, at least to really be able to. Your uncle and I both agree that if you stay at your school, then it will be much, much more difficult. I know you're one of the best there, but the schools are just not as good. It's late to transfer you in your final year, but it's the only chance we have. Plus you're smart, I know you are. You'll just need some help catching up and Muzi will help you, you'll have to move but it's really not that far, is it? And since he teaches there, he can really help and talk to the other teachers too." My head was spinning. *Live* with Aunty Sli and the girls! Go to the fancy school. I wanted to...to...I don't know what I wanted to do. Burst maybe. "Ma, you have a lot of catching up to do. I don't think you realize how much. Muzi says that if you want to really make the most of next year then you have to start now. He wants to see you every weekend." She stopped talking and looked at me again. She was right, I definitely needed time to digest.

"Every weekend?" I croaked. She nodded.

"You're lucky your cousins are a grade below and above you. He wants you to study with Zinzi first and see if you can keep up with her. He thinks you're most likely at a level between what she is doing and what you are currently learning at school. So you'll have to come every weekend until you 'pass grade ten' and then Muzi will take you through his school's grade eleven curriculum. He thinks you can do it, but it will take every weekend and very hard work from you." She kept quiet then. I was quiet too. "Well then, what do you think? You think you can handle going to two schools at the same time?" I looked at her, studying her face. When had she had the time to discuss and plan all this? My cousins also didn't know, they would have definitely brought it up. Zandi didn't know what 'secret' meant. Were they also being told now as well? Were they also excited at the idea of living together? Was this all real? I knew it was because Mama was incapable of a joke and this one would rank as very, very elaborate.

She was looking at me expectantly and I knew she was waiting for the jubilee I had hinted at earlier. The more time passed, the more I felt a sinking feeling at the base of my stomach. What would all of this mean for all of us? For Aunty Sli and Uncle Muzi, I knew Zandi would be leaving home to go to university by the time I would be starting my matric year, but were they really ready to say goodbye to one child only to say hello to a new one? Maybe that worked out rather perfectly in their household, I would simply be slotting myself into the space that she left. But what of my household, my leaving would have much more of an effect there. What would it mean for Mama?

Should I rejoice that we were doing so well that she felt she no longer needed me there all the time? That she had organized all of this for my future. Would she be fine without me? If I was gone every weekend then I couldn't help her with her pots. Maybe Sizwe could take over and help her paint. His face flashed across my mind. My brother, what would this mean for him? Would he hate me for the opportunity I was being given, an opportunity he never had? And my father, would he be alright with this? I doubted that he knew what Mama was planning and I couldn't imagine his reaction. I thought of the fragile peace we had just brokered and how devastating a blow this suggestion would be to it. Baba had not wanted Mama to sell her pots, because it made him look like he couldn't provide for his family. How much more, having his daughter leave to be educated in a different household. How would he react to that?

Mama was still looking at me, a slight concern entering her eyes. "What is it, Ma?" she asked softly as she lowered her now half-empty packet of *niknaks*. I struggled for the words to explain what was going on in my head. I was so scared of her thinking that I wasn't grateful for everything that she had done. The fear crippled me into silence, what if I told her what I was worried about and she took the offer back. I desperately wanted to go, but I wanted it to be alright for me to go.

"Are you worried about your father?" She asked, not breaking eye contact. I nodded, lowering my gaze to the plastic bags that occupied the space between us. "And your brother?" she continued, I nodded again. "Are you worried about me too?" I looked up and nodded again. I was grateful for not having to say it. She held my hand then, without taking her eyes off my face. Her palm was warm and loving. "I know this must be a lot to take in all at once, but I hope you see how important it is for you to go." She breathed in and out silently, looking away as she did. I could tell she was thinking about what she was going to say next, finding the perfect way to say it. "Makhosi, life is very different for a young woman than a young man, especially in our village. If you stay there, then your life will be like mine. And you might not have a wonderful daughter like you to keep you going." She stopped then, giving ample time for the elephant on my chest to settle down comfortably.

She blinked back what I knew was the start of tears I would never see. Her palm was still warm and loving. "This is your chance, Ma. We don't have a lot of opportunities and we will not get another like this one. *That's* what I want you to think about the most. You can be anything you want, you can be in control of your own life. I couldn't do that, but you can." I wanted to cry, so I blinked back my own tears. "Your brother and your father, they know that too. They want the best for you too. I know you think Sizwe will be upset that you get to leave, but he loves being home. That is the perfect life for him, it's the life he has always known and he has never wanted anything different. All he wants is to be like his father and you know what? He is better than his father. Your father too, could you picture him anywhere else? But you, this was never going to be the life for you. You would die here, slowly."

Those words tore into my soul because I knew she was describing her own life. This should have never been the life for her either and I knew from the way she was speaking that she had given up on the idea of us escaping it together. "Come with me Mama," the words were feeble. I wanted to add '*like we planned*' but I simply couldn't. She brought her other hand to cover the other side of mine, so my hand was sandwiched in hers. I felt the warmth radiate from her, circling me in love.

"No, sthandwa sam". *My love*. Her voice was a whisper now. "It was so nice to dream with you, but this is my life. And you must go and find yours."

She looked out the window for a long time before turning back and carrying on as though she had never stopped. "Your father and I.." she trailed off before starting up again. "Your father, he understands. I told him he has to let you go, or I will go too." I felt heady, why had she done that? I opened my mouth to protest, but Mama stopped me abruptly. "Shhh nana. *Baby*. This is my choice. You might not understand it now, but this is the way it has to be. And your father and I, it's different. He's different." She looked out the window again and somehow I knew this time she wouldn't turn back around. She was lost in a world of her own thoughts and I dove into my own. She continued to hold my hand all the way to our stop.

Over the course of that week, I was exposed, separately, to the thoughts held by my brother and father on my going away. Sizwe caught me in the early afternoon on Tuesday, alone in the kitchen with my tea. I had been avoiding him, afraid of what he was thinking of me. Afraid that he saw me as deserting him, leaving him to look after our parents alone. I looked up when he walked in and my heart sank, there was no running away now. This was judgment day. He made his tea and I looked at the floor. It was suddenly so awkward to be around him again. His cup ready, he walked to the door and I took a silent deep breath, holding it to exhale when he left. He hesitated and then turned around. Unable to continue holding it, I exhaled, my eyes on his face.

"So...when do you go?" he was looking back at me.

"On Saturday, I'll be there for the rest of the school holidays. And then after that, I'll be going on Fridays after school and coming back on Sunday afternoons." He sipped his tea.

"Hmm okay, that's good. Good luck, Khosi." He smiled, turned around, and left. I exhaled again, long and deep, aware I'd been holding my breath again. I had been let into heaven. With that smile, my brother had kicked off the elephant that had made its home on my chest since that bus ride with Mama. He had given me the right to be excited about my future without guilt. I knew then that I didn't really need Baba's approval. Somehow, it had all rested on my brother for me, but I got Baba's blessing too, on the same day no less.

I carried his dinner to him, walking the tray through the already open door. He was playing his harmonica, he played a lot now, but he put it down when he saw me.

"Sawubona, Baba." I greeted him as I put the tray down. He gave me a nod and a smile. He stopped me as I was turning to leave, "Makhosi." My father said my name so little it always surprised me to know that he knew it.

"Yes, Baba," he looked at my face, another thing I wasn't used to, so I looked at the floor.

"Look after yourself at your aunt's home. Listen to them and do everything they ask. Now that you're going to be learning from the fancy township schools, I expect you to be number one at the end of the year. You can't be number two to any of these village kids now, right?" He was laughing. A third thing to shock me, I couldn't remember the last time I saw him laugh. His face was nice when he laughed.

"Yes, Baba. I promise I'll be good." I left his room in a happy daze. It was really going to be okay, I could go and it would be okay.

CHAPTER 16

T hat Saturday morning when Mama said goodbye to me at the bus stop, I wanted to fling myself into her arms. She was the only one that came with me. I know Sizwe would have but I think he sensed our need for this moment. In a deviation from her character, Mama chatted to me the entire way. More like instructed me the whole way. "Be respectful, don't ever talk back, okay? Be respectful to Zandi and Zinzi too, even Musa. Even if you are family, it is their home and you are a visitor. Just do everything they ask and most importantly you must apply yourself. Don't ever give them a reason to think twice about taking you in." She was rambling, which meant she was nervous in a way I had never experienced before. I watched her and my heart was weak, but I said nothing, she needed to say all this. I listened and nodded to show my understanding even though I knew all of it and it didn't need to be said. When we got to the stop she held my hand, finally silent. We heard the bus before we saw it and then came the cloud of dust it was kicking up on the gravel road as it sped to us. This was it. Mama put her arms around me and kissed my cheek. "Alright Ma, it's time to go. I will call you once a week, make sure you're there. Say hi to everyone for me. I'll see you in three weeks."

I squeezed her tight, "I will Mama. See you soon." She tucked a hundred rand note into my hand. She had already given me money to travel and fifty rands on top of that in case I needed anything. I protested and she waved me off, "get on, quick." She was lucky I had no time to fight her because the bus was right there, caked in a permanent layer of brown dust. I stuck my head out and waved to Mama until I couldn't see her anymore. I waved also to my home, I could see it from the bus and it felt like the right thing to do. I settled back down, feeling every type of strange. It was really happening. I was going to spend the next three weeks being taught by my cousins and my uncle, hopefully catching up to where Zinzi was and maybe a little bit past it.

I had three bags with me. One was my school bag with all my books, the next was a bag for my clothes, and the last was a plastic bag full of *imfino* for Aunty Sli from Mama. She had slipped a small plastic bags full of treats for me in there too, She packed me lunch even though I was going two and a half hours away. I smiled as I bit into the banana, the *niknaks* would be next. She'd also given me a sealed envelope to give to Aunty Sli with the instruction to say "Mama said to thank you" when I handed it over. She didn't say it, but I knew it was money. I was glad I had it too, I knew Aunty Sli would protest, but it made me feel less awkward about staying with them. Like the money bought me the right to be there and I wasn't just going to breathe their oxygen and eat their food for free.

It was weird traveling on my own, but also very liberating. I stopped at one of the stores that Mama and I always passed when we were in town, but she never looked at. It was a shoe shop run by an Indian man. He said 'hello' when I walked in and I smiled and looked at the ground, and didn't look up again until I was safely out of sight. There were so many shoes, I must have spent fifteen minutes walking through the store. The ones I loved were a pair of white sandals. They had gold finishings and the sole had a flower pattern drawn in white. R60. I marked the price. I then walked over to the men's section and marked the ones that I would buy for Sizwe. They were brown leather slip-ons, with two horizontal bands on the top. R140. I left the store and made my way to the taxi rank. If I saved all the money that Mama had given me then I could buy Sizwe his shoes when I went back home. I almost had enough for my shoes from the money I saved from Mama's weekly pocket money too, but I hadn't thought to bring that with me. So I would buy Sizwe his shoes when I went back home, then I would buy mine after the four weeks it would take me to save enough. There was a taxi already waiting, I climbed in and waited for it to get full.

I was welcomed to the kitchen by Zinzi's excited face, "I thought Mama was just pulling my leg, I'm so glad you're here, mzala." *cousin*. That brought Zandi peeking in from the dining room, "So it's true! This is going to be so much fun." I greeted Aunty Sli and Uncle Muzi who were seated in the dining room, with Musa on the floor.

"So happy to have you back my dear, go put away your things and change into something comfortable. Are you hungry?" She turned her head and shouted into the kitchen, "Zandi, will you boil some water?" It was a statement, posed as a question.

"Yes, Mama." I heard Zandi's reply from outside the door as I changed my clothes. I looked around as if for the first time. This was the room we would share for three weeks. I hoped we still liked each other as much as we did now at the end of it. Being in my home clothes made me feel at home. I liked that Aunty Sli told me to change into them, that she knew which were my home clothes. I had the tea that Zandi made for me and then we got started on the washing. It was easy to be with them, easy to fit.

We started working straight away, I didn't even get that first night off. Uncle Muzi came into the kitchen as we were washing dishes and called Zinzi and me out. In the girl's' room he asked her to take out all of her books. "Last year's and this year's please, Zinzi," he said. I was a little offended. Did he think that my grade eleven was equivalent to her grade *nine*? I must have worn it on my face because he smiled at me then, "I just want you to read over it, that's all, and confirm that everything is familiar to you. If you want to go over any of the material then you can ask Zinzi." I nodded. I felt embarrassed. He was taking time out of his life to do this for me and I was acting like a brat.

"I expect this to go rather quickly. It should just be a recap. We really want to spend our time efficiently, right?" I nodded again. He left us then, Zinzi giving me her books from grade nine, a stack of ten books.

"I'm going to help Zandi with the dishes," she said. Call me if you need anything'" I was actually glad she left. I worked best alone. I got started.

By the end of the three weeks, I was done with the grade nine recap, having covered all the material, but I was shocked to find that I had only covered some of it in my grade ten syllabus. The biggest gaps were in Maths, Physics, and Biology. I was far ahead of her in IsiZulu, but that was the only subject where I had the advantage. I was also through half of her grade ten year, which seemed to put us on par. I was roughly exactly a year behind where I should be in terms of what I knew. Although Zandi and I were a year apart, she had learned the same things that I had and in some cases, she had even learned more. It was no wonder that in my school and in the schools around me, a fifty percent matric pass rate was seen as something to celebrate. Of those matrics who passed, most barely just made it. Except in IsiZulu, if an A was received by a student then it would be in IsiZulu.

I knew then just how lucky I was to be able to get out of that pool and into this one. I thought of my friends and felt a pang of guilt like I was doing something wrong by leaving them behind, yet happy to be doing it nonetheless. I went back home with Uncle Muzi's words still ringing in my ear. "I had no doubts, but you've proved me right. You're a smart girl, Makhosi, and with enough time and the right help you'll be just fine here." I played the words over and over as the bus made the two-hour journey back home. Despite the excitement of learning and the fun I had with my cousins, I was really happy to be going home. I had never been away this long and the weekly calls from Mama had done little to close that space. "Just make sure you work hard, okay?" I still remembered Sizwe's words from the one time he went with Mama to the container so she could call me. I did work hard and I couldn't wait to tell him.

I arrived at the bus stop at a quarter to two in the afternoon, it was Friday and I was the only one to get off at my stop. I'd told Mama on the phone that I would come back on Saturday but had asked to go home a day earlier and surprise them. Aunty Sli was happy to keep my secret. This way I would arrive with no fuss and as I walked I pictured what I would probably find each of them doing. Baba would not be home, Friday's were normally a gathering day at the courts. It was difficult to decide if I should place Sizwe out with Baba, or at home with Mama. I decided he was home with Mama, tending to her fire. She was outside, under the shadow cast by the kitchen, making her pots. There would be a fire, so I could just drop my bag and make my tea after greeting them.

Home was in sight now and I felt my heart quicken. Nothing in the world made me as happy as seeing the outline of my hut through the fence. I saw the chickens, and even they made me happy. Nobody had chickens in the townships, or animals of any kind really, maybe a dog. They didn't have the space. Mama saw me, she had just walked out of the kitchen.

"Hhawu!? Ma, usubuyile!" *You're back.* She wiped her hands on her pinafore as she walked towards me. I walked towards her too, wanting to run but reminding myself I was no longer a child. Her arms around me were heaven, my world was once again complete.

Sizwe came out of the kitchen as I was hugging Mama and released me of my bags when I finally let her go. "Ya," he flashed me a smile as he expertly carried everything I had divided into both hands, in one, his cup of tea in the other. "Ya," I said it back. The greeting was so informal it made me feel warm like I never left. Like I hadn't been gone so long that I now required formality. I was home. I changed into my most homely clothes that I had missed dearly and I joined the two of them in the kitchen. Mama had already made me a cup of tea and she fired her questions at me instantly. "How was it? What did Muzi say?' Did you like it, Ma, they were nice weren't they?" She sipped her tea, making it possible to get a word in.

"Yes Mama, they were all very nice. Zinzi really helped me catch up to where she is now and Uncle Muzi too. It's a lot of work, but I like it." Sizwe was quiet, but his face was happily relaxed, content to just listen to us. Mama nodded continuously, looking at me for so long I thought she was looking for new signs of growth that she had missed in three weeks.

"How are the pots?" I asked in an effort to redirect her attention. She beamed then, "Oh you should see them. Since you've been gone Sizwe has been painting them and I have just never seen anything like it. You must have seen them, the spare hut is full now so I started using yours for extra storage."

I *had* seen them and she was right. They were spectacular. My brother painted the same way he drew, with such precision and a lifelikeness that was captivating. I thought of that lioness, I wondered if he had painted that on one of the vases yet. Compared to his work, mine was suddenly childlike. I tried not to make the comparisons, but even Mama had declared his better. Aside from my wounded pride at being demoted to number two, I was actually happy that Sizwe had started painting Mama's pots. In fact, I felt relieved. The anxiety I had been experiencing at holding back the thing she loved most because I couldn't be around, was suddenly dissolved.

Why hadn't I thought of Sizwe to paint the pots before? Why hadn't he volunteered himself? Even though *we* didn't, I'm sure he must have thought of it? I remembered then just how jealously I had guarded our pots, guarded them against him and Baba. Perhaps he knew I wouldn't have been ready to share it then, but now, now I found myself ready to give it over completely. I couldn't come close to doing what he could with them, and we could sell his designs for so much more. I was proud to see how my brother had stepped in. "I have seen them, Mama. They are stunning." I directed the last part to my brother, who was looking at me. "I can't wait to see the rest." We all three of us smiled.

When Baba came home just as the sun was

setting nobody had to tell me, but I still smiled when Mama said, "Take your father his tea, Ma". I set the tray carefully, wanting him to be pleased with it and pleased with me. I had to remind myself yet again that I was no longer a child as I concentrated on placing one foot in front of the other to stop from running, an already foolish idea because running would spill the tea. "Baba," I announced my arrival as I stood at the door, so he could look at me.

"Ah, Makhosi. Ubungashongo ukuthi uzobuya kusasa?" *Didn't you say you would be coming back tomorrow?* He was smiling and his face was nice again.

It had healed too, with only the slightest reminders of what had happened that night all those weeks ago.

"Yes, Baba, but I missed you all too much." He laughed then, showing slightly yellowing teeth.

"Is that so? Well, you are back now and I am sure we are all happy to have you home. Your mother especially, I'm sure. Did everything go alright, then?" he lifted the top side of his sandwich to reveal what awaited him inside, closed it and took a bite. I had seen him do this many times and no matter what was in his sandwich, his face never registered any emotion.

"Yes, Baba. Very well." He finished chewing and swallowed. "Good, good. Very good, my girl." I closed the door behind me, content. I was happy serving him once again.

The next day I was struck for the first time about how quickly things can change in just three weeks. I truly was happy that my brother had taken over my place as Mama's artist for her pots, but that Saturday I saw what that really meant. Forced to, they had developed a new bond, and despite myself it hurt to witness. After lunchtime Mama went to her favorite spot in the shade cast by the kitchen to begin working on her pots, I watched as with unspoken understanding, Sizwe got up to start up the kiln fire.

He stayed there as he began work on the pots from yesterday that had dried and cooled completely. I caught more than once, a gentle look shared between them as they worked separately. A look like Mama and I used to share. I realized then, that I was not needed. If at all, Mama's distress at my not being there was overcome when she found a better replacement. I finished washing the dishes and went to my hut. I was ashamed at the hurt tears as they fell, but I knew I was powerless to stop them. I wept for the pain of realising that life had gone on without me. I stayed there until it was over, my selfish tears completely done. That was the third time in two days that I had to remind myself that I was no longer a child, but that was the first time I felt it to be true.

I walked out with a fresh face, ready to be an adult. With each new step towards my brother, I felt the weight leave my chest. I was not around and Mama was lucky to have him here. He looked up when my body cast a shadow on his face. "I saw these and thought of you," I blurted. He put the paint down and wiped his hands on his shorts, something I could tell he had done a few times already. He unwrapped the white plastic bag and the joy on his face melted my heart. There, it was all gone and my heart had made peace with my replacement. "These are so nice!" He got up and tried them on, smiling all the while. "Thank you, Khosi." The sandals fit him perfectly, and I was happy a hundred times over that I had decided to buy his shoes instead of my own.

"Don't worry about it." I could feel myself blush, so I turned around and left him with his shoes and his painting. Our exchange caught Mama's attention and she was smiling at me. "Thank you, *nana*," she said when I was close enough to hear her. She received the same smile I still had from witnessing my brother's happiness. I walked into the kitchen and made myself a cup of tea. Adults deserved tea.

CHAPTER 17

The next term ran through July to September. I spent it in its entirety in a state of constant exhaustion. I had my school throughout the week and on Fridays I caught the bus to Aunty Sli's to catch up with my new syllabus. I would catch the bus back on Sundays only to start it all over again on Monday. Although tired all the time, I found my joy in the progress I was making. I didn't like to dwell on it, because there was always so much more to learn, but I couldn't believe just how far I had come in a few months. I was at this point completely caught up with Zandi's grade ten syllabus, and had worked with both her and Uncle Muzi to where I currently was in my own school. That's when it began to get tricky, although I had in a sense been working towards this I was unprepared for when it came. I was suddenly ahead of all of my classmates, and more uncomfortably,

NONJABULO SANGWENI-ARAHILL

my teachers.

I was now acutely aware of the bad habits of so many of them, having experienced something different. Mr Mpanza, our biology teacher, had the habit of skipping entire sections and some-times entire chapters that he was not comfort-able with. His English was poor and so rather than to embarrass himself by getting stuck on words he didn't know, he would skip that part altogether. "We'll come back to this section," he would say, but we never did. When he set his tests, they were tailored to the parts he taught, so most students passed and didn't see the problem. He was not the only one, although he may have been the worst. This was the reason we did so poorly in matric. Those exams were standard-ised and not set by our teachers, so all the sec-tions that they chose to skip could be asked and we wouldn't know the answers. There was no real structure in place to evaluate the teachers, so they got away with it. Our teachers were the reason we were failing.

If I had had any reason to think that maybe there was something I could do about it, they were shut down very quickly.

"Sir, you said we would go back to the lymph-atic system after that chapter. I was wondering when we would do it?." The room went suddenly quiet as I put my hand back down. All the soft murmurs from my classmates, gone. They were all looking at me, shocked I think from hearing my voice given voluntarily, and not as a result of having been spoken to first. Shocked even more, by the line of my questioning. Although I didn't mean for it to come off that way, it sounded like a challenge. Nobody questioned the teachers -we just didn't, and doing it had broken something. Mr Mpanza was looking at me, his expression unreadable.

He was quiet for a while and when he answered he was calm. "We will not be doing the lymphatic system. It won't be covered in your next test." He turned to write something on the board and I don't know what it is that possessed me right then, but it boiled all the way inside me, giving me courage I never had. The courage to speak up.

"It's in the syllabus, Sir." I saw his hand freeze, stopped mid-word on the board. I felt my heart pound, cursing myself for my stupidity. I felt forty sets of eyes on me, taking turns between me and him.

"Excuse me?!" the composure was quickly leaving his voice. I was quiet, looking at the desk, unsure of what to do next. "MaMthethwa, khuluma." *speak*. And speak I did. When he called me by my surname, he ignited that fire inside me again. It made me think of all the people I shared that name with, my family. I thought of Mama, and all the sacrifices she was forced to make so that I could get out of this school and go to a better one, because she knew there was no hope here. I thought of Sizwe, who matriculated from this very school, who was taught by this same man and how it had failed him. He was passed by a school that had not really taught him anything and he was not sure of his future as a result.

I looked around at the faces of my classmates who would suffer the same fate and it was all because of the unchecked power of teachers like the man standing in front of me. Men who went into a profession that held within its clutches the futures of so many children and just did not care. Men who were used to being worshipped and listened to even though they did nothing to deserve it. I thought of my father, another man who fell into this category, who only through his absolute humiliation had found his way out of it. I thought of the benefits of that for those around him, for me and Mama and Sizwe. It was with that burning in my belly that I fired back, "Sir, it's in the syllabus, and it continues on in matric. That means it could get asked in our finals. So we should cover it or we won't be prepared for it."

My peers had stopped moving, but for different reasons now. They suddenly realized how all this pertained to them as well and it made them listen with sharper ears.

"I AM THE TEACHER HERE!" Mr Mpanza screamed the words at me, each one loud and clear. He regained control with visible effort, lowering his voice back to normal, "I decide what we learn and what we don't. Your teachers in matric will teach you what you need to learn in matric." He was looking straight at me and I was looking back. That was the first time that I looked an adult straight in the face while they shouted at me. I always looked down out of respect, but I didn't feel that Mr Mpanza deserved my respect and I wanted him to know that I was no longer a scared child. I was an adult. His gaze shifted from me and he slowly scouted the entire room, resting his eyes for a few seconds on some faces. Then he turned and looked back at me, "Outside." I got up and went outside, my head high so my classmates would never guess how scared I was. I had never in my entire schooling career been in trouble, teachers only ever called my name to either answer a question or in praise.

I walked in front of Mr Mpanza, snaking my way in front of classes of kids whose eyes followed me until I was out of sight. My pounding heart was my only companion as we made our way to the principal's office. The moment was both destabilizing and empowering. I stood outside while he went in to talk to the principal, awaiting my fate. He reemerged with a thin red pipe in his hand. The horror stories I had heard for years came flooding into my head, stories from other students who had experienced the pipe. I held out my hand and thought about the irony of getting hit for standing up for our education.

The pride I'd always taken in my blemish-free

record evaporated as the pipe connected with my skin. The pain gave me validation. I knew I was right and as I looked at his face full of contempt, heaving from the effort of punishing me, I knew he did too. I received four strokes in total and I have no clear idea how that was worked out. I wiped the tears from my face and massaged my hand as he walked away to give the pipe back.

"You're a good student, Makhosi. I like you, but I can't have that kind of display in my class. Just stop this nonsense about the syllabus and we'll forget about this. Come back to class when you're ready." He didn't wait for a reply.

Back in class, I could feel the shift that had happened. My shell of perfect student had been shattered and I felt an acceptance from them that I hadn't before. I looked down at my still throbbing hand and realized it was the price I'd pay for the change I wanted to make happen. If the school didn't care about us, then what other choice did I have. I was the only person who was now in a position to help us, I had the knowledge and I could pass it on. I could help and more of us would pass if I did. By the end of day I was ready to tell them about my idea. Mr Mpanza strolled out ten minutes before the bell rang, but everybody stayed inside because we knew the trouble that exiting prematurely would bring. I stood up in front of the class, before the quiet was completely gone. Lungi and Sanele were also standing, and I hoped they would act out of character and just be quiet as I spoke. They often made snide remarks about me and how I thought I was so smart, remarks I had perfected the art of ignoring over the years.

They were looking at me now, the entire class was, and I was already standing so I had to say something. I took a deep breath trying to quieten my once again pounding heart. 'I've been having lessons with my uncle, who is a teacher from a school in Ngwelezane.' The eye rolls I got from Lungi and Sanele told me that I said the wrong thing. I must have sounded like a snob, but it was out there now. All I could do was carry on because they were still listening. 'I meant what I said earlier about the syllabus. They will ask us those questions in the exams and if we want to pass then we have to learn those sections.' It was quiet, but even Lungi and Sanele were actually listening to me now. 'I'm proposing to hold classes and teach what I learn from my uncle. He teaches matric and we're already behind compared to their grade eleven students.'

The silence was longer than I hoped, but I was patient. I could only offer my help, I couldn't force it on people.

"I heard you're leaving this school at the end of the year. Is that true?" I followed the voice, turning my head to look at Mthunzi. He was an okay student, mostly known for his soccer skills. I wasn't expecting that question. I didn't think that was the kind of thing people would have heard. I had told two of my friends, and maybe they had told other people, but there were so many degrees of people separating Mthunzi and me that I couldn't imagine anyone ever thinking to talk to *him* about *me*. But, he had asked the question and I had to answer it.

"Yes, I will be going to the school my uncle teaches in." I lost them. That attention that I had held was slipping and there was nothing I could do.

"So even if you teach us this year, what's the point if you won't be around next year when we really need it? There's not even that much of this year left." I saw the nods that accompanied his every word, because he was right. I would be gone and they would be stuck here, but did that mean we should not even try? Was that not worse?

"'But I could teach as far ahead as I can learn so by the end of the year, we'll be well into our matric syllabus. We could really do it if we're focused. My uncle has taught that syllabus for years, he knows it." I watched Muzi slowly pull his bag over his right shoulder and stand up. "Your uncle, is your uncle. You should keep him to yourself." He was tall, taller than most of the boys in our grade, and I felt a knot in my stomach as he walked right to me, eyes on mine and then past me and out the classroom. He didn't look back.

"How long have you been doing this, Makhosi?

Going to study with your uncle, I mean?" Londi asked, she was a sweet girl who took excellent notes. On the days that I missed school, she was always my first choice to catch up from.

"Since the beginning of the June holiday," I answered her, already seeing where she was going.

"That's over two months ago, Khosi, and I'm sure you worked fast because it was just you. But how much time would we need just to catch up to you? All of us." I knew she was right and I was starting to feel weary from this entire experience.

"Okay, so it would take a little longer-" the look on her face stopped me flat.

"When do you see your uncle?" she asked me calmly. She was one of the people that I knew was aware of my schedule, so she was asking this only for the benefit of the class.

"I go there on Fridays after school and come back on Sundays." Saying it out loud made me aware of it again, I hardly had enough time to do everything as it was. I exhaled slowly, focusing on Londi, "What are you saying?" My voice came out more tired than I intended. She looked down at her desk and then around at our class and then back at me. "I'm saying that this is a very nice thing for you to offer to do, but maybe you should think about it first. It sounds like you have a lot going on already without teaching us too." She had made her point and she was right. I watched my classmates get up and start to file out of the classroom and I couldn't wait to be one of them.

I was walking silently to the school gates, following part of the route I had walked earlier to the principal's office when I felt somebody fall into step with me. Londi. We carried on in silence for a while before she finally broke it.

"I'm sorry, Khosi, but I had to make you see you were being foolish in there." I carried on walking, not upset with her, just tired. She wasn't discouraged by my silence in the least.

"Khosi, I was thinking, I know how you can make the difference you want to make." I stopped then. I liked her, but I really wanted to walk home alone and if I carried on walking then she would take it as an invite. She lived close enough to my house that, that would be a long walk. So I stopped, ready to listen to her speak and then walk home, alone. "You want to help as many people as you can pass, not only grade eleven but get ready for matric as well. The same way your uncle is doing for you right?" She paused, so I nodded.

"Well you have a great idea, you just have to make it smaller. Shrink it to the group of kids that can actually learn that fast and that way there's a much greater chance of success. Teach the top ten kids and then we can self study with your books and we'll teach anybody who wants to learn, but this way your job is manageable and the responsibility is shared. I've already discussed it with Sphe and Sli from our class and they are interested, I know the other kids from the other classes will be too. We can just start there, and see what happens? What do you think?" She was waiting for an answer, the excitement all over her face.

"Okay, okay. Let's do it." The more I thought about it, the more sense it made. That should have been my first approach all along, it's always better to start small. I walked home with Londi that day, the two of us feeding into each other's energies and developing our plan. We didn't need teachers who didn't care, because we had each other and we cared.

I woke up earlier now, meeting with the smartest kids in my grade an hour before school started and an hour after it ended each day. There were twelve kids who came by invite to the first few classes and by the end of the week six more had asked to join. We made it clear that we were open to anyone who wanted to come, but they had to take it seriously and keep up with the work. It worked wonderfully, because the sheer amount of work covered and the time it demanded meant that only the most dedicated joined. We didn't allow people who didn't come in the morning to join in the afternoon. We had a few incidents of the rowdier bunch coming in after school trying to disrupt us, but they stopped when they realized we would pay them no attention. My class, I never called it that except to my family, now had thirty-two students. It was small compared to the total of a hundred and fifty-eight students in the entire grade, but it was manageable. More importantly, it was thirty-two students who wanted to be there. I told Mama of all the milestones that I reached with them and how I felt a bigger sense of accomplishment with them than I did when it was just me. They were finally on par with where I was with Uncle Muzi at the end of the short September holiday, a feat of immeasurable proportions.

CHAPTER 18

Uncle Muzi displayed just what a great teacher he was as we ploughed through the official grade eleven syllabus, filling in any and all gaps that my teachers had left. He was easy to listen to and follow, and I felt both special and lucky that he taught only me. I had struggled to talk to him at first, having only my father as a reference, but with him teaching me I found the freedom to ask questions and the courage to share my opinion. I flourished under his praise, which he gave freely and often. I still couldn't quite define it, but I was acutely aware of the relationship developing between us. It was official in a way similar to relating to Baba, but also friendly in a way that not.

"I'll do it," he said calmly and decidedly. Like it was not only possible but also definitely going to happen. Unable to come up with a response, I stared at him. How could he do it? There was no way to get the entire class, *my* class, all the way here so the only way would be to get him there. Get uncle Muzi to my village and teach my class himself. Even the image of it that I tried to conjure up in my head seemed ridiculous. I saw him clean and perfect in a dirty classroom, out of place. It just wouldn't work.

"If we just go over it one more time, then I'm sure I'll get it. I'm sorry it's taking me so long," I didn't mean to whisper the last part, but it seemed to highlight just how sorry I was. We were doing the lymphatic system that Mr Mpanza had deemed unnecessary and skipped, and I was struggling through it like nothing else before. I found myself in the moments of my greatest frustration wishing I never told uncle Muzi about my encounter with Mr Mpanza, or about the formation of my class. But I had to, that class wouldn't exist without him, it was in fact his class. I wasn't sure what to expect when I told him at the end of our lesson one evening, and the possibility of him thinking I was a silly little girl ate into me as I finally did it. "Well, I guess I'll have to make thirty-two photocopies now," he said with a smile, but a real smile, one that touched his whole face and showered me with his approval.

"Makhosi, you are not slow. You are one of the smartest students I've ever had. The way you've picked everything up is amazing. You are an above-average student, so you struggling with this chapter tells me that most of the other students will too. I know you'll get it, but I think that maybe having a teacher who is comfortable with the material teach it would be best for them. Right?" he was looking at me and his face was poised in a question although we both already knew he was right. I was nowhere near being able to confidently explain the lymphatic system back to him, let alone anybody else. It would be nice to not have to be responsible for that section, it would be more than nice. What I was really afraid of was him coming to my school, into my space. They were such remote parts of my life, that although connected, were absolutely separate and I wanted to keep them apart.. My class existed, because of the lessons that uncle Muzi gave me, but I would never have dreamed of putting uncle Muzi in front of my class.

"Right," I muttered in response. It felt like admitting defeat.

"Find out if it would be possible for me to come in and teach a class from one of the teachers. Two classes, Saturday and Sunday and then I'll come home. Which means for a change you can host me, huh?" he laughed. I wished I found it funny too. I hadn't even thought of that, he would be at my house. With Baba, Mama and Muzi. He would be in my space. Our space. I don't know why it bothered me so much, I practically lived in their space, weekend after weekend. I should feel honoured to be able to return the favor. But I didn't feel honoured. I felt nervous, sickeningly so.

"I'll ask the principal and I'll tell Mama about the visit." I tried to smile and act natural at his questioning face, but I must have failed.

"Are you alright, Makhosi?"

I nodded with unnatural vigour. "Yes, uncle. Just tired."

He nodded gently as he packed up his file. "It's been a long lesson. Alright then, we'll resume tomorrow. Goodnight."

I told Mama that Sunday when I got back home and she was overjoyed, "That's wonderful. Muzi is such a good man, coming all the way here to teach those children." I wanted to remind her that I was one of *those* children and I wanted to complain to her that I didn't want to share my amazing teacher but I knew Mama had too much sense for such a ridiculous complaint. That was my own selfish issue to deal with in private.

"Will Baba be alright with it?" I thought back to the last time the two men saw each other when Baba came to fetch us, the murderous look on Baba's face and the anger on Uncle Muzi's. It seemed so long ago.

"Yes, Ma. They will be fine," she stood up, "come, we have to prepare his room."

The guest hut was a room that I hardly ever went into and it was one that we seldom had to prepare. Walking in now we saw the first problem, it was *full* of pots. They were set out in clusters of similar designs, like the families that I had created and you could move around each cluster. It was designed to give access to the entire room, with pathways around clay pots. But the entire room was full so that very little floor could actually be seen. I marvelled yet again at the talent of my brother, all of the images were so beautiful.

There was a cluster, which had the face of the same woman, caught in her many various emotions. I looked at them so long the face started to look familiar, until I realized it was Mama. It was not obvious, such was the abstract nature in which he drew her, but I saw it. Once I realized that, I couldn't pull my eyes away from them. The gentle strokes showed depth, moments frozen in time captured perfectly. How the sun caught on her skin in the one where her head was thrown back, in the middle of a laugh. The fine lines around the corners of her mouth as he captured her sipping a cup of tea. The hollow look in her eyes, in the one of her smiling. These were all glimpses he had seen, special moments they had shared, that I had missed. It was like a window into my brother, that showed me the way he saw the world, and the way he saw Mama.

"These are so beautiful Mama, you are so beautiful." She had been looking at them too, captivated as I was.

"Thank you, nana. Your brother, he has a true talent." I heard the pride in her voice and it made me swell with pride too. "Alright, we can leave half of them here, there is nothing to do about it and I think they make the room look nice. We'll just have to divide the rest between all of our rooms." She carefully walked a little further into the room, "here, we can set up a bed for him on this side. Maybe put in that small table from our dining room next to it so he can put his things somewhere. That should do it, right?" I looked around, envisioning everything she was proposing. Even in my head the room looked bare. But then I pictured him walking around it to study the different images that Sizwe painted on the pots. I imagined him as captivated by them as we were and suddenly he had the most interesting room imaginable. It would do.

"Yes, Mama." We had an entire week to prepare for him and while that was more than enough time for the room, I was not so sure about everything else. I had to actually ask the principal for permission to bring another teacher into the school for extra lessons. I told uncle Muzi that I would call Aunty Sli by Thursday to tell him what the response was. I couldn't imagine the principal actually saying no, so long as he didn't need to personally do anything. I *could* see some of the teachers possibly being opposed to it if they found out. So I would wait until the last minute to actually ask, I would wait until Thursday. It gave them less opportunity to find out and ruin everything. I would only tell the class after I asked the principal. Meanwhile, I had to make sure that we were all caught up to where uncle Muzi needed. I wanted to fling myself into a wall from all of it, I wanted to sit someone down and complain to them, in detail, but there was nobody to complain to.

As the week went on, I started to feel the dread build. Everything was running smoothly which was stressing me out even more. I wanted something to break, so I could have a real reason for my sense of panic. By Tuesday the class was ready for uncle Muzi and we spent the rest of the week working on Maths while we waited. By Thursday I could no longer push it back, it was time to be an adult yet again. I lingered in the general vicinity of the office towards the end of second break. I had spent the break telling Londi about the plans for the weekend and to say she was excited was an understatement.

"Your uncle? The teacher? Really? Wait 'till the class finds out, they'll be so excited," she practically squealed.

"Please don't tell them, not yet, okay?" She agreed reluctantly, but she agreed. I could hardly handle her excitement, what more that of thirty more students! "Just wait until I confirm with you in class okay, I still have to ask the principal. Okay?" she nodded. The bell rang and she went back to class and I was on my own.

I knocked on the open door and waited to be acknowledged. Mr Shezi was busy on a call, but he looked up and saw me before looking out into the distance as he listened to what the person I couldn't see was saying. He was a bit of a legend, our principal. He was feared by absolutely all students, even the matric boys. The power of his legend was multiplied by his being a bit of a phantom. He hardly spoke, even at assembly, choosing mostly to gesture when he wanted things. "She-she" as he was known in the spaces where students could speak freely, had built his reputation over the fifteen years that he had been at the school. First as a deputy and then in the last six years as principal. Rumour was that he had been fiery in his early years and a pipe from him meant your hand was numb for three days. Other teachers would threaten to send you to him instead of punishing you themselves, and the threat always worked.

Then, as the story goes, he was in a very bad motorcycle accident four years ago that left his head gruesomely scarred. He'd left for six months, leaving Mr Masondo in charge. He returned with a new accessory- the traditional fila hat that he got from his Nigerian friend that sat on the top part of his head, covering the worst of his scar. He also came back with a new attitude. No longer the fiery punisher, he now seemed to quietly operate in the shadows. He left most things of a verbal nature to Mr Masondo, who more than made up for the principal's silence. I could hear his voice when I closed my eyes, loud and high. I saw Mr Shezi put the phone down and then look up and motion for me to come in with a slight movement of his middle finger.

"Miss Mthethwa. How can I help you?" I was stunned. He spoke so little that I had forgotten what his voice sounded like. It was soft, at least, it was much softer than you would expect for someone of such a reputation. That was the first thing, the other thing was that he knew who I was. I had never spoken to the principal, ever. I had shaken his hand countless times at the beginning of each new term when the top ten was announced. We'd all stand as Mr Masondo called our names and shake She-she's hand, but he never spoke, not even then. He just shook your hand and nodded his acknowledgement. I had learned to appreciate and look forward to that nod. I guess maybe it wasn't so ridiculous to think that he had heard my name called so many times that he knew it, but I was still shocked.

"Good day, Sir," I shifted on my feet, the little presentation I had prepared and practised throughout the week suddenly wiped from memory.

"Er, Sir, I was wondering if my uncle could come and teach an extra lesson on Saturday. And Sunday." I addressed the entire sentence to the desk, afraid to look at his face or worse, his head. I shouldn't have said *uncle*, I should have said 'another teacher', but then wouldn't he ask what was wrong with our teachers? Maybe I should have said uncle. He was quiet for so long I finally looked up to see if he heard me. He was looking at me, clearly amused and only when my eyes were on his face did he start speaking.

"Do you always talk to the furniture, Miss Mthethwa?" I felt the blood rush to my head. Was he *mocking* me? It seemed unreal. I stared blankly. I heard the slight chuckle before he continued, "I hope not. As for your uncle, would this be for the superclass that you've been building?" I felt my knees go weak. How did he know? Well, we were hardly keeping it a secret, so I guess he must have known. It was so unnerving to think that this man knew so much about the things I did, even though they *were* common knowledge.

"It's..it's not a superclass, Sir, it's just students studying together after school. And before school and sometimes on weekends." I hadn't meant to say it like that, but I didn't want to leave anything out in case he thought I was hiding something and trying to be smart with him. I looked up at him, suddenly aware that I had said all that to the desk as well. He was clearly amused by me, again. I felt like such a child, a weird feeling after all my recent achievements in the category of 'adult'.

"Have your weekend lessons, it's fine. Arrange for the class key from the caretaker and make sure you lock up and leave it on the premises each day." He motioned for me to leave him with another quick motion, this time using his whole hand.

"Yes, Sir. Thank you, Sir." I walked back to class feeling strange. I guess that went well.

On the call I made to her that afternoon, Aunty Sli told me she missed my face even though she had seen it just last weekend. She also told me to hug Mama for her and to tell her she missed her face too. I was about to tell her that the principal said it was okay, when she told me to hold. I expected Zandi's high energy voice to burst through the phone so I was extra surprised when Uncle Muzi's low, calm tone came through instead.

"Makhosi, I won't be able to come on Friday anymore."

My whole entire heart stopped and I think he heard it because his reassurance came quickly. "I'm still coming. But I have some marking to do and the marks need to be in before I go home on Friday. So I'll probably get home late, which would mean getting to you at night. I'd rather just get up early the next morning, plus this way I get one more night at home. I know there's an eight o'clock bus leaving from town, so let's arrange to meet at your school at ten o'clock. Is that alright?"

I couldn't help my long exhale. "Yes that's perfect." I could hear the steady rhythm of his breathing.

"It's the last stop, right?"

That's right, he hadn't been here in years and he'd never come alone. "Yes, Edebe. Say that to the driver." The sound of him clearing his throat came through, but distant sounding so I knew he had moved the phone away to do it.

"Alright, see you on Saturday then." *click*.

Ten o'clock on Saturday morning saw me waiting for him with my class. Nine thirty that morning had seen me do the same, just in case the bus did something it never did and came early. I had hoped to welcome him alone and then for us to wait together for the rest of the class to come, but that was a dream. I sat on the desk with Londi next to me as some of the girls revised notes. We sat quietly and waited for 'the uncle'. He had stopped being *my* uncle somewhere from the time that word spread that he was coming, to now. At some point during that time his 'uncleness' stretched from only covering me, to all of us. I actually heard someone refer to him as 'Uncle Teacher,' and that cemented it.

I had with me a small picnic basket from home, after failing to protest hard enough to Mama. She had packed him a lunch, "Makhosi, how can you expect the man to teach you on an empty stomach? Hmm? I wish there was a way to make him tea. Is there a kettle in the office? Can you get hot water?"

I hadn't seen her this excited in a long time, apparently neither had Sizwe who was watching her with the most amused expression.

"Does Baba know you're making tea for other men, Mama?" She made a face at his teasing and we all laughed, but she didn't slow down.

As a result I had a cup with a tea bag inside it, in the basket. I put the basket on the teacher's desk, assuming he would serve himself at his leisure. There was enough in there to feed an army; sandwiches, scones, biscuits, two packets of lays chips and a small chocolate. There was also a small bottle of coke that she'd sent Sizwe to buy when I couldn't give her a definite answer about the tea.

"I don't want the man to choke," she'd said, aghast as though she could see it happening.

He arrived at a quarter after ten, and I could see him through the window. I stood up to go fetch him, giving the class a look that said "He's here. Don't embarrass me," before I left. He was carrying his big file that he always taught me out of, and a backpack. I waved and stopped as he smiled and walked towards me.

"I forgot just how long that ride was. I feel like I've aged," he was relaxed. Even his clothes were relaxed. He had on blue jeans, a black golf shirt and a pair of black Nike sneakers.

"You haven't aged a bit. The class is all here, they're a bit excited to be taught by you."

He smiled, "I'm excited to teach them." We walked into the class and everybody stood up. "Good morning, everyone," his voice filled the room as he looked around. I liked that he said 'everyone' and not 'class' like our teachers always did. It made him different, and special. I watched the excited faces, still standing next to him as they chorused, "Good morning, Sir." He gestured for them to sit down and I took advantage of the noise to fulfil my duty.

"The basket is from Mama, she can't wait to see you."

He followed my eyes and smiled with his whole face, "What a sweet woman. I'll be sure to thank her later." I sat down in the very front row.

"Alright, my name is Mr Makhubu. I am a Biology teacher for grades 10-12 and I am also a Maths teacher for grade 11 at Khombindlela High School, in Ngwelezane. I will be your teacher for the next two days and we will be covering the following topics," he turned and went to the board and wrote it all down in point form. "Transport systems in mammals, which includes the lymphatic system; gaseous exchange and excretion in humans." He walked back over to us, standing in front of the desk occupied by Londi. She flashed me a sideways smile and I couldn't help rolling my eyes, but I smiled back.

"Transport systems in mammals is actually a section that you should have covered in grade ten. Now I understand you had some issues doing that, so we'll go over it first. It does require a lot of time, so you'll all need to pay very careful attention. I think though that we can get through all three sections in two days, after which it will then be up to you to do your own self study. I will be leaving questions with Makhosi that I want you to complete over the course of the week. Right then, before we get started, I'd like to learn names. Let's start here." He pointed to Sphe, on his far left who got up and stated her name before sitting down again. We went through the whole class like that, the only person who didn't get up was me.

It was so different watching him teach from this perspective. It was wonderful. I thought that he was great as a personal tutor to me, but seeing him now truly in his element, was wonderful. He was so engaging and he knew the material so well that he hardly looked at his notes. If he did it was for structure and not because he needed to copy things down word for word like so many of our teachers. That was it, he was a real life challenge to the teachers we were used to and although he was great regardless, he was even more spectacular in comparison. It wasn't just me either, I drifted a few times when he covered parts I felt comfortable with and studied the faces of my classmates. There was a sense of wonder and excitement that they all had, the same wonder and excitement that I had. He made us *want* to learn and he cared about our learning. That was the moment I knew I wanted to be a teacher and in that moment I couldn't picture doing anything else. I wanted to create that sense of wonder and love for learning in someone the way he had created it in me.

We took a break at two o'clock. Thirty minutes, we still had so much to cover. Although we were free to roam, most of us stayed inside. Little groups formed and lunches were shared. He called me over to his desk and I went happily.

"Your mother packed me quite the lunch here, it's really wonderful, but there is just no way I could possibly eat it all. Did she happen to pack you a huge feast as well?" I looked at the food as he had it spread out on his desk, it looked even more ridiculous that way.

"No, I made my own lunch." He smiled. I didn't know a person who smiled more than he did. Rather, I didn't know a person who smiled as much as he did *at me*.

"You see the thing is, I don't want to offend your sweet mother by not finishing the lunch she so carefully packed for me. I was thinking you could find a way of distributing what I can't eat amongst all of you?" I felt myself smile, I had been eyeing those biscuits. I walked around carrying the basket, letting anybody take what they fancied. They took for granted that I was not just distributing food, I was also distributing my beloved uncle. Like the lunch Mama had packed, he was ours now. I felt like I had just taken another difficult, but definite step in the direction of being an adult.

When we finally finished the lymphatic system it was five o'clock and compared to how he covered it with me, uncle Muzi had gone through it quickly. I looked around at the faces around me, knowing that their brains were very close to being mush. We had two options, stay and go through excretion in humans, which he said was a nice and quick section which we could finish in an hour and a half. This way we would only have gaseous exchange left for tomorrow, which we would start at eight o'clock to be done by three o'clock comfortably. The alternative was to leave both sections for tomorrow which meant we would only be done at five. Unanimously, we opted to stay. We had a quick ten minute break and this time most of us decided to leave the classroom. He was right about the relative ease of the excretion in humans section, but by the time we left I knew none of us ever wanted to see a book again.

I hadn't thought about the fact that we would walk home together. We were going to the same place, from the same place. It would be foolish not to, but I hadn't thought about it until now. As we walked out of the class, the group fractured into smaller ones with people gathering themselves with those who lived closest to them so they could walk together. There were about eight students in our general direction, four of which I knew would fall away quickly. I was glad Londi was with us, she would be with us the longest, which was about two thirds of the way. Although I often found her constant chatter annoying, I was counting on it today. She would fill the space between us after everyone else was gone and that was just what I needed.

I was carrying Mama's basket which was empty now. I knew she would take this as encouragement and pack another one for tomorrow. Not that I was complaining, nor my classmates for that matter.

"Did you enjoy your first day, Mr Makhubu?" Londi asked for all of us. We wanted to know how we compared to his township students.

He was quiet for a while as if he was thinking about it, "Well, I'll be honest, it was definitely the most challenging time I've had in a while, but I absolutely enjoyed it. You are a wonderful bunch." I thought he knew how to play to his audience, but I also knew that he meant every word. I could tell by the smiling faces that they all felt the same pride I did.

"Did you enjoy my first day?" he threw it back.

Two of the kids fell off with a wave, as Londi answered for the group. "You are the best teacher we've ever had. Sorry Makhosi." We all laughed, continuing on down the road.

The conversation in the group had been so pleasant and easy, like soft music I was listening to in the distance, that the space left between us even after all the kids were gone was comfortable. Quiet, but comfortable. We had only about seven minutes left before we got home, and I neither wanted them to rush by or drag on. We let the silence take a comfortable seat between us before he finally pushed it out.

"So you have no questions for me then?" he didn't turn to me and I liked that. We spoke, both of us addressing the empty space in front of us. It had just gone past six o'clock and because it was winter, it was getting dark. In the township the street lights would be on, but not here and I was glad of it.

"No, no questions. But a statement." I felt him turn his head to me and then look forward again.

"Oh? And what statement is that, Makhosi?"

I felt that funny feeling in my knees again, where on earth had I gotten the confidence to be so bold? We passed the old store ruin that served as our bus stop. We would be home in five minutes. "I have decided that I want to be a teacher because of you." I wanted to stop then, but it didn't seem complete and I knew I had to finish it. "I want to be a teacher like you." He was quiet for a while, so I was quiet too. Our walk was synchronised perfectly, I focused on the steps. I thought I wouldn't get a response out of him, because I could see home now, I could see the light coming from Baba's room. I could make out Mama's figure moving in the yard and as we approached the side of the fence that ran along the road, I could see the fire from the kitchen. I realized I wasn't holding my breath for his response. When I practised telling him in my mind, I imagined he would say something amazing afterwards that would have sealed this moment as special for the two of us. He said nothing as we walked through the gate but the moment had still been sealed as special for me. I admired him and what was important was that he knew.

As soon as Mama caught sight of us, she was a ball of energy.

"Finally! I was starting to get worried, I was about to send them out to look for you two. Muzi, how was your trip? I hope those kids weren't too much trouble, eh?" I wanted to laugh, but I knew Mama wouldn't appreciate it. She had to let the man get a word in if she wanted a conversation.

"Sawubona, MaBiyela," he addressed her by maiden name, a respectful and oddly endearing term. "First things first, I have to thank you for that basket. I don't know if I have any room left for dinner."

She beamed, "Don't be silly. Of course you do." We had met in the sort of center of our home, in the yard, and I knew uncle Muzi was waiting to greet Baba as would be the respectful thing to do. Talking to Mama, was a gentle way of letting Baba know he was here and was awaiting his reception. On cue, Baba opened the door. One look at him and I knew what he had been doing in those last few minutes. He had on a clean t-shirt, one of his newer ones, a courtesy for his guest. I peeped through the door to see how neat everything was inside, I knew that was Mama's doing. We really should have more guests.

Baba walked out with his hand held out, "Hhawu, Makhubu. Sivakashelwa yiikhulu namuhla." *We truly have important visitors today*.

"Ngaze ngajabula ukuba nani, Nyambose." *I'm so happy to be here, Nyambose*. Nyambose, he had referred to Baba by his clan name. I was suddenly grossly out of place and acutely aware of it. Mama called me to her with her eyes, so we could leave the men to catch up in Baba's room.

The fire was already going and Mama had set up the tea trays long ago in anticipation of our arrival, such that when I reemerged from my hut, she was already carrying it out to them. It was nice in that I could relax and just enjoy my own tea, I needed to relax and stop using my brain. Sizwe was in the kitchen as I expected, and when I walked in he handed me a ready made cup of tea, which I had not expected. I nearly cried at the simple gesture.

"You look tired, Khosi. How did it go?" His face right then at that moment, was a treasure I imprinted in my brain. The concern on his face was all I needed and I was so grateful that he knew. While our parents were fussing over our guest, a guest I myself had been fussing over for most of the day, it was priceless to have someone fuss over me. I sipped his tea to taste it, it was stronger than I liked, but I didn't care. It was good, it was perfect.

"It was a long day, but we got a lot done. A lot. My brain is dead. Uncle Muzi, he's a really great teacher, the class loves him." He was quietly sipping his own tea, looking at me.

"Okay, well that's good." I really hoped that was the last thing he would say to me, because it felt like I had used all the words I had left in me. I knew Mama would be gone for a while, talking to Uncle Muzi about Aunty Sli and listening to his account of the day. Although I knew it was a little rude to dish first, I did it anyway. She'd made chicken stew, which I dished with a little pap and ate right away. My body was shutting down and I couldn't wait for them. I finished eating with their distant laughter in the air and then I heard the clink of empty dishes as Mama prepared to come back. I deliberately shot out of the kitchen then, not wanting to explain myself to her. She wouldn't be mad, but she would want an explanation. I heard Sizwe say, "Khosi's gone to bed. She was really tired Ma, she ate," as my head raced to meet my pillow. My hero.

...

It was strange being up so early on Sunday, but my body thanked me for giving it sleep. I was passed out for a full twelve hours and I felt like a new person. Only Mama was up and Uncle Muzi was bathing in his hut. "I'll take his tea when he's done, go ahead and make yours," she was in good spirits again. Dressed and ready, I sat down to my breakfast. I wanted to leave by half seven, which would give us enough time to walk to school and open up so we could have everybody settled and ready to start by eight. Mama had made us both lunch, packing my smaller package inside the basket as well.

"You must have been so tired last night to just go to bed like that. How are you today?" We watched as uncle Muzi walked outside with his dirty bath water, disappearing behind the hut and reemerging with the plastic tub, which he placed next to the door. He was dressed similarly to the day before, but this time his golf shirt was a light blue. I would have to answer Mama later as she wiped her hands on her apron and took the tray in her hands. Serving him would most likely have been my job, but she was just so happy to have a visitor. Especially one who had showed us so much hospitality in his own home, this was her way of saying thank you. We had twenty minutes before we had to leave, which was more than plenty. I ate quickly, wanting to give myself enough time to take a quick look over my notes before we left.

With ten minutes to go uncle Muzi walked into the kitchen carrying his tray of empty dishes. Mama got up and he stopped her protests before they left her mouth.

"Please stop it, you're too good to me," he placed the tray on the table, "believe me I can carry my own dishes, your sister has taught me well."

"Good morning, Makhosi. Ready for day two?"

I nodded, tea cup still in my hand. He came over and sat next to me. I could see Mama's head about to explode and I slipped her a smile. She smiled back and settled back down, finding her cup. It pained me and I felt the disloyalty to my father gnaw at me, but I couldn't help wishing that Mama had married a man like my uncle.

"I was hoping to chat to you last night about the day, but I heard you retired early." I was so comfortable around him now, a shocking truth for my mother. I could feel her watching me. Still she said nothing and in true Mama style her face gave nothing away either.

"I was exhausted, I just had to sleep. I'm sorry I didn't come say goodnight.' He was studying the page I was on in my notes.

"It's fine, we have the whole walk to talk about yesterday. I think we should get going soon." The small clock in the kitchen revealed he was right. "MaBiyela, you are the best host I've ever been lucky enough to be hosted by. I'm already thinking about lunch. Thank you for everything."

"No, thank you, it was so nice to have you stay with us, even if it was for such a brief time," Mama said, flushed. I had forgotten that for them this was goodbye, he would catch the four o'clock bus from the school directly to town. Although we hoped to be done by three, he said he would stay the extra hour to answer any questions the class might have.

As I waited halfway to the gate he knocked

gently on Sizwe's door and I saw the disgruntled face I was so used to come out. They shook hands and exchanged words I couldn't hear, which ended in a laugh that I could. Lastly, he walked over to Baba who was now standing outside his door, ready for his goodbye. I was afraid Baba would keep him for too long, but they managed to keep it brief. When he reached me he turned around once more and waved and they all waved back. I knew they were really sad to see him go. I was surprised by the familiarity I saw between him and my brother, had I missed a lot last night?

"Sorry, I know I've put us behind schedule, but you have long legs, we can rush a little." I pictured myself as a praying mantis, it was the image I got when he said 'long legs' and I wasn't quick enough to suppress the giggle. I got that questioning look I was so used to now and gently shook my head, he didn't need that visual.

"Did you see the pots in the room you stayed in? My brother painted them." He smiled then, like I had brought up something he wanted to talk about.

"I did. I was actually just saying to him that I was serious about those art lessons. His work is excellent, and to think he taught himself?!" I was starting to realize just how much I'd missed last night, and it made me sad. Not because they had spent time together, I was rather happy that they did, I wanted my brother to know a man like that. I was sad that I missed hearing my brother talk about his talent. It was the kind of talk you could only hear from your sibling if they were talking to someone else and you happened to be there. Even if I asked him, I knew I wouldn't get the quality of story he had given uncle Muzi.

We were walking much faster than yesterday, although being a few minutes behind had something to do with it, it also seemed to just happen naturally. Yesterday we were exhausted and lacked the energy to move any quicker than was required, and we were engaged in a group discussion. Today it seemed like we were flying, we were already halfway to school *and* we were going uphill. We didn't talk much after we spoke about Sizwe's paintings and evaluated how the first day went. We both seemed to think it went well and more importantly, the class did too. I knew they would all be there again today, energized from a good night's rest and ready to learn. "Makhosi, I just want to say this before we get to the school." We could see the school now, not the students so I assumed someone opened the gate and they were waiting outside the class, which I knew was still locked.

I allowed myself to steal the side of his face, wishing I could draw like Sizwe could. If I could, I would draw him from this angle. His skin was darker than Mama's, much darker than mine, it was even darker than my brother's. It was so rich that I envied it.

"I wanted to say it yesterday, but I wasn't able to. I think you will make a wonderful teacher. It is in fact what I've always seen you as in the future. You have the right...personality." I felt uncomfortable and excited and I knew I was blushing. I had to get my face under control before we got to the school. "What you said yesterday is something I will always cherish. Thank you." I wanted him to keep talking, or for me to think of something to say back. I wanted to ask why he hadn't been able to say this to me yesterday, but I didn't. As we walked through the school gate, all I could think to say was, "thank you."

The day whizzed past, and compared to the lymphatic system we tackled yesterday, gaseous exchange felt rather easy and almost fun. We were done at ten minutes to three, which I thought was amazing. When he said, "alright. We're done," there was an actual cheer that rang throughout the class for at least two full minutes. I felt a relief that I thought only uncle Muzi felt too. We had set a goal, a very ambitious goal to get through all that content with the class. The act of which may prove to be the difference between them passing, or failing at the end of the year and more importantly at the end of next year. I knew they truly appreciated it, but not in the way that we did. Not in the way only teachers who truly care, can. Following a ten minute break, the class could either stay for questions or go home. Nobody left and when we settled back down, expectedly the bulk of the questions were still on the lymphatic system. Something wonderful had happened for the group of us, I knew that even though they wouldn't be seeing Mr Makhubu again, he had further bonded us to each other.

We were done with everything by half past three, after I thanked him on behalf of the class the applause for uncle Muzi lasted even longer than that first cheer. He walked down with the group of us, saying he could catch the bus at our bus stop instead. I floated most of the way, held up by a deep sense of accomplishment. We did it! I half listened to the conversation that was taking place, more of the students had found their voice today. Sli and Thulani were quizzing him on his school's pass rate. It was so strange to think that we would all be at school again tomorrow after such a weekend. We said goodbye to Londi and once again fell into a silent walk. I felt a sense of relief, alone we could finally just be quiet. I could see the store now and knew that soon it would be good bye. Was I supposed to wait with him until he boarded the bus? Unsure, I decided to let him decide when we got there. There was a woman there, around Mama's age I guessed. It was a while before I realized it *was* her and then I was confused. Why was Mama at the store? Maybe uncle Muzi forgot something, but then wouldn't she have just sent Sizwe?

"Is that your mother?" he sounded as confused

as I was. I nodded as we closed the distance between us.

I could see the bus in the distance coming our
way, but we still had plenty of time because it
first had to pass us and go up the hill to the school
where we had just been before turning around
and coming this way again.

"Did I forget something? I'm so sorry you
had to come all this way," he really did sound
sorry, his voice soft. Mama waved him off, "oh
no please, you didn't forget anything. I wanted
to give you something and I couldn't this morning." She looked down as she said that, and then
pulled an envelope from her pinafore, expertly
concealed. She handed it to him and I knew from
his face that he had no idea what it was or why he
was receiving it. He took it and placed it safely in
his bag between two books.

"Your sister will be happy to receive your
letter, MaBiyela." It was a question, disguised as
a statement. We waited for her response. Mama
shook her head, and I felt my hands get moist.
It was a letter for my uncle. As the atmosphere
around us changed, I knew then that the right
thing to do was for Mama and I to go home and
let uncle Muzi wait for his bus alone. We said our
goodbyes again, briefly this time.

"I'll see you on Friday then," I said, it came
out almost as a question and when he nodded
and smiled, I found the relief I was looking for.
I'd been sure about it before, but now I needed

reassurance that, that letter hadn't changed things. His nod and smile gave it to me, even though I knew he hadn't read it. Mama and I went home.

That letter hung between us like a cloud, dark and heavy, ready to pour down on us at any moment. I was dying to ask her what had just happened, what had she done? Why would she ever want to write uncle Muzi a letter? And give it to him like this, in this shroud of secrecy? There was a vow of secrecy that we three had just taken, unspoken but understood. Mine was to never ask Mama about it. These questions were my own and I could never voice them, and even if I did she wouldn't tell me. Uncle Muzi would know the extent of his secrecy when he opened it. Would he tell Aunty Sli? Mama's wish was for him not to, but didn't his loyalty belong first to his wife? I wondered if he was opening it right now, seated by the window of the bus, on his way home. Mama hadn't known that he would walk down to the store with me, so she must have hoped to stop the bus and give it to him when he was already inside, without me present. That she had gone on and given it to him anyway, in front of my watchful eyes made me feel trusted. She could do in front of me what she wanted to do in secret. This time the trust didn't feel as good as it normally did. This time it felt like a burden. We walked the entire way in silence.

We arrived home to reveal what I already

knew, Baba and Sizwe were gone. Our secret. I changed my clothes and dished the food that Mama had made for lunch. My favorite dish of *imfino* and *uphuthu* tasted bland in my mouth. Mama and I moved around each other like silent energies, neither of us knowing what to do with the other. The silent walk home with her had cured me of the burning questions in my head, now I was sure of only one thing. I did not want to know. It manifested itself in my not being able to talk to her. No words formed themselves at the back of my throat asking to get out. She busied herself with the chores of the day, perhaps no words formed at the back of her throat for me either. I left the kitchen after I washed the dishes. Air hit my nostrils when I stepped outside, in a way that I felt. There had been no air in the kitchen, but I knew I could breathe in my hut. I would stay in my hut, head against the pillow, and wait for sleep.

I woke up to the faint sound of distant voices, drawing nearer until I could hear my brother talking to my mother. I sat for a while with my eyes closed, just enjoying the animated sound of his excited voice.

"You should have seen it Mama, that woman can drink. Eh!" I heard Mama's soft laugh and I pictured her face. Sizwe was her connection to the outside world. For a time I was too, but she hardly saw me now, so that role belonged fully to my brother. I imagined too that she was bored with my stories, because even I was bored with them. My life consisted of reliving the same week over and over, but my brother's life was exciting. He had court visits with Baba where they got to oversee the endless disputes of countless people.

He also served as Baba's companion to all social gatherings where they got to enjoy the benefits of their sex. Even if Mama and I found the time to go, the experience we would have would be so much different. He always came back from a wedding preparation, or coming of age ceremony or whatever event was happening that weekend with stories for her. He would build them up, and colour them in so that she had a full image. Like he was doing one of his paintings, only with words. Sometimes the experience through his stories was better than what it would be in real life. Mama was lucky to have him. He was lucky too, she was the perfect audience for him. She listened without interruption and when he presented points I knew he had heard discussed by the older men at the courts, she looked at him like they were his own. He could say so much to her, so easily and I had no words for her. If I walked in there now and still had nothing to say to my mother, would he notice? Would he find it strange enough to ask? We were often quiet, but would he smell that this silence was different?

I made my tea and watched my mother and brother. Mama and I were still silent energies moving around each other, deliberately not touching. We had a meeting point, a safe zone, in my brother. It was our job not to let him see our invisible dance.

"How was today?" he asked, breaking from Mama with a full face smile.

"It was good, much better than yesterday." I wanted to say more, about how talented uncle Muzi thought he was, but I wanted to say it to just him.

"She has enough energy for dinner with the rest of us today, so that's good," Mama's voice was light, her intention to make a joke, I knew. But it fell flat and even though for my brother I wanted more, all I could manage was a polite upturn of the corners of my mouth. We spoke in circles like this, around and through Sizwe for the rest of the night. If he picked up on it, he didn't tell us. I retired early, claiming tiredness. Nobody pointed out that I had slept all afternoon. The game was getting too much for everyone and it could only end if either Mama or I left, so I volunteered. As I sat alone, reading over my work, I hoped they were grateful for my sacrifice.

I hardly spoke to any of them that week. Throughout the week we were swift avoidance warriors and school was my saviour. On Friday I was saved by my other family. Uncle Muzi and I were back to work. We had caught up fully to where I was at my school, so I would bring him what we did that week and he would go over any issues that I or any of the other students in our class had. I would teach them what I learned in our extra lessons during the week. There was less to do now that we had caught up and often we just met as a study group or homework class. Even then, not a single one of them stayed away. If uncle Muzi felt that our teachers hadn't done a thorough enough job in a section, then he would and I passed that along too. We fell back into our old rhythm, it was almost as if we hadn't experienced that weekend together. Almost, the easy comfort I still felt in his presence was the only proof I had. I was happy that had stayed. I didn't talk about the letter, I tried my hardest not to think about it. I wanted my knowledge of it to go, but that stayed too. We were heroes to my aunt and cousins and although I tried to explain how uncle Muzi was really the hero, they wouldn't take it. Whatever account of the weekend he told to them gave me a much bigger role and that was the one they believed. I tired of protesting in the end.

...

It was over a week before I was able to form a word at the back of my mouth for my mother. Every evening we would do our dance for the benefit of my brother. School took me away during the day and I was gone for the weekend, but on Sundays I came home. On Sunday evening I was sitting with my cup of tea, my second to last. After this I would have my last, the one I would take with me to my hut, that would be my companion as I read over my work, consolidating. It was just after dinner and we were all deliciously full, quietly nursing a cup of tea. Mama had her legs stretched out straight with her skirt flared above and beneath them. The very tip of the pale green pinafore she wore over it had landed on a tiny stray coal, which had burnt its way through. It was so small that the little smoke I was seeing would die out and it wouldn't amount to anything.

But I wanted to tell her. If only to find out if I could. I wanted to say something to her and observe how the words felt, how they tasted. If I could talk to her again. "Mama, your dress," I said it looking at her straight in the face and I thought about how proud Principal She-she would be. She looked up at me and I registered surprise. Not from what I said, because my words lacked the tone, the urgency. She was surprised to hear my voice, directed at her. I pointed to the small hole now in her pinafore and she flicked at it, achieving nothing. She smiled at me and the smile was real. Full and whole, and I let my heart start beating again because so much had been hinged on that smile. I could talk to Mama again.

CHAPTER 19

The rest of the year seemed to go like that. I blinked and we were getting ready for our final exams. The rest of the grade was engaged in a panic that only exams could bring, but my class wasn't. We had put the time in, we had put the work in and when we were with each other we were free to admit the truth. We were looking forward to the exams. We sensed the daggers that flew our way, shot from the eyes of students that didn't feel as settled in their preparation. Their panic brought them to us and we answered whatever questions they had, but it was too late. They knew that and we knew that and they hated us for it, and about that there was nothing I could do.

I let the knowledge settle me. I had no stress for these exams, I had studied the material and taught it so much that I knew I *knew* it. Not in a way that could be forgotten after a while, but in the way that stayed and I could build on in the future. When exams started in early November it was the loneliest time I'd had in a while. There were no more study groups, or travelling back and forth. We saw each other in the mornings before each exam, distancing ourselves from those whose panic was like a disease, shouting answers back and forth to show how much they knew but also betraying how much they didn't. We sat quietly and chatted about what we would do after the last paper.

For the first time I wanted to stay, stay and continue what we had started here. Stay, relive this year and carry my class through matric. We could all pass together like I knew we would when the results for these exams came out. It would only take two weeks for the teachers to complete all their marking and finalise our reports. They didn't have to mark the matric papers, those were marked externally, so we took preference. In two weeks we would know the fruits of our labour. It was a thought I pushed out of my head as we walked home on that last day. Our last exam was History, a comfortable paper whose greatest challenge was getting everything down in the allocated time.

"I can't believe it's over," Sli who was walking a little ahead of me said, not really to anyone. I couldn't believe either.

"Whoo!" the shout caught all our attention, it came from another group of students who were behind us. When I looked back my eyes connected with Mthunzi, but I could tell the girl next to him, Luyanda, made the shout. Her fist was still in the air, her pretty face stretched out in a broad smile. Their group wasn't a part of my class, they were not really a part of anything except each other. I watched as Mthunzi put his arm around her shoulder, and remembered how he had walked out of my meeting that day, "keep your uncle to yourself," he had said in his self assured voice. I turned back around.

...

It was strange to once again have time, to not have to be somewhere or prepare a section. I had been feeling more energetic since exams started because I had less responsibilities, but now, I had *no* responsibilities. I was free. I had left everything on the paper. I now had time to just be with my family, for the last time before I moved to my Aunty and Uncle's house. It was halfway through November and the heat confirmed it, so I had two full months before the next school year started. This was the last time I would have with them as a real member of my family before I turned into a visitor. The shift had started to happen already with how much time I spent away from home, but my things were always here. When I went to Aunty Sli's, I packed a small backpack from home. Now I would be packing a backpack from Aunty Sli's when I wanted to come home. These next two months were going to be the last of an era in my life and the heaviness of that reality hit me as I walked home. I could see the kitchen now, from where I was on the road. I felt like I was seeing with fresh eyes, how nice our home was, how the green paint of every building just seemed right, how much I liked the yard. I pushed the gate to walk through and I was met by Mama's ululating. I could smell the chicken she made, my celebration chicken. Today I didn't mind the prematureness of her celebration.

"Usebenzile, Nyambose," *You worked hard*. Mama rarely referred to us by our clan name, and when she did it made my insides melt. Her hug was warm and tight, I could feel her braless breasts on my stomach. When she let me go I felt like she had taken away most of my weight and worry along with the scent of onions.

"I made your favorite," she said as she turned and walked back into the kitchen. I followed, deviating only to go and change out of my uniform for the last time. I looked at the black skirt and white shirt, and felt a funny tingle. I would not be wearing that anymore. Londi had asked if I would give her my extra skirt and I agreed, I told her she could take both. I would keep the shirts, Uncle Muzi's school also wore white shirts but the skirts were navy like the jersey.

"Sho Khosi, you're done now. How was the last one?" Sizwe was topless in the midday sun, I thought I was starting to see some definition in his stomach.

"It was good, long, but that's history."

The first two weeks were torturous. I was ready to relax, to calm down and enjoy the break that I had earned, but every time I sank into the comfort my brain would send jolts of shock up my spine. I would remembered that I was still waiting for my results and even though in my family everybody had already celebrated them and gotten over it by now, I was stuck with the truth. I still needed to see my report. I loved them for how easily they accepted that I aced all my exams with no proof, but I still needed it. I imagined that the only other people who felt as I did were the other members of my class. I imagined Mthunzi and his friends playing soccer in the afternoon sun, not a single thought wasted on how badly they did on exams they hadn't prepared for. I pictured the rest of my class, like me, unable to fully enjoy a single day, plagued by the question of just how well they did.

After about two days of milling about and trying to enjoy having nothing to do, I knew I had to find something. I started doing my old chores again, disrupting Mama's new rhythm which she had formed around my unavailability. I woke up early to fetch water and joined her to get wood. I washed the floors of my hut and the kitchen too, I even asked if I could cook more. The only thing I didn't touch was the pots. She had slowed working on them during the winter, saying the weather wasn't conducive. In September when spring rolled around again, she resumed with my brother while I focused on school. The pots were now firmly their thing and I was respectful of that. The same way Sizwe had been when the pots were firmly our thing, but it was also more than respect. I couldn't offer her what Sizwe could. Mama would never stop me painting her pots, but if I picked up my brush I wouldn't be able to stop myself comparing it to his work, so I let the pots be. By the end of the two weeks I was an efficient cleaning and chore machine. I felt like I made up for all the work I'd missed over the last few months.

I was first in all my subjects, and despite everything, I was still shocked. In IsiZulu I was tied for first with five other students and in English I was tied by three. The only two distinctions that came from students who were not in my class, were in IsiZulu. The thirty-two of us passed every single exam, but with varying results. Between us we attained seventy-two distinctions, distributed unevenly. There were a few of my students who, although they passed everything, received no grade of eighty percent or more. Somehow they were the ones we all felt the proudest of, because their improvements were astounding. Thulani had gone from being a fifty to sixty percent student to passing all his exams with merit. His highest was in Biology, where he received a seventy-four percent. That evening, I ate the beans that would give me gas later awash with pride. For all my students, for my uncle and for myself.

Mama cooked me a second celebration dinner the following night, she hadn't planned to but when she saw my report she insisted. My brother looked at it and whistled, holding the note for a while until he handed the report back to me.

"Well done sisi," he was looking at me with admiration and I floated. When Baba got home I took it to him and watched him study it quietly for a few minutes. Then he folded it back and gave it to me, a smile on his face.

"Hhe? So my daughter is a genius?" I couldn't help the way my heart fluttered. "Well done, Nyambose. You have made us very proud. Very proud. Have you told your uncle what your results were?" I shook my head. He had been the first person I wanted to tell. I would have climbed on a bus and gone to show him straight away if I could, but I would have to wait, I would be seeing him very soon.

"You should, he'll be proud to know that all his hard work paid off." I left Baba's room thinking that he was right, if I was so proud of my class I could only imagine how Uncle Muzi would feel when I told him how well I did, how well we all did.

I got my opportunity a few days later. Mama was ready to start selling again, they had built up enough inventory. I was excited to sell again and to see my other family again, I was equally excited to do something that wasn't cleaning or related. My brother and I were sitting in the kitchen, happily and silently coexisting.

"I can't wait to see how you sell tomorrow," I said, ending the silence. I imagined he would be cool and smooth and not struggle at all. He looked at me blankly and when I met his blank stare with my confused one he was prompted to say something.

"I'm not going." He said it very matter of fact, like it was all he needed to say, but I continued to stare at him blankly and he finally caved into an explanation I could tell he felt he didn't need to give.

"Selling, is not my thing. Or town, I don't like it there. There's just too many people going this way and that way," his head followed his words like he could see the people in front of him right now. "You guys have fun, I just like to paint the stuff that's all." I was disappointed, but the more I tried to picture him in town the more out of place he looked. Mama was right, this was his element. It had never occured to me that someone could love staying here so much that they would choose it over the city. Perhaps older people like our parents, who had established their lives here and were comforted by the familiarity, but not someone as young as my brother. Yet, he was content here, this was not only what he knew and what he was comfortable with, this was also what he would choose if given the option.

...

Although Saturday was more of a reunion than anything else, it was also very much still about the pots. When the girls and Aunty Sli saw them they gasped. I volunteered that my brother had painted them before they asked if it was me and then I was forced to say no. I thought their looks of pure amazement and endless remarks about his talent would annoy me but they didn't. A strange thing happened when someone new saw my brother's work, it forced me to look at them and for a second I saw them through their eyes and experienced the wonder of his talent all over again. It was a magic I found I enjoyed very much. After the initial wonder, they would still look at the pots and just marvel at the beauty.

His designs transcended the actual pot they were on, such that we stopped selling the pots for their uses along with their beauty, because with his art on them all anybody saw was his talent. They didn't want to buy Mama's pot, they wanted to buy Sizwe's painting. Uncle Muzi said that we should add R100 to the biggest pots, R50 to the medium ones and R20 to the small ones that Sizwe painted! Which Mama should then split with Sizwe, which would only be fair. It was the highest markup we had ever had, but people bought them. People bought all of them and if they didn't they picked them up and I recognised on their faces that look of amazement I was getting to know well. It was a look that said, 'I can't buy it now, but I will one day.'

Where my brother excelled in art, I got a chance to show my own excellence a little later when Aunty Sli asked about my results. Mama's quiet smile made me feel warm inside, because it said she was proud of me and she knew that they were all about to be proud of me too. I didn't want to sound like I was bragging so I opted to just hand her the report. She didn't disappoint, her face lit up and she clapped her hands together.

"Ha! And I thought *my* girls were little geniuses. Wait until your uncle sees, he'll be so proud of you!" She hugged me to her and I could smell curry powder and fresh sweat. "All distinctions! Well done my girl! Nyambose! Ha!"

By now my cousins had gathered around and Zandi reached for the report card, which her mother handed over. Musa was excitedly jumping around, clearly not understanding the commotion but enjoying it. Zandi studied my report for a long time, her hand on her hip. Zinzi was behind her and I realized I had done it too. I had managed to induce in them, all of them, the same sense of wonder and amazement that my brother had with his art. This was my art.

"Well done, *mzala*! I did really well at the end of my grade eleven year, but not like this. And in *everything*! You killed it!" She reached her hand up for a high five and I happily imitated the action. Zinzi was looking at me in shocked amazement, "I'm going to have to start borrowing *your* notes now," she said smiling at me, "well done, cuz." My insides were happy jelly, swishing around.

As happy as I was at all their praise and excitement, the person I really wanted to show was not there yet. He had come to help us in the morning as always, but then he rushed somewhere with the van. I hadn't asked because I knew he'd be back to pick us up in the afternoon and I would just have to show him then. He came at around four o'clock and I waited quietly for someone to bring up the results. It was old news by now, so I found myself waiting for a while. If it was just uncle Muzi and I, I would have brought it up with no issue. But in the presence of my Aunt and cousins, that somehow seemed rude. It was Mama who finally saved me from my anguish, "Muzi, Makhosi brought her report to show you."

He reacted instantly, like he couldn't believe he hadn't asked yet. I understood from his face how much more he cared about this, because he had worked so hard to help me achieve it. He had a nervousness as he reached for the folded paper that the rest of them hadn't, and he carried me with him through every second of him computing my marks. He jumped up, straight in the air and when his feet hit the ground again he clapped his hands together. He hugged me, no he wrapped himself around me squeezing tightly for a second before he was gone again. It all happened so fast that for a few seconds we all forgot about my marks and were captivated by his rare burst of emotion. "This is brilliant! Well done! Well done!"

I wanted to live in that moment forever. I saw a look from Zandi that wasn't as happy as before, like she had never seen her father that excited about results and it didn't deserve to be directed at me. I looked at Zinzi, who was also not quite as excited. Uncle Muzi seemed oblivious to the change in the air, but all the women felt it. Subtle, but definitely there.

"Yes, she did really well, didn't she? They all did," Aunty Sli corralled him, expertly.

"I'm so proud of all of you girls, wow! Now we're just waiting for Zandi's results, did she tell you? I know they'll be good though, that's why she isn't even stressed. Right, Zaza?" Uncle Muzi continued, joyfully. That at least managed to get a weak smile from her, and I was grateful. I didn't want to bring up my results ever again. I watched Zandi and Zinzi walk to the grilled mealies stand. I didn't join them.

"Can I hold on to this, Makhosi? I'll need to make photocopies for the principal. You know your acceptance was conditional and I was waiting on your results." I nodded, he had come over to where I was standing next to Mama and Aunty Sli. He paused to flash me a smile.

"I knew you would do well, but this is out-standing. I meant it, well done." He went back to where his bag was and he slipped the report inside.

Outstanding. I liked that word. Mama and I were ready to go, I was just waiting on my mealies from the girls. When Zandi handed it to me I wanted to smoothe things over. They seemed to be back to normal, but nobody said anything so I decided to try.

"I couldn't imagine what you're going through waiting for your results, Zandi. I was going crazy after three days and I only had to wait for two weeks." She shook her head in a way that said, *you have no idea*, and I knew I was about to get one.

"I'm losing my mind. I would give my left arm to have waited two weeks. We have to wait two *months*! Can you begin to imagine?! It's a fate worse than death, I swear." She had such a flare for exaggeration, it was really almost a skill. I couldn't help laughing and when Zinzi rolled her eyes and started laughing too I felt like we were okay.

"It's seriously not that bad," Zinzi said and it struck me how she had always seemed like the older sister.

"You know Zandi, I really think you would be a great actor. On stage, or maybe even on tv," I said. Zinzi shook her head vigorously and shot me eyes that said, *oh no, what have you started?* On cue, Zandi dramatically caressed her face saying, "Well, I mean, I definitely have the face for it." We parted happily and when Mama and I sat on the bus, snuggled by our plastic bags, I was ready to go home.

We sold over the rest of the summer and in the weekend just before Christmas we sold together for the last time, capitalizing on the buying spirit this time of year brought up in people. I was most excited that Sizwe was finally coming with us, even if it was the last day. Uncle Muzi had asked him to come, he wanted to show him something in town. He had asked Mama two weekends ago too, but Sizwe had been tied up in an important case with my father. It wasn't the last day that we would sell, but it was the last day that *I* would. In a week I'd be making my move, and it somehow still seemed far. None of us brought it up.

We set up and were settling down to sell when uncle Muzi revealed what he asked Sizwe to town for. I only heard it in passing as he told Aunty Sli where they were going, "we're off to the art gallery now then okay," he said as he gathered up his bag. Aunty Sli nodded, her eyes on my brother, "have fun, dear." An art gallery, I wasn't exactly sure what that was, but it must be a place with art. He wanted to show Sizwe the works of other talented people? This time I *was* jealous, I wanted to go to an art gallery too. I wanted to see if other people's art was like his, or would it be completely different? I went over to join the girls where they were standing, getting ready to start shopping for customers. It was much easier since my brother started painting them. We just had to display the images to the crowd and somebody was bound to come for a closer look. They practically sold themselves.

"Your brother is much older now, he got really tall," Zandi sounded strange, or maybe she didn't and it was just strange to be discussing my brother.

"Yeah," was the only thing I could think to say. But her bringing him up gave me a window. "So where's the art gallery?' I tried my best to sound casual, unsure whether I succeeded or not. 'It's in the center for the Department of Arts and Culture on the other side of town, Baba mentioned it last week. Have you ever been there?" Zinzi asked, looking up at me through her long lashes. I shook my head, prompting her to continue. "We took a field trip there last year for Arts and Culture class. It was a little boring to be honest, but some of the art was very good. I think since your brother is an artist he'll really like it."

I had never given that title to my brother, not even in my head, so it was a bit overwhelming to hear someone say it out loud. An artist. I guess he was, wasn't he? To be an artist was simply to be someone who created art and Sizwe certainly did that. My brother was an artist, and he was going to a building that celebrated art.

When we finished selling Mama went to go

deposit all the money we made from the start of the spring in the bank. She carried a bag and I couldn't help imagining it was full to the brim with money. She carried in that bag our entire year's work. I wanted to know how much we made, how much we had in total, but it felt wrong to ask. When she came back she looked pleased and that was enough for me. That was Mama's money, even if I did still have the other bank card. Sizwe was making a mock sketch of Zandi, and Zinzi was laughing at the comical way he exaggerated some of her features. I wanted to join them, but I didn't want to ruin the moment so I stayed with Mama, who was starting to pack up. It was almost time to go. We said our goodbyes and separated into two families. Theirs happily going home, and ours begrudgingly following Mama to the mall.

She wanted to make use of us both being in town to buy us new clothes and was deaf to our protests. And protest we did, Sizwe because he said he didn't need new clothes and me because I knew the weekend before Christmas was the worst possible time to shop for anything. Stores would be unbearably full and uncomfortable. Not to mention, all the good things would be gone. Mama didn't care and we ended up in the huge Jet store. It was cool inside, so that was nice, but that was one of the only comforts. The line we would have to join after we picked out the clothes we wanted was already snaking its way out of the store. Mama didn't need too much convincing after that. We agreed that she would shop for Sizwe in his absence while I did my shopping, when she accompanied me to Ng-welezane the following week. She forced Sizwe to walk around and point out what he liked before she would let us leave. I know the sole reason he indulged her was to buy our freedom from that store and I was grateful for his sacrifice.

On our way to the bus rank she more than made up for our torture by stopping in front of the women who sold mealies. The smell had long since called to me and when Mama reached into her purse I wanted to dance. My brother was all smiles too. We ate them all the way to the bus stop, walking slower to enjoy every bite. In the bus, I sat next to Mama and Sizwe sat in front of us. My eyes were fixated on the back of his head, wanting to be ready when he turned around to tell us about his excursion to the art gallery. I knew Mama wanted to know too and I was glad that I was sitting next to her with nowhere else that I could possibly go. At some point my brother would turn around to shower my mother with the story of his trip, dripping in all the details that only she could inspire out of him. And I would be here to benefit from it, free of charge. I fought the urge to open a pack of *niknaks* to help me with my wait, I didn't want the crunch of possibly the world's loudest chip to deter my brother from starting his story and

I wasn't quite ready to completely kill the last of the taste of mealies still in my mouth. I realized we wouldn't be getting this story on the bus when the old thing started up. It was so loud that now we would have to pay extra attention and he would have to damn near shout, and my brother would not be shouting on this here bus.

...

"I saw the work of so many great artists, Mama, so many. I didn't know that people could do things like that. That there was a place where people went just to see other people's work and creativity. There was so much, there was *tin*. Did you know you can do so much with a tin? And it all looked good too." I watched him sip his tea, and understood why he had had to wait to get home before he could talk about it. He had needed all that time to wrap his own head around what he saw and heard. He was so vulnerable in that moment, like a child who just discovered they could fly and we were there to witness it. It felt like we were hearing his every thought as it came to him, his brain not bothering to filter anything. I saw in my brother for the first time, the same sense of wonder that his work gave everybody else. Mama and I didn't say a word, both content to be his audience. Where he was, I don't think he would have heard us anyway.

"Uncle Muzi took me to see the man who runs the gallery, can you believe that? I didn't know, he just looked like an ordinary man, so I thought he was also just admiring the art. I was such an idiot. But, Mama, Uncle Muzi told him he had to see my work and that I should be in the gallery. I nearly died, he didn't tell me he was going to say all that. And the man said I should put together a portfolio and he'll take a look. He said if I'm good then he'll display my work in his gallery." I don't think my brother meant to cry but he had no control over it. He was caught in the moment in a way so grand it captured us too. We knew we were lucky to have witnessed this moment in his life. The moment he realized his wings when before he had never dared to think he could fly. I couldn't recall getting up, but as I clung to my brother I hoped my own tears showed him that his were okay. Twice now I had seen my brother cry, captured by the extremes of his passion. This time it was beautiful.

We didn't speak about it again and I knew we wouldn't, but it coloured my brother's life so that just seeing him felt like talking about it. Even on Christmas day he was outside under the tree, working on a sketch. His life revolved around putting together his portfolio and we all happily respected the space he silently demanded. If I caught him not working and asked how it was going I knew the answer to anticipate.

"I don't know if I should show him my best work, or just some good work to start and then give him the best if he asks me to display?"

He had been asking us this in different forms ever since we got back and Mama and I had stopped answering him, because we realized he wasn't really looking for an answer. He asked because he enjoyed how it sounded. "Please just make sure you include the lioness," I'd respond. That was my only solid piece of advice. That sketch remained my favorite and I knew that whoever that man was, he would love it too.

I had my own dilemma that I didn't have a solution for, perhaps that I also didn't want to find a solution for. How could I thank Uncle Muzi for what he had done for my brother, and for me? I mulled it over as I whacked the potatoes, trying to make them smooth for the side dish of mash potatoes I was making. It was Christmas and the one tradition we had for the day was a plate of food worthy of the gods. 'Seven colours' as it was known, was the standard and Mama and I had managed to get it right every year. We made pumpkin, spinach, beetroot, a cabbage and carrot salad, a potato salad, mash potatoes, a bean salad, pap and that wasn't even including the stews. Mama made her chicken curry and I made a small beef curry that I knew Baba liked. It was a ridiculous amount of food for four people but that was its genius, we cooked such that we didn't have to for the next few days so that Christmas' gift to us was being able to relax. It was also wise to overcook so we had something to offer unexpected visitors who dropped in more than usual this time of year. After lunch when we thought our stomachs couldn't take anymore, we served the sweets. The official Christmas biscuits, choice Assorted, and the fancy chocolates Mama had hidden all week finally came out as we had the best tea time of the year. I served Baba's tea, and he rewarded me with unconcealed jubilee when he saw the contents of my tray.

I cried the night before I moved. I sat in my hut, alone, and wept. I cried more because I knew there would be no other time to do it, this was my absolute last chance. I couldn't do it tomorrow, because I didn't want to look like a child in front of my father and brother. I couldn't do it on the bus in the safety of only Mama's company, because I didn't want her to think she had any reason to worry about me. I needed her to know that I was capable of taking care of myself and that I would. I couldn't do it once I arrived because I didn't want Aunty Sli and Uncle Muzi, or even my cousins to think that I didn't love staying with them, or that I was ungrateful to be there. I had to cry now because when the sun came up tomorrow, I would no longer have the option.

It wasn't difficult to cry, I was scared that planning it so much would kill the need, but I found my tears were real and plentiful. I cried because I did not want to leave home and because I did. I cried because I knew after I left things would never be the same again. I didn't know how they would be, but they would be different and that was enough to make me cry. I cried because I would miss Mama and Sizwe and even Baba. I cried because I didn't know how much they would miss me and for how long. I cried for a long time until I was completely done and it felt like my body was drained. I sat quietly for what I thought was long enough for my face to no longer look puffy, before I walked to the kitchen. If Mama and Sizwe could see that I had been crying they said nothing about it. I made a cup of tea and drank it silently, as I enjoyed the gift of being in their presence. Satisfied, I made my last cup and took it to my hut.

The goodbyes were brief and I was grateful. My brother gave me a quick hug and told me he'd include the lioness for sure. I nodded, taking in all of his face. The flaring nostrils that flared more as he returned my smile, mouth full of white teeth.

"Good luck, sis," he said as I was walking away. I turned around, happy he said it, "you too." Baba shook my hand and repeated what he said to me the first time I went over to study for a weekend. I took in his face too, narrow eyes with thick eyelashes. His cheeks balled up when he smiled at me. I smiled back.

Mama and I made the entire trip to the bus stop in a silence that wasn't uncomfortable, and remained so until we arrived at the Mthethwa's.

I went to put our bags away and Mama came in the room with me. She sat on Zandi's bed, and watched me pack everything away as easily as if I lived here. I watched her get comforted by how easily I slotted in. I changed into comfortable clothes and Mama stayed in her travelling clothes. She was a guest, but I was not. I had been coming here every weekend for months, each weekend bringing me closer to crossing the threshold and being treated like family. While Mama was loved, she still received the politeness given to visitors. It made me feel strange, but not in a bad way.

Having them in the same house made me think about the letter that Mama had given uncle Muzi and I couldn't shake it. I observed them for any signs of weirdness which would tell me if they were thinking about it too, but they were perfectly normal. As the three of them enjoyed tea, I heard their continuous chatter accompanied by spells of laughter and sometimes silence. I wondered if Aunty Sli knew, or maybe the girls. Maybe I was the only one who didn't know the contents of that letter. I focused on the orange I was peeling for Musa, his big eyes looking up at me impatiently. I cut it up into chunks and placed the pieces in his little plastic lunchbox. His smile was the only 'thank you' I received before he dashed once again to his mother's side. He had taken a liking to me over the last few months, allowing me to slowly become his chosen big person to ask to do all things he still couldn't. When we were lounging on the couches he would hold onto my thigh with his fat hand. Zandi and Zinzi had stopped apologising for him when they realized that not only did I not mind, I rather liked being a big sister.

Mama and I cuddled up in bed that night, and I felt that feeling I had been afraid I wouldn't. The feeling of being connected, loved and protected. I thought that I wouldn't feel it, because Mama and I hadn't been as close as we once were and I thought that feeling only existed in that close-ness. But as she held me, hugging me with her entire body, I felt it again. It was a strange sort of parting gift, that I think Mama came all the way here to give me, to remind me. The next morn-ing when she left me to go back home, her gift remained.

CHAPTER 20

On the first day of school, I walked through the school gate next to uncle Muzi, feeling the looks of the other students and feeling proud. I was immaculate in my navy blue skirt and jersey, white shirt and socks and shiny black shoes. I knew my uniform was too bright, a consequence of wearing it brand new in the final year of high school, but I didn't care. Students always knew things and I wondered how much they knew about me. Did they know about my old rural school? Did they know that 'Mr Makhubu' was my uncle? I looked through faces, trying to figure out which ones looked kind, or smart, or rude and mean. Which ones would be friends and welcome me in, which would hate me for being new and exciting and stealing their spotlight even if just momentarily. We made our way to the principal's office, he had asked to see me. I was looking forward to meeting him, from the way uncle Muzi spoke about him I knew he was a very kind man.

Mr Mkhize was a jolly looking man and all of his features were round, as though he had been constructed using only circles. He looked like he should have been short, but somehow he wasn't, standing level with uncle Muzi. His smile seemed permanently fixed on his face and I just knew he was a happy man.

"Khabazela," that uncle Muzi addressed him by his clan name, told me just how familiar they were. "Hhhoo...so this is the clever niece?" he motioned for me to sit down in one of the chairs, smile in place. "How are you today, miss?" I knew he was talking to me, but it took me a second to come up with an answer, thrown off by how relaxed everything was.

"Fine, thank you, Sir," I said finally after a very noticeable silence.

"Good, good. Your uncle has spoken very highly of you and I thought he was just being nice until I saw your report. Those were some excellent results." He looked up at me, smiling now more from his eyes, which I liked more.

"Thank you, Sir," I turned to look at uncle Muzi and was comforted to find him with a relaxed smile too, looking like a proud uncle.

"Right then, there's not too much to discuss, I just wanted to put a face to the name. Your uncle and I have discussed everything and if you have any questions I'm sure he can answer them. Welcome to our school, I look forward to seeing your progress throughout the year. You've spoiled me with that report, I expect great things from you now!" His short, loud laugh was infectious, I felt my face turn up in a smile as I stood to leave.

"You will be in Miss Khuzwayo's class, we just thought it would be best if you weren't in mine. I will still take you for Biology and Physics, she teaches Maths, but since she's your register class teacher, you will start everyday in her class for the register period. You'll get to know your other teachers soon too." He paused to smile at me as we neared what I knew was Miss Khuzwayo's door.

"You'll be fine and you'll get the hang of everything in no time. If you don't know something, just ask. They're good kids." I felt the warmth of his hand on my shoulder for just a second before he urged me on with a gentle tilt of his head. I had been perfectly fine until now and I could feel the nerves build in my entire body as I walked towards the door. It was open and I was grateful Miss Khuzwayo saved me before I had to make a decision between just walking in or knocking on an open door.

"Miss Mthethwa, come in. Class, this is Makhosi Mthethwa, she'll be joining our class." I heard the murmur of voices, I saw the questioning looks, I saw the looks passed amongst friends. "We're happy to have you," she smiled as she pointed to a desk with just one girl in the third row. It was further back than I liked to sit, but the girl had a kind face and that was comforting. I smiled at her as I sat down, and she smiled back. She had a small gap in between her teeth, a feature that instantly became my favorite.

The first day went insanely fast and painfully slow, there was no other way to describe it. The girl I sat next to was Thando and she was a godsend. Perhaps she'd been instructed to be, and even so I was still grateful. I learned the names of some of my other classmates as Miss Khuzwayo took the register, trying to tie them to faces in my head.

"Is Mr Makhubu your uncle?" when Thando asked me I simply nodded and so did she and I was glad to see it wasn't a huge deal. "He's my favorite teacher," she volunteered. I didn't say, 'me too,' because I thought that might sound strange so I smiled and nodded. I liked her very much, she didn't talk too much, but she also didn't need to be prompted to talk. She didn't prompt me to talk either. Sometimes I would say something to her and she would offer no response outside of nodding to show that she had in fact heard me. I loved her for this.

By the end of the day I had met all of my teachers and spoken to maybe a third of my register class, mostly just a few girls who came over to say hi and some others who wanted to know if I was really Mr Makhubu's niece.

"I heard you're really smart," a pretty girl with

cornrows and a rather short skirt said to me. I had no idea how to respond to what she said being that it wasn't really a question and there was no way to respond without either sounding arrogant or stupid. So I shrugged my shoulders and hoped she would accept that and go away. She did, but when she turned I noticed the girl just behind her. She was looking at me in a questioning way that was rather standoffish. She'd caught the pretty girl's comment on my being smart and that look told me that *she* was the smart girl in the class and she didn't appreciate the confusion. I was the new threat. Strangely, I liked knowing this, I liked having bits of the hierarchy revealed to me.

"That's Nonto," Thando said with a major eye roll, "you'll get used to her." I didn't know what that meant, but I was sure I would find out.

We had Biology with uncle Muzi, and I could feel the entire class looking at the two of us from time to time like they expected us to do something that would validate our relationship. I hoped they would get over it quickly. Thando introduced me to her two friends from a different class at break, Sindi and Thobeka and we all spent both breaks together. At day end I waited for uncle Muzi to gather up his things so we could walk to the staff car, the car I already knew so well from the times he had borrowed it to help us carry our pots. It was a good day.

...

In the third week of school, I finally felt like I fit. Not only that I now knew how things worked here and where everything was, or that I knew all the names and personalities- it was more than that. It finally felt like everybody else had shifted or shrunk themselves just a little so that they could make space for me. I *fit into* their world and they were okay with it. That week as I sat in uncle Muzi's after-school class, where I would wait until he was ready to walk to the staff car, I felt ready to ask him the question. It had been inside me, sitting quietly and waiting for this moment when I would finally give it life by lending it my voice. What determined that *this* was the right moment, I have no clue, I knew only that I had to ask. "Uncle Muzi," it was actually amazing to me how my brain switched between 'Mr Makhubu' and 'Uncle Muzi' so effortlessly depending on our surroundings. I never got the two mixed up. "Yes," he stopped ruffling through his papers to look at me.

"The letter that Mama gave you, was it about me?"

A cloud moved in front of his face, and I knew I caught him off guard. "I don't need you to tell me what it said, I won't ask, but I just need to know if it was about me. Please." He was looking down at his papers now and I heard the sigh that came from deep inside him. I think he had been waiting for this question and when he looked up at me again, I found comfort in knowing that he would answer me. I had been preparing my next pitch to force him to give me an answer, but his face told me there was no need. He would answer and he would be honest.

I waited, feeling the thud of my heart, which seemed to be getting louder.

"I won't tell you what it said, because your mother asked me not to. But I won't lie to you either. It was about you." I felt relief, even though his confirmation only filled me with more questions. I think it was relief from knowing I wasn't crazy for thinking that in the first place. "Thank you," he nodded in response and the look he was giving me made me feel self conscious. I felt pitied, and I hated it. "She loves you, Makhosi, very much," was what he decided to say. I wondered what other options he discarded before settling on that. I nodded, not quite knowing what to say. I waited silently for him to pack up so we could go home.

...

I went home for the first time after a month, and it was nice to be home. It was so nice to walk barefoot and feel the sand beneath my feet, it was even nice to spend the first ten minutes in bed crying because my eyes were trying to get rid of the fire smoke they weren't used to anymore. It was nice to serve Mama and Baba. It was nice to see my brother turning into a man. It did feel like life had gone on without me, like I feared it would, but I found I could just as easily still fit into this space again. I was like family and a visitor at the same time and Mama and Sizwe blessed me with stories about what I'd missed. Sizwe had handed in his portfolio and the art gallery owner really liked it. He'd gone during the week like the man asked him to, which meant uncle Muzi wasn't able to accompany him. I assumed that meant he went alone and I was shocked to find out that Baba went with him.

"I asked for bus money and he said he was going to town too that day and that we could just go together. He really liked the art," my brother's face was as happy as I remembered. It was so nice to live in his stories again. He had not been offered a space in the gallery, but he was asked to add his work to a month long exhibition called 'The youth and Art' alongside six other young artists. "He didn't say it exactly, but I think that he'll pick a few of the artists to have their own real exhibition. Or maybe just one, the best one, I don't know. I just have to give my best work." Mama was listening to him with a quiet smile, her eyes finding mine every so often as if she were checking to see if I was as proud of him as she was. I was. "I've been working on a few pieces for it and Mama has been helping me a lot. Maybe later I can show you some and you can tell me what you think." I beamed at being consulted.

I was enjoying my brother, and his passion and his excitement, but I was longing for my mother. My need for her was satisfied on Saturday when I was free to have her selfishly all to myself, because Baba and Sizwe were at the court. We fetched water before the sun came up and fetched wood as it came down. We sat down to tea in the afternoon and I enjoyed just being in her presence. My mother proved to be more shy than my brother, or even my father who both asked me questions, or offered me their own news as soon as they saw me. Not Mama, she watched me from what felt like a safe distance for most of the first day I was back. Kind and loving, but somewhat far. I knew I had to be patient and she would open up to me again when she was ready. As we sat under the shadow of the kitchen like we used to, I was finally rewarded.

"So how is it, Ma?" I told her about the new school and the principal. I told her about my new friends and all the different characters in my class. I told her about how Zandi had done really well in her results. She hadn't slept a wink the day before they came out, waiting for the first newspaper she could buy to see them. She received 4 distinctions, in Biology, Physics, Isizulu and English. She was a bit disappointed, because she thought she would get at least five, but I thought her results were amazing. In the end she chose to study electrical engineering at the Durban University of Technology, which she said was hard, but she was surviving. Zinzi and I got on really well and Musa was like a little brother to me.

I told her that at first having uncle Muzi as a teacher was both strange and nice, equally, but it just wasn't a big deal anymore. She listened and took it all in and when I was done I thought she looked satisfied. She even rewarded me with a little news of her own. She was still selling, but she was back to being focused on just the neighbouring villages.

"It's just too difficult to sell in town without you. If I stay closer I have more time to still keep up with everything and still sell on two weekends per month. I'm very happy with that. I think that on holidays when you come back, then we can sell in town again. We'll see. And I've also needed to focus more of my time on helping your brother with his exhibition, the things he asks me for are time consuming, you should see them!" I felt the sense of pride as she spoke and it made me happy. I was happy she had just reminded me of his new work too, I still hadn't seen it. "Can you please show me, Mama? I'm sure Sizwe won't mind," she smiled, clearly happy to.

They were in the guest room, which had some new space because a lot of the extra pots that had been there were moved to my old hut. I chuckled at seeing that my room was being used as storage. Nothing says 'you don't live here anymore' quite like that. Mama opened the door and I watched as the light entered, bringing to life everything it touched. I was blown away first by the sheer size of them. They were *huge*. I had no idea that Mama could make vases that big, one of them came to about half my height, and was also fat. The tallest was about a full head taller than that one, but was skinnier. There was a third one that was the smallest, but still far bigger than the pots I used to watch Mama make. The three were grouped together so that they resembled a family, and there was a beauty in just seeing them next to each other. And then after being hit by Mama's craftsmanship, I received my second blow from my brother's talent. The three pots were painted with wild cats, all in various stages of motion. The tallest one had a cheetah, while the fattest one had a lion. The little one was decorated by the image of a leopard, just about to pounce. The genius of these pieces, what really captured you, was how he really captured them. It felt like they were really in motion, an effect compounded by seeing the light hit the animals. The colours were natural and realistic, Mama said he spent days mixing them to create the perfect shades. I found that I couldn't speak, there was nothing I could say that could express what I was thinking or feeling. I wanted the whole world to see my brother's work and my mother's work too. Stronger than anything else, was the pride I felt. I don't know how long I stood there just staring at their work.

Sizwe's exhibition was chosen, along with that of the artist who used soft drink cans as his medium, to join the other artists at the gallery who had their own exhibitions there. I wasn't surprised at all and it struck me as odd that my brother was. The entire family went to see it one weekend. Mama and Baba came with Sizwe and I came with Aunty Sli and Uncle Muzi, Zinzi and Musa. Zandi was still away at school, but she would come see it when she came down to visit. I walked around the well lit space, focusing as much on my brother's work as the other artists. It was all so wonderful and I couldn't believe that people had thought to do these things, to make them. There was a painting of a girl that I loved most, but I didn't say that to anyone. She was looking up into the sky and her face was in a huge smile that reached all the way to her eyes. Her skin was dark as night and for her hair the artist had used cotton wool, dyed black. It was the way it seemed to come alive, like she was jumping out of the page, that captured me and it made *me* feel alive. It reminded me of when Sizwe had painted Mama.

"It's beautiful isn't it?" I hadn't seen or heard him come up and I felt slightly embarrassed because he caught me looking at another artist's work. He smiled, "I like it too. I met the lady who did it, she kind of looks like that," he said as he bounced off somewhere else. I was looking at the picture again with new found love, I loved that a lady had done it.

Back home, I dove into my work, given new

fire by the events of that day. I was both inspired and fueled by my brother's growing success; by the way that our parents looked at him
in the gallery; by the tone they took when they
spoke about him, the unmistakable pride. I was
inspired by the way he included them and me
in everything. He wrote both his and Mama's
names on the pieces that were painted on her
pots and I knew how happy that made her. He
asked me to help him write descriptions for each
of the pieces, and as I walked past them and read
my words, it made me feel like I was a part of his
success and his talent. I wanted to be like that, I
wanted my parents to be proud of me in the same
way and to talk about me like they spoke about
my brother. My art was my books and I ate, lived
and breathed them. And if I ever found myself
losing steam, I just thought back to how my parents' eyes shone brightly as they watched people
marvel at their son's talent.

...

The end of the first quarter saw us all together
again for the first time that year, selling our pots
in town like we used to. Zandi was back too
and I couldn't help notice how she seemed to
have grown! She sounded so sophisticated talking about the places she'd seen and the things
she's done. Every second I was around her made
me crave the end of my own schooling career. I
wanted to go to university, where I would finally
dive into the glamorous world of sophistication

that my cousin now knew. She'd just come back from Sizwe's exhibition, it did so well that it was still running. She came back with a newfound appreciation for my brother. She spoke of him like he created the very oxygen we breathed, like he wasn't just the same cousin she left a few months ago.

Tease her though I did, I was happy that in her Sizwe had found a true fan. She went to see his exhibition three times before she went back to Durban. Schools were only closed for ten days and after that weekend selling, I spent the rest of it at home. I used every day of that week going to my old school and meeting with my class, teaching them as much as I could and letting them make notes from all of my work books. It was strange at first, a fresh layer of resentment- although thin- existed with some of them. Resentment that I had left and that I was going to a better school. I was aware of it as I taught them, they no longer treated me as an equal because I was no longer one of them. It stung even though I had tried to prepare for it. Still, I woke up everyday and did my best to help them learn as much as I could in the week that I had. Perhaps as a form of appreciation, I felt the resentment dissolve and acceptance form as the week went on. But it was never the same, we weren't quite friends or peers anymore, I was their teacher.

I did this again at the end of the second quarter, this time bringing the beloved Mr Makhubu back with me. He stayed for a weekend while I continued to teach for a week after he left. I did it again in September and for the last time in the last weekend of October, in preparation for the final exams starting in November. It was hard to know if I did enough for my former classmates, if I dedicated myself enough to their success, but from now on it was each of us for ourselves. "Good luck, guys. This is the last time I'll be seeing you before we start writing. We've gone over everything, just give yourselves enough time to go over it again. And, study hard." It was my attempt at a motivational speech, but it didn't quite hit the mark.

I could hear the fear in my own voice and I could see it on their faces. Was this really enough? I had come out here four times in a year to teach them what I had been learning consistently over the course of the entire year. Was there any version of reality where that could really work? Did we all just come here to make ourselves feel better? Me, so I didn't feel like a sell out for going to a better school and having better opportunities. And them, so they felt like their situation was better than it was, because they were working to change it. But would it really change? I knew half of them had never *really* thought about university, because that just didn't happen here, while I had applied to six different universities already. Was I being more cruel in my effort to be kind? I wanted all of them

to pass and apply for bursaries and get them-
I brought them the bursary application papers
myself. I had done everything that I thought I
could and now that we were at the end I couldn't
help wondering if it was worth anything. And
worse still, if they didn't do as well as we all
hoped, would they blame me for making them
hope in the first place? They gave a gracious
round of applause, but I walked all the way home
with a heavy heart.

I think Mama knew. After I'd changed my
clothes I went into the kitchen and lumped into a
chair. She made me a cup of tea and I felt her eyes
linger on me while I desperately tried to avoid
them. She waited. When I finally looked up at her
she was waiting.

"Nana, you can't do this to yourself." She sat
down next to me and gently brushed my hand.
Her skin was warm and I could feel her gentle-
ness was about to bring me to tears. I looked
away, not wanting her to see me tear up. This
was not the time to be a child, I had been doing
so well. She continued brushing my hand, strok-
ing gently. I pulled my hand away to wipe the
tear I hadn't been able to call back. There was a
slight relief in having that one tear fall, and in
having someone see it and care, a relief so good
I couldn't stop myself from crying then. I felt
Mama's body over mine, her warmth covering
me. I could smell her, the familiar smell of home.
It felt like all my other senses were coming alive,

because I couldn't see, blinded by my own tears.

She held me until my shaking lessened to slight tremors before stopping all together. We were quiet for a while as I let the relief wash over me. I felt good and light. It was only once I let it go, that I knew the true weight I'd been carrying and I felt now like I could fly. Mama's kind face was there for me again when I was ready to look at it, her own eyes slightly glossy, but soft. "You did everything you could and those kids are lucky that you kept doing it. I'm sure they are very grateful to you and if they are not, baby, that's not your problem. You are a wonderful child, Ma, and I won't let you think otherwise." She was quiet for a few seconds, perhaps thinking, perhaps giving me time to let her words sink in.

"It's time to focus on yourself now, okay? You can't be two people, you can't be in two places. You've done everything you can and now you need to focus on your own results. That's why you left in the first place, isn't it?" I nodded. I was thankful that Mama had removed the burden from my shoulders and made it alright. She'd set me free from a prison of my own making and I wasn't sure I knew how to thank her for that. As I thought that, the answer came to me. All I had to do was my best. Without guilt of making anybody else feel bad, because like she said, that was not my problem.

...

I was a girl possessed in the weeks leading up to our final exams. It was wonderful. When the day came for our first exam, I felt that familiar feeling I had felt the year before. I was ready. As we filed into the hall, I looked for Uncle Muzi and found comfort in his face. He was one of the invigilators and it was nice to have him close by. He gave me a nod as I sat down, the only communication we would have until we heard the ominous, "Pens down." But that nod was all I needed. It was calm and ready and it made me feel that way too. It said, '*you know what to do,*' and I did. Exam after exam, I knew what to do.

...

On the day that Matric results were out, Baba woke up early in the morning to go and buy me a paper in town. I knew it would have been easier just to walk to the container and call Uncle Muzi who I knew would already have the paper by now, but it was special to have Baba be a part of it. The rest of us waited awkwardly for him to come back. He was on the noon bus, Sizwe spotted him by standing on the water tank and looking out toward the bus stop.

"I see him," he shouted excitedly. My heart was a drum, excited and scared. Mama was looking at me, the excitement having spilled to her too. The paper only printed the names of the students who passed, and next to them, symbols showed just how well they passed. There was no question of *if* I passed, not for a single member of my family, it was all a question of how well.

Baba came through the gate, walking much faster than I had ever seen him do it. We were all on our feet, outside his door in a second. It was the first time I'd seen his arrival not met with tea, but rather by the entire family. The paper was misaligned, so I knew he'd looked at it already. "Excellent, my girl," was all he kept saying. It was great, but it did nothing for me, I still had no idea how I did. He opened the paper to where he'd marked my name and lay it flat on the floor as we all huddled around it. I saw the name of my school and I looked through the long list of 'M" surnames until I found the list of 'Mthethwa' surnames. I think I forgot to breathe as I identified my name, following it to the symbols side with my finger. My brain was dead and I couldn't compute. I heard Mama's ululating and my brother's loud

"Whoo!" in my ear, but I still couldn't fully wrap my head around it. Six distinctions. *Six*. I had never actually known of anyone that had gotten that, sure I'd read about students who got all seven distinctions or even those who got eight or nine by taking extra subjects, but I had never *known* those people. And now, I *was* that person. The only subject that I didn't get a distinction for was physics, for which I got a B, which I still thought was great. We sat like that, my family engulfed in a moment I knew I would treasure forever. I looked at each of their faces and knew

I had done it, I had made my parents and my brother look at me in *that* way. The awe and pride dripped from them and I felt like I was an artist too. Mama cried and as I held her hand as we walked back to the kitchen, I cried too. I understood that she was proud of me in a different way, in a deeper way. My world had just been opened in a profound way and maybe only Mama could understand it and appreciate it, because she had lived what it was for that not to happen. I fell in love with her again as we made Baba's tea.

She took the walk with me to call uncle Muzi. Aunty Sli answered the phone and the joy in her voice was heartwarming. "Usebenzile, sisi," *You worked hard.* She was right about that, she had seen all my effort and I knew she was happy for me. She spoke to Mama for a while and at some point I heard uncle Muzi come through. Mama handed me the phone after she gave him a repeat performance of what she had just said to Aunty Sli. "Its wonderful...yes, so proud. Sky's the limit now." I knew she meant every word, but it was funny hearing it again. I was excited to speak to uncle Muzi too, not for the congratulations I knew were coming, but because I needed advice I could trust about what to do next. I got every bursary that I applied for and now I had to choose which direction to go. I had narrowed it down to two options; a full bursary from Eskom for a degree in electrical engineering at the Durban University of Technology, or a full bursary for a degree in teaching from the Department of Education, also at DUT. It should have been an easier choice given that I was certain I wanted to be a teacher, but I kept thinking about the opportunities that could come from having a degree in engineering. That degree could still allow me to teach, if I really wanted to. I needed to secure my place soon, so I had to make a decision. My family had been open to both but had not really leaned in any direction. They were ready to support whatever decision I made, but they would not be helping me make it. I knew it was in part because they wanted me to feel free to make my own choice, but also because none of them had gone to university so they felt unqualified to advise me. When I suggested talking to uncle Muzi about it, they had championed the idea.

His voice came through the phone, calm and steady. "I know it's tough, it's a big decision. I've thought about it a lot and I really wish I could be more helpful but in the end it has to be your choice Makhosi." He was silent for a while, "you've thought about this for a while now. What do you want to do?" I *had* thought about it at length and I didn't know what I wanted to do, which is why I was making this call.

"I don't know. I know that I love to teach, I really do, and I think I'd be good at it. But I could also be an engineer and I could make so much more money to take care of everyone. I think if I worked as an engineer for a while, I could always come back to teaching. I could teach Maths or Physics, which I would understand so much more." He was still quiet and I would have started to wonder if the connection was lost, but I could still hear him breathing.

His voice came through at last. "Well, it sounds to me like you've made a decision." I took in a deep breath and slowly let it out, aware that he would hear it in detail. It sounded like I had made a decision to me too. I was getting ready to say goodbye when I heard him speak again. "Makhosi, just...just choose the one that makes you happy. Your family is fine, are they not? Is there a desperate need for money in your home right now? I don't think so. Your brother is doing well. You know his exhibition is going to Durban and possibly Johannesburg after that. And your mother still sells her pots and she's saved all the money that she thought you would need for university. You have a bursary which means you won't need it. So, take money out of the equation and see if that changes things. I hope that helps." I felt him draw in his own deep breath and let it out slowly. I had the feeling that had been difficult for him to say, but I was so grateful that he had. It certainly did help. I was going to be a teacher.

CHAPTER 21

I had three weeks at home before I would start university at the Durban University of Technology. I chose it, in part, because Zandi was there and the idea of having someone there who I knew was very comforting for me and my family. The idea was that we would keep an eye on each other. When we spoke on the phone she sounded excited that I would be joining her. I was excited, thrilled in fact, but I spent the last three weeks hardly thinking about moving. I spent those last weeks with Mama, we'd spend almost entire days in her garden. We fetched wood, a chore I'd always hated but endured, and I found that I didn't hate it this time. I found that I enjoyed being outside with her, free and happy. Tired, but happy. We cleaned, and I even scrubbed the floor of my brother's flat while he was away, an act he noticed and thanked me for.

He hardly painted Mama's pots now, his time

taken up by new works that he was always thinking of. He bought painting canvases in town and
whenever he had a moment to himself that was
what he was doing. It was mostly landscapes for
now, but they were magical. Sitting outside in
the shade one day, Mama coaxed me to paint one
of her pots again, "Just do one, I know how much
you enjoyed it," so I did and she was right. It was
no masterpiece, but I really did like it. It didn't
look like my painting was art, because it wasn't,
but I realized that was in itself a gift. It forced you
to look past the painting and at the pot. When
Sizwe painted on them people bought the pots
because of what he had painted, but with me,
they bought the pot because *it* was beautiful and
they could really see it. The realisation gave me
the push I needed to paint as many of her pots as
I could.

As much as I tried to be present in every moment and fully enjoy every day, the days rushed
past. I had packed all my clothes into one suitcase, a new big one that Aunty Sli had given me
as a gift. We decided that it was best to buy most
things once we got there, because we didn't really
know what I needed and we didn't want to travel
with excess baggage if we didn't have to. They
would all come, Mama, Baba and Sizwe, all the
way to Durban. When I told uncle Muzi this, he
suggested that we all go together.

"It doesn't make sense for you all to use public
transport when a week later I was going to bor-

row the van, so that your aunt and I could drive Zandi back up there. Why don't you all just come here and we'll all go together. The van has the space and I'm sure Zandi won't mind going back a week earlier. Your aunt and I want to see you off too, you know. It makes sense." There was very little arguing with him on that, he was right, it did make sense, and it made everything so much easier.

It was nice that we were all going, and it was strange. I don't think my family had ever all left home at the same time. We could all be excited about getting up early the next day and seeing a new city. Durban was only a two hour drive from town, so it would be a four hour trip for us, which was not bad. We met the rest of them in town, to save time. Not because going to their home would take long, but because if they welcomed us in it would be at least an hour before we were ready to leave. I could tell we all shared the excitement for tomorrow as I sat with my mother and brother in the kitchen, quietly drinking our night time tea. It was a ritual that was as natural to me as breathing and one I knew I would miss dearly.

...

Baba and Uncle Muzi rode together in the front, and the rest of us rode in the back. It was perfect, it allowed us at the back to relax in a way I knew that Baba's and to a lesser extent, uncle Muzi's presence would have disturbed. The two of them were getting on well enough too, we could hear them talking through the small window between our two sections. Mama and Aunty Sli were having their own soft conversation, which left us young people to carry out our own. I was grateful that Zandi and Sizwe were having their own conversation, a conversation that didn't need me. I looked up in time to catch a look that was shared between them, a look that made Zandi cover her mouth in an effort to suppress a giggle. I was happy to be a wallflower. I just wanted to take it all in. Every so often Musa's shifty little body would pull my gaze from the window, but it always found its way back.

The thing I saw first was the ocean. It was the clearest sign that we were somewhere completely different. It stretched out to the left of us, sometimes hidden from view only to reemerge a few seconds later. It was a game of peekaboo and everytime it went out of sight I patiently waited for it to return. It had the same effect on all of us, there was a silence and a calm in the car, attention directed outside. Even uncle Muzi would turn every so often from the road to take it all in. We whizzed through the changing landscape, the vast openness of the sea giving way to the buzzing of the city. It was nothing I had ever seen, the noise, the smells, the endless supply of people. The colours, I had never seen such a colourful place. I saw yellow bananas for sale by tall, dark men on side streets. I saw green and blue *doeks* on the heads of big hipped and big bottomed Mamas walking slowly down the road. I saw young kids, younger than me, who walked with an exaggerated spring in their step. I saw filth on the streets, the waste from all these many people collecting on either side of the streets like decorations. I saw little boys who needed a bath and vaseline and a comb. I saw little girls who needed longer skirts. I saw mealies roasting and I imagined the smell, my tummy rumbling. The landscape changed again and I saw peace and calm; quiet streets which looked like they had just been swept just this morning; lawns with green grass, which looked like it had just been cut. The air smelled clean here, but there was still that hot, sticky feeling. The humidity covered the entire city like a blanket, equally and fairly.

The university was abuzz, thousands of other students doing exactly what I was doing, and thousands more doing what Zandi was. I felt the divide of the newcomers and the returners, the way they rolled their eyes and smiled at us as if to say, 'kids.' I didn't mind, I was used to being new at this point and I was grateful to have Zandi point out all the things I needed to know. I had gotten into one of the better residences, according to her and I was really lucky. I would have to share a room though, because I was in first year. She was finally getting a room by herself.

"My roommate was nice, but I just want my

own space, you know?" I nodded to most of the things she said, trying to take it all in. It felt like a thousand different things were happening all at once and I had to somehow remain aware of all of them. I kept my eye on Mama and Baba, knowing they were out of their element. I didn't worry so much about Sizwe, he would be fine and if he wasn't, Zandi seemed to have his back. Uncle Muzi was already my hero, he had the added benefit of having done this last year with Zandi so I trusted him to fix everything. We all did, I could tell by the way everybody looked at him when there was a moment of uncertainty. "It's alright, they just have a lot of students, but it's all under control. Makhosi is in the next block, they're next."

The girl who took us to my room was very excited, not about me per ser, it just seemed to be her natural disposition. I liked the way her hair swooshed this way and that as she led the way, the same way her hips did. I was to spend my first year living in Block G, towards the rear end of the residence, on the second floor.

"You're going to hate fire drills," Zandi's voice penetrated my thoughts briefly before I zoned everything out again. I wished we were back in the van, whizzing through streets and time. Being bombarded with stimulation for all my senses, distracted. As we climbed the stairs, uncle Muzi and Sizwe positioned themselves on either side of my black suitcase, bracing the weight with each new step. I felt exhausted, but more than that, I felt the anxiety creep higher up my spine with each step. They could only stay for two hours at most, so they had enough time to head back and for Mama, Baba and Sizwe to still catch a bus. I would be left alone with Zandi, who I didn't want to be left alone with right now. "G 22A. You should get a padlock for your door. Your roommate hasn't arrived yet." She opened the door, and we walked in. I followed her as she showed me the good condition of the windows, the door, the floor and marked it all down. There would be another inspection when I left at the end of the year.

"See you around kid, if you need anything, Find me. Name's Linda, remember this face." I was happy when the door closed behind her.

I trailed behind as we took a tour of the entire residence and then the campus. It was all so big, and so wonderful to think that this would be my new home. It was all so *overwhelming*. I wanted just one of those faces I came with to turn around and say, 'are you okay? This must be so much to take in,' but that was a selfish hope. They were all so happy and excited, happy and excited *for me*. Mama looked at everything, where I would wash my clothes and was amazed to find actual washing machines. When she heard that there was staff hired to clean the residences, and all I would have to clean was my room she looked dismayed.

"You're going to come back lazy, I'll have to make you clean at home so you don't forget how to." Baba was talking to another man, another father, the two of them with faces awash with fresh pride. My brother was talking to uncle Muzi and I could hear Zandi talking to her mother, who seemed concerned, "She's okay, it can just all be a lot the first day. She'll find her groove." They were behind me, so I decided not to turn around, choosing rather to walk towards my brother and uncle. When Sizwe saw me he lit up, putting his one hand inside the pocket of his new black jeans. I remembered him choosing them at the store and they looked good on him, contrasted by a clean white t-shirt.

"Khosi, we want to go take a look at the Durban gallery where my work could be coming to. It's not too far from here, apparently. Mama said you have to buy things for your room, so Uncle Muzi said he could drop you guys off and then take me. We won't take long and we'll pick you guys up after."

I wanted to protest that I was going to be stuck picking a bedspread while he went to a gallery, but I didn't. I should be happy for my brother and for myself, everybody was getting what they wanted. I offered him an upturn of the corner of my mouth and hoped he accepted it as a smile, I added a nod for good measure. I caught a concerned look from Uncle Muzi but turned before I had to acknowledge it. We discussed the plan as we all got into the car again. The invite to join the trip to the Durban gallery was extended to Baba and he accepted. I saw on Zandi's face that she wanted to go too, but she wouldn't ask. When the lines were drawn this clearly, it was silly to argue. She had to come with us. Musa was the only one young enough to defy gender roles and get away with it.

It was nice how clean and cool the store was and it lifted my mood.

"Which one do you like?" Mama was looking at me gently and I knew this was important for her too, all of it. I picked a white one with light grey and pink flowers that came with two matching pillowcases. It was reversible with the other side having a pink base with grey and white flowers. It made me feel happy and calm and I liked that. We bought the inner for the duvet as well as the pillows. Aunty Sli picked out a woven mat for my floor, a bright orange one she said would 'wake me up'. That reminded Zandi of the alarm clock she said I needed, picking out a bright red one. I looked at all the things and wondered how well they would all go together in the small space but didn't have the heart to say anything. I wanted them to be a part of everything and I knew the various pieces would remind me of them when they were gone. Mama came carrying a kettle and an iron, both black and part of a promotion special.

"You need these," she said with no room for a

real response.

"What else?" I looked around and had no idea. I knew I would need food, but that would come later.

"Coat hangers," I was grateful for Zandi being here now, I would never have thought of that until I didn't know where to hang my clothes. "And a bin, then she should be pretty much ready to be a university student," she winked at me and I smiled at her. I *was* a university student. At the till Mama paid for everything and my heart swelled with the pride I knew she was feeling too. She paid in cash, the idea of paying with a card made her uncomfortable. She would draw money from the ATM and then pay using the notes instead of swiping. It was perhaps tedious, but it made sense to me.

We bought food and Mama surprised me with a cellphone. It was cheap and small, with a tiny screen with strange colours. It was the best thing I'd ever owned and I couldn't believe I had a phone.

"It's my gift to you, nana. You're too far now and we should be able to talk to you" She bought a cellphone for herself too, cheaper and more simple than mine. She could have easily bought a better one, for us both, but that would have been a waste of money. Hers had a small black and white screen that lit up green as the man tried to show her how she could play a game of snake on it, but Mama showed no interest. She paid cash for all of that too and it made me proud all over again. I wished Baba and uncle Muzi and Sizwe were there to see her do it, slowly counting out the notes before she looked to me to confirm she had done it correctly and then handing it gently to the man. She held the furthest part of the note, I think to make sure their fingers didn't touch accidentally. Her eyes were on the counter the entire time, looking up only for the second she held out her hand for the change, which she gave to me.

Standing in my room for the last time before they left, I was grateful I didn't have a roommate yet. As they prayed for me, in a tight circle of interlaced hands, I knew the moment was too precious to share. I listened to each of their prayers as far as I could follow a single voice before it disappeared into the choir. It was easy with Uncle Muzi, he was used to leading prayer and being the loudest, "We come to thank you God for the opportunity you have given our child. We ask for you to protect her Lord and let your spirit shine through her in her studies..." It made me warm to hear him say 'our child'. Baba didn't pray, but he showed his respect by quietly bowing his head. If he did pray, I had no idea what he would pray for. Sizwe didn't pray either and when I peeked to steal a glance I saw that he also didn't close his eyes, but he did bow his head. I tried hard to hear the soft prayers of my mother, aunt and cousin, but they were lost in their own gentle chorus. The only thing I did manage to hear from Mama, who was right next to me, was, "..thank you, Lord. Thank you." It was a bit of an awkward scramble after we all said "Amen" because nobody seemed to know what to do. Rather nobody wanted to get it done. As the mass of bodies tried to find new and exciting things to keep themselves busy with in my tiny shared room, I picked up Musa and held his little, warm body to mine. It was my own attempt to do something new and exciting to escape the awkwardness floating all around us, but I was glad I did. His warmth and easy acceptance of my affection made me both happy and sad.

"Khosi, this is for you." I looked up from the little body embedded in mine to find my brother's face. His hand was behind his head, positioned for a scratch that didn't exist and I knew he was embarrassed. Embarrassed to be doing something sweet for me and embarrassed that he was forced to have an audience. He handed me a painting, on an off white piece of canvas like the ones he had been practising his landscapes on. Only this wasn't a landscape. It was me and Mama. It was a painting of me and my mother, sitting under the shadow of the kitchen on a grass mat. I had a cup of tea in my hand and Mama's was within reach, but not in her hand. I had my face turned toward her, the soft lines on my face showing that I was smiling. Mama was looking ahead, although her head was tilted towards me. Her face was open and she was in the beginnings of what was about to be a big laugh. The background was there but it was just that, background, negligible. It was a simple painting for my brother, but it was immaculate. He captured perfectly the warmth between us, the ease, the love.

I didn't know I was crying until I felt a tear fall. The room was silent with everybody caught in the same moment I was, but differently. Perhaps the only other person who felt it quite like I did was Mama, who I saw wiping her own tear, only she wasn't looking at the painting. She was looking at me. I don't know how long we stayed like that, but I know that, that part of the silence wasn't awkward although I think it should have been. It was beautiful. I mouthed "Thank you," to my brother and he nodded, I knew wanting me to not make it into a big deal. Awkward, I knew, at what a big deal it had already turned into. Goodbyes were long and hugs were tight and when they left I fell on my freshly made bed and cried. I was grateful Zandi said she had something to do and left me alone with a promise to see me for supper. I think she knew I needed her to go for a while and I was grateful.

The next day when I opened my cupboard to pack some things away I noticed the pot on the top shelf. It was a small one, that I had painted a very long time ago and I remember Mama remarking on how much she loved it, the two of us just staring at it. It had an impala on it, an impala and her calf and they were grazing peacefully. Their fawn bodies stood out in the warm sunset colours I painted as the background. It really was beautiful, so much so that I thought we had sold it ages ago. I guess Mama had kept it and I knew she had left it here for me. I moved it from the corner in my cupboard and placed it on my desk. I wanted to see it everyday, the same way I would see the painting of us done by my brother every day from where I hung it on my wall.

March

I went home in March for the first time and I knew as I sat sandwiched between a man and a woman in the taxi, that the two weeks we had off would not be enough. The man who sat by the window leaned his head against it and went to sleep. I was glad, it made me more comfortable. I could look past him and to the ocean without him thinking I was looking at him. It had only been nine weeks since they left me, but it felt much longer. I felt like I had aged a decade in those short weeks, I felt like I had done so much. It was the biggest adjustment of my life and it was challenging, but I loved it. I enjoyed the work and it was nice to focus in a direction I knew I wanted to go. Zandi and I saw less and less of each other, which I knew our families wanted us to do more of, but I knew we didn't. I liked her, loved her in fact, but it was becoming glaringly apparent that we were just different. No longer bound by the confines of the same house or the wishes of our parents, we explored our freedom in the directions we wanted to go- and they were different. I would see her from time to time and the kids in my class could never believe we were related.

She seemed to always be at the center of the crowd. She thrived in it and I liked to watch her as much as everybody else did. I just liked to do it from afar, and I preferred to hang out with her when it was just us. She stopped inviting me to all the parties I wouldn't go to and we learned that when we saw each other on campus a wave was often enough. There was one event that she invited me to that I agreed to go to. We had a date for the gallery about halfway through the semester, Sizwe's exhibit had moved to Durban. I knew he would have added new material and I couldn't wait to see it. Even if it was still exactly the same, I would have gone just to marvel at his talent. "Wow," it was all Zandi and I could manage to get out of our mouths. I saw her watching the other people looking at Sizwe's art, like I was. We smiled at each other when they said 'wow' or just looked at it in that way people always looked at his work. We smiled because we *knew* him, this person they were in awe of was my brother and they had no idea. It was a nice secret.

Sizwe himself hadn't seen his Durban exhibition at all nor would he.

"I don't see the point, I've seen the gallery and I've seen my work. I can put the two together in my head." He'd sent me the text with his new phone when I'd asked him about it. We didn't talk often, but we talked. Strangely enough we spoke most often at the end of the weekly calls I made to Mama. "Say hi to your sister," she would say as I heard the phone change hands. Sizwe bought his phone himself, with money paid to him by the gallery for one of his sales. Someone bought one of the huge pots that he painted. "A hotel I think, to display in their foyer." He had told me the news on one of those phone calls and I was so proud of him. I nearly dropped the phone when he told me how much they paid for it.

"Hhe?! *R7000*?! For *one* thing?" His laugh on the other end made me aware that I had been shouting and I was grateful my roommate was at supper.

"Yeah I know right! And the funny thing is, apparently that's nothing. Bra Mike, the owner, sold a sculpture for R18 000, says I'll get there one day. Can you imagine?" I couldn't. Not at all. I was struck dumb and I'm sure my face showed it. I was grateful yet again for my roommates absence.

Sasha. She was the most delicate girl I'd ever seen, there was simply no other way to describe her. She had hair down to her back, thick and healthy. "I've never cut it," she'd told me in the sing-song Indian accent I'd gotten so used to. I had learned so much about Indian culture just by observing her. We didn't talk too much, sometimes if we managed to exchange a single 'hi' the entire day that was an achievement. Slowly our silences changed from awkward to comfortable. It was like we lived in two completely separate worlds within the same space. I envied people who said their roommates were like their sisters, the pairs I saw walk together, eat together and do their laundry together. The ones who chose to spend their free time together. I felt that Sasha and I happily tolerated each other. It was comfortable, even nice sometimes, but not like that. We did have our moments, a collection we were growing. I woke her up when she overslept on the day of her presentation and one night she offered me her pimple cream when I had a surprise breakout. It smelled like it should never touch skin, but it worked. She had a boyfriend, Devon and whenever he came around I made myself scarce. I would find a need to go to the store, or have a sudden urge to take a walk, get some fresh air. They were always gone by the time I got back. Sometimes she didn't come home and on those days I would make my tea and sleep in just my underwear on top of the covers. I lived for those days.

The bus ride was long and bumpy, just how I remembered and every bump made me happier because it brought me closer to home. Walking through the gate, I let the feeling of home wash over me.

"Khosi!", Sizwe saw me first and his voice drew Mama out of the kitchen. Released from my bags by my brother's muscular arms, I was free to hug Mama. That smell, her smell, made me float. I was home. Baba wasn't home yet, but I was looking forward to seeing him too.

"I like your shoes," my brother smiled as he dusted off the black adidas sneakers, with the iconic white stripes.

"Thanks, I bought them after I got paid. They

are my work shoes." And that they were, I would have kept them pristine, but his were decorated with splats of paint. It didn't look horrible, on him it looked honest. We were having our first cup of tea together and I forced my brain to slow down enough to enjoy the moment I was in. I pushed aside the questions about what he did with the rest of the money, about where his exhibition would go next, about all the important things that could be important later. I focused just on being with them. Mama was on her grass mat, and I gave my eyes the pleasure of caressing her skin, and taking all of her in. I think it was my intense focus on her that jerked me to the realisation of how thin she was. Her darker-than-caramel-but-lighter-than-chocolate skin was clinging to her bones a little too tight. I looked then at her face and the lines around her mouth seemed deeper. She caught me staring and smiled. I smiled back, but couldn't help noticing how when she did, it only made her face seem more hollow.

"Your hair, it suits you." I stared at Sizwe blankly for a second. I had forgotten that my new style of braids was something they had never seen me with before. Zandi and her friend put the thin long twisted braids in my hair, an excruciating process that took two days and made me wonder if hair was really worth it.

"Thank you," I had to admit though, I did like it. I looked at Mama again and wondered if my brother didn't see how frail she looked. He was talking to me about my hair. People didn't discuss hair when one of them looked so weak. Had she started to disappear so slowly that he hadn't noticed it? Or had he seen it for so long that he no longer saw it?

The question plagued me but I couldn't ask it in front of Mama. So I just looked at her, trying my best to make it seem casual. She caught my eye and held it.

"How is school, nana?" It was the first real question she'd asked me. I knew she knew how school was going from the weekly updates she made me give her every time she called. But it was different having her ask me in person, everything was different in person.

"It's going well Mama. I like it very much and I like my teachers." My brother was listening too, his ear turned to me with his eyes on the floor.

"So when do you start teaching then?" It was the question I received most often and it was the one I hated the most.

"That's only toward the end of our degree, we're still doing all the foundation work for now." I said that exact line so often I sounded like a robot to myself, but it always sounded interesting to other people.

"Hmmm," my brother nodded. Well maybe it didn't sound interesting to *all* people.

My father came home and his face lit up when he saw me behind his tray. "Makhosi, isibuyile ingan' yami." *My child is back.*

"Yes, Baba," I said as I set the tray down. He motioned for me to sit, so I did. He had never asked me to sit down before, I realized with the shock of not knowing what to do. It felt so strange to be invited into his presence. It felt important. I waited.

"So how is it there at the university?" I shifted in my chair. I desperately wanted this to feel natural, but it didn't. It felt like an interview.

"It's nice Baba, I'm doing well." He picked up the spoon and stirred the tea that Mama had already stirred.

"Very good, very good." It was a strange conversation in which we were both present and both absent. He brought the white cup to his lips and sipped. It felt like looking behind a curtain into a world I didn't know. I was never around long enough to watch him sip the tea I served, or eat the food I brought. Except that night when he had been drunk and I brought him water. I blushed at the thought and fixed my eyes on the beaten brown rug so he wouldn't see. I wondered if he ever drank again after that day with Sizwe.

"Makhosi?" I had completely missed his question, or comment.

"Baba?" was all I could offer in a gentle, apologetic voice.

"Your hair is different. Is that what the girls do there in Durban?" He was not upset.

"Zandi did it." I shifted in my chair again

knowing I must have looked itchy. "Do you like it?" I don't know why I asked him that, but it had found its way to the tip of my tongue and then made the jump. By the time I thought about it it was too late. He looked at me, intentionally, and I knew he was really thinking about it. It made me nervous to hear his answer, even though I had not been serious about the question.

"Hmm, it looks nice on you, but I think I like your short hair a bit more. It makes it easier to see your face." I couldn't help smiling and suddenly I wanted to leave the room, but I also wanted to stay. I was smiling too because this was the longest conversation I'd ever had with my father and it was a nice one. I looked at him too now, looking for traces of what I saw in Mama. The fatigue, the strain, the hollowness. They were there, but different. Whatever was eating Mama was kinder to Baba. He looked tired, but not unhappy. I stood up slowly to leave, because the moment that had been perfect was starting to shift and I didn't want to allow enough time to ruin it.

...

"Is Mama okay?" I asked my brother in the kitchen while Mama was hanging the washing. I offered to do it for her, but she shooed me away. At least it provided me the opportunity to speak to my brother in private. His eyes darted to the left when he heard my question, before quickly coming back to focus on the floor. He seemed uncomfortable which made me uncomfortable. I drew a small circle with my foot while I waited for him to answer me, feeling the silence get awkward.

"She's just tired I think," he was still looking at the floor and I felt my heart rate pick up. "Tired?" My tone made him look up. He let the breath out slowly.

"I don't know, Khosi. She's just been...like this for a while. She won't tell me what's eating her and I don't know how to fix what I don't know." I felt the anger evaporate from my insides when he said that, I saw a little boy who really didn't know what to do. I imagined him trying to make her laugh with his stories and being frustrated when that didn't work. How long was a while?

"Why didn't you tell me?" I asked, but I already knew why. Because I was away and he wouldn't want me to worry, so he would just try to deal with it himself. I let out my own sigh, slow and deliberate.

"Has Baba..." I trailed off, not knowing how to continue. Not knowing what I was really asking. Had he beat her again? Had he been seeing his mistress? Was he drinking again? Sizwe shook his head. I didn't know if that was a no for all my unasked questions or just some, but I didn't ask him to clarify.

When Mama walked in I wondered if she sensed the weirdness of the room. She gave nothing away as she made her tea.

"Mama, are you going to make any pots today?" It had always been the one thing that was hers, that had always had the potential to make her happy. I remembered a time when even that hadn't been enough and I dug my thumbs into my palms as I waited for her response, silently praying that we weren't back there again. She gave me a weak, quick smile and shook her head. "Not today, nana." The rest of our tea time was spent in silence, until she finished her cup, which she placed on the table before leaving. I shot the question at my brother, knowing I didn't have to ask it. His voice was sad, low, "it's been a while. She started making them less and less and then she eventually just stopped. Maybe about two weeks ago. I asked her and she said she's just taking a break, because she has enough for now. I don't know, I didn't push.." I wish he did push. Maybe I would have to push.

The next day after tea in the afternoon, I pulled up some of the pots she made that had never been painted and I set out to work. Sizwe had gone with Baba and I helped myself to the paints in his hut. I sat on the mat as I often had, in the shadow of the kitchen. Mama was in there, finishing her tea and I knew she could see me. I wanted her to see me. If she saw me then maybe it would spark something in her. Maybe she would see me painting and remember how we used to do it together and how much we loved it. Maybe she would think about why she started selling her pots in the first place and how I was living the dream she had worked so hard for. Maybe she would remember just what she had accomplished and she would be happy again. And her face would break into a smile, a real one that took over her whole face and lifted her spirit. I worked and I waited. I finished two pots. I looked in the direction of the kitchen as much as I looked at what I was painting, but she never came out. I started the third pot, my last, with dread. I was giving her one more chance to come out and I knew that would make it worse if she didn't. She didn't come out. In the kitchen when I walked back in, she didn't say anything to me. I sensed her wanting me to leave and it was a familiar sensation. That thing, that had repelled us before, that silent odour of sadness was back and I wanted to ignore it and stay with her, but I couldn't. I spent the rest of the afternoon outside, in the shade.

The silence hung around us like a dark fog, the only sound coming from our teaspoons clinking against the cups. Sizwe seemed unbothered by it and he also seemed unbothered by the messages I was trying to give him with my face.

"It was a good day," he said suddenly. It was so random it made me stare blankly at him. Mama gave a 'hmmm' that would serve as his reply. Is this what it was like then? Did he state things sporadically so it felt like they were having a conversation, so it felt like he was trying? *But he was trying.* The thought silenced the chatter in my head for a minute. He *was* trying. What was I doing? I had been here a day and I had already run away from Mama to the safety of outside, protected by distance. He still tried.

"Mama." It came out louder than I planned, sharper, but I had to do it then or I knew I'd lose my nerve. She turned her head towards me, my brother too. "Mama, you should let me do your hair." I wish I thought about what I would say before I said it. Only, just then all that had mattered was that I say something. *I* was trying. I looked at my brother, because I wanted him to see. I was trying too.

I looked back at Mama and she was just looking at me, head tilted slightly.

"My hair? I don't have any hair." She spoke slowly, taking her time with each word. But she spoke, and it gave me courage to continue, to try even harder. I got up to sit next to her, "yes you do, I've seen it. You have beautiful hair and I can braid it now, Zandi and her friend taught me." I reached my hands up gingerly to her *doek*, gently unwrapping and then pulling down the silky brown and orange fabric. I was holding my breath waiting for her to pull away or to tell me to stop, but she didn't. I exposed the thick mass of hair which she had braided into four thick braids. I undid them, heart racing, suddenly aware of myself in a strange new way. Who was I? Who was this brave new person who could do what I was doing now? Loose, her hair was a soft, tightly curled cloud on her head. It reminded me of the painting I had fallen in love with that day at the gallery, the dark skinned woman with a radiant smile and a cloud of hair. Only Mama was missing the radiant smile.

For what I wanted to do, I needed a comb, but I was too afraid to get up and fetch it. Afraid that if I left then the spell would be broken and I'd come back to a rewrapped head and a cold layer around her. A layer I had broken through for the moment, a moment I wouldn't waste. Sizwe was looking at us and I saw hope in his face as I finger combed Mama's hair. It was the same warm hope I felt in my belly. I massaged her scalp and saw her close her eyes, It was the first time since I arrived that I could describe her as peaceful. I styled her in medium sized two strand twists, so that in the end her hair looked very much like mine, just shorter. When I was done, I was a bit lost about what to do next. I lowered my hands, and they patiently waited for instructions on the mat. The stillness threatened to get awkward again, but my brother shifted before it did. "I'll get some more water for tea." I stood to wash my hands, knowing we were safe at least for another cup of tea. My brother and I were involved in a very intricate game of balancing the sadness around my mother. Maybe all it was, was a distraction, but the point was we were trying. Sizwe left after his cup of tea and I stayed. We didn't talk, but I felt like that was okay. I made us each one more cup before we went to bed.

...

It wasn't until a full week passed that I could get the words out of my mouth. I thought about them almost every second of the day, how I would say them and even what she would say back. But every time I had the opportunity, when it was just us, the words would catch at the back of my throat. I don't know what set them free that morning, before sunrise, as we walked to the water pump, but they gushed out of me.

"What's wrong, Mama?" it had come out almost randomly and out of the blue, disturbing our silence abruptly. But it wasn't random at all, because something was obviously wrong. Maybe it was the pump, maybe that's what finally inspired the question. It reminded me of the time we came to the pump together and that woman had...done what she did. I looked at Mama, feeling guilty for thinking about it and checking for signs that she knew. She walked on, unbothered by me, unbothered by anything.

"Mama?" she had given no indication that she heard me so I started to think that maybe she hadn't. We reached the pump and filled up our buckets, put them on our heads and walked home. "I'm so proud of you, nana," her voice was a shock, because I had given up on her saying anything. I shifted my head to look at her, feeling the water swoosh above me. She was still looking forward, her pace steady. "So proud," she turned to look at me and smiled, her eyes penetrating mine. "You're going to be such a wonderful teacher. I have dreams about it." She turned back around, leaving me to deal with my butterflies.

"Thank you, Mama." I don't know what inspired that from her, but she said it and was done. She didn't say anything else directly to me for the rest of the day.

...

I went back to school that Saturday, leaving behind a set of instructions I knew wouldn't be followed. "Call me when she gets really sad, and I'll talk to her," an instruction I whispered to my brother behind Mama's back. I said the word 'sad' extra softly, because that was the bad word. He nodded, but I knew he wouldn't. At what point was she *really* sad? And what would I say to change it? Still, I said it and he nodded. We were still trying.

"I'll call you more often and you should call me more often too," that one was for Mama and I knew that wouldn't be done either. We spoke once a week and I already struggled for things to say after she asked me how school was and I asked her how she was. In those moments I wished for the thing I hated in other people the most, the gift of blabber. I wished I could talk endlessly about nothing, barely braking just long enough to make sure the other person was still listening to me. That way I could fill the silences that often engulfed us, silences I didn't mind sometimes, because I liked silences. It was because I liked them so much, that I was acutely aware when they shifted, and they had shifted more and more with Mama. "Be good and do you best," I smiled at Baba, that was an instruction that I knew I could keep.

June

I took the trip down in June with Zandi. She hadn't gone home in March and had teasingly called me a baby for doing so. It didn't seem to matter that she had gone home in March in her first year too.

"Baba will be waiting for us, I've texted him that we've left," she said as she tossed her thick 'boom shaka' braids behind her back. They were a loud hairstyle that I knew I could never pull off but it somehow fit on her. They could easily have been understated if they were either just long or just thick, but they were both. Her longest braid almost touched the top of her bum, I had no idea how she could stand it. As if the size and length weren't enough, she added blonde streaks to a few of them, "for an extra pop, I can't just be having braids like everyone else." She was right about that, it seemed like everybody had them, which only added to my list of reasons for *not* wanting them. Even the idea of looking like everybody was one I could still bear, but what really threw me was the practical element that everybody else seemed to look past.

"Isn't it heavy?" I asked her, hoping for a real answer.

"Yesterday I tried to wash them," she confessed, " I nearly fell in the shower from the weight. I'm not washing them again." My laughter prompted the entire row of people in front of us in the taxi to turn around and look at me, but I couldn't help it. I imagined her not being able to hold her head up in the shower, boom shaka braids pulling her down and I just couldn't stop. She started laughing too, and her laughter started up a fresh bout of mine. I hadn't had a laughing fit in ages and it felt good.

Uncle Muzi gave us big hugs before hurling our bags into the van. We had a whole six weeks of holiday and we packed for it. I would spend the first two weeks of mine with them before I moved on home. When I told Mama I was thinking about doing that over the phone she had championed the idea. Maybe not championed more than she said, "yes, go see them." In response to my instruction she had actually started calling me less, every two weeks now. My brother gave me nothing and no matter how I phrased the question all he said was that she was fine, that everything was fine. I wanted to go see for myself, but instead I went to Aunty Sli's. She hugged me and I smelled the spices, her gentle belly soft against my skin.

"Look at you," she said squeezing me all over. It made me laugh and I quickly moved out of reach of her hands, picking up a much heavier Musa. I saw some Uncle Muzi in his face and it was heart-warming.

"Now what is this on your head?" I turned in time to see Aunty Sli examining Zandi's hair like it was a disease. Zinzi was at a Saturday class and would be home late.

"Ja, that's matric for you," Zandi responded. She was right, matric seemed so much more intense than university.

"How is it going?" uncle Muzi flashed me a smile, as he sat down next to me on the bench outside. It was the first time we got to talk since I moved to Durban. When I called Aunty Sli, which wasn't often, he would come on in the end to say hi and ask how I was and then wish me luck. I had been looking forward to really talking to him again.

"It's going well, really well. It's still all foundation stuff and most of my class thinks it's boring, but I really enjoy it." It was more than anybody else ever got out of me, but I didn't think anybody else would understand like he would. He smiled and for a second he was far away, I wondered if he had travelled back in time to his own university days. He came back with a smile. "Yes, I remember something similar. I loved every minute of my degree." He *did* get it. "Wait until you start shadowing teachers and then get in front of a class yourself." His face was animated, and I knew I could have had this conversation forever.

"That must be amazing, I can't wait." He gave me a skeptical look and scratched his head, "it's scary, I won't lie to you. At least it is for most people, but hey, you might just be a natural. It was scary for me, that first day, but you live past it, and if you can live past the first day, then you can do the second." We sank into a comfortable silence again.

I went home at the end of the week, the guilt of being so close and not going eating at me. I told Aunty Sli that I just really missed Mama and she touched my cheek and said that she completely understood, sending me with her love. I had to go home and I had to see whatever it was that I would see. I had to know how everyone really was and I couldn't hide at my Aunt's anymore. I tried to not imagine the worst, as I sat on the bus squeezed between the produce Aunty Sli made me take for Mama and my suitcase. Sizwe was waiting for me at the bus stop, I was carrying so much stuff that I called to tell him that I needed an extra set of hands.

"Unjani?" *how are you?* he was calm, casual.

"I'm okay, you?" he slowed his normal walking pace to match mine, the weight of my suitcase probably helping.

"I'm alright.' It was nice being with him, *outside.* It hardly happened so it was strange, it felt like a stupid thing to notice, but I couldn't help myself.

"How's Mama?" that centered me. I took advantage of being safely out of earshot and that was what I wanted to ask.

"She's okay, you know?" I tried to study the contents of his tone, the way I'd learnt to, because his words often left me with so little. He was like Mama in that way and like her, he gave me nothing, so as with her I'd have to push.

"No. what do you mean?" He let it out then, the sigh that always accompanied his conversations about Mama.

"I don't know what you want me to say, Khosi, she's...she's okay." I was quiet, because I didn't know what to say, but I knew I wanted to say a lot. I was trying to organise my words in my head and it turned out my silence was the right thing at the right time. "She doesn't eat much..anymore. Maybe once a day, but I have to force her and she doesn't talk that much either. I'm glad you're home because maybe she'll listen to you. I don't know what's wrong and she won't go to the doctor, I've asked. She cleans and does the washing..I don't know, Khosi." I still hadn't organised my thoughts into words as I wiped the tears from my face and followed him through the gate. I was home.

I put my bags down and changed into my home clothes and made my way to the kitchen. She hadn't come out to receive me and that hit me harder than anything Sizwe said. She had seen me and not been moved. Sizwe was building up the fire, preparing the water for my tea, tea I needed. "Hi, Mama," I tried to make my voice normal, free of the hurt from her ignoring my arrival and free of the shock I received from her appearance. This woman, whoever it was that sat in her space and wore her clothes, wasn't Mama. It wasn't *my* Mama, so much so that talking to her like she was my mother was difficult.

When I left her a few months ago she was thin and had looked weak, but she was still in there and a good day could turn her around. This woman looked like she hadn't had one good day since I left and the bad ones in their place had eaten at her gently, piece by piece, day by day. Her clothes swallowed her up, but where I could see her skin, I could see her bones more easily than before. There were no parts left of her that were rounded, not in her wrists, not in her fingers, and not on her face. Her face, I tried to gloss over it casually, to take it in without making her self conscious. I tried so hard and I couldn't. Her face was hollow. Not like before when from time to time she would travel into the place inside herself that left her face vacant, and we knew she wasn't there. The place we would try to pull her from, frantically and desperately. It was no longer just metaphorical. Her face was actually hollow. I felt like if I reached out I could have sunk my finger into the hollow beneath her cheek bones. Her skin looked old, much older than her, dry and loose around her.

I wanted to wash her whole body in warm water and then cover it in vaseline. To restore it to life, to make it soft again. I knew I was staring and I didn't know how to stop. She was still covered in the scent of sadness. It wasn't so much a scent you could smell, more than it was one you could feel. Mama actually smelled like a good scrubbing, like she had felt the dark, sad scent on herself and tried to wash it out. I was hit then by the reality of what it must be for her to be stuck in her body. It was difficult for all of us to be around her, to want to be. It was uncomfortable, but when we reached the very end of our tolerance we could still walk away and leave her alone with her sadness. We left because the darkness that covered her threatened to engulf us too and only when we ran from it into the safety of the sun were we safe again. What if she wanted the protection of the sun just like we did, but was trapped by the dark? Maybe if we pulled hard enough the shadows would let her go. She was staring into the space right in front of her and my greeting didn't reach her. I sat down, waiting for the water to boil, waiting for the whistle that would fill the room. Maybe that was a sound that could reach further than I could.

It was a few hours before I saw my father and the sight of him shook me to my core. Why hadn't it been like that with Mama? I had been shocked, of course, but it hadn't almost stopped my heart. Maybe because Mama's demise had been steadily building. So much so that I had been secretly preparing for it in the depths of my psyche, because I was expecting it, but not Baba's. His shrunken frame hit me like a ton of bricks. I set the tray on the table and couldn't help notice how much smaller he looked in this space. It was so clean, too clean, I knew Mama had scrubbed it too. The scrubbing had stripped it of all traces of home and now it just looked and smelled clean, but sad. I felt with a tightening feeling in my chest that this room was a metaphor for Mama herself and I suddenly had to get out.

Outside, I watched my father drink his tea through the window and wondered if that was why he had become affected too. His only space at home was the one he shared with Mama. He lived in the cave of her sadness, sharing it with her everyday. Had he been reached by the darkness? At night when they lay next to each other, had it crept from her and wrapped itself around him too? Had he given in? Was it possible for him not to? He had spoken to me, he even made a joke, about my hair.

"So you got tired of the snakes I see?" His voice was low and his laugh short, but when he spoke I still sensed the light in him, a lightness Mama was missing. It wasn't him I couldn't stand, it was the actual room he was in. As I carried his old dishes, I wondered how he could.

I toured Sizwe's latest works after lunch the

next day, my mind separated from my body. He was next to me, I knew watching for my reactions.

"Do you think Mama is sick?" I wouldn't have any reactions, because I wasn't really looking at his art. He made his way to the door of the guest hut, if I wasn't going to be an audience then there was no point in showcasing it to me. I was glad to be outside, the sun touching my skin, reminding me I was alive. My brother spoke gently, his voice deeper than I remembered, "I think she is, but I also just think she's sad. It's like, one day she just got sad and didn't stop. And everyday she got sadder. I think she got so sad it made her sick and she won't get better, because she can't stop being sad." It was a statement that told me he had thought about it before, at length. And it made all the sense in the world to me, because it was true. Mama was sad, deeply and perhaps thoroughly now.

"Do you think Baba is sad too? Like Mama is?" His pause told me that he had thought about this too, also at length. It made my heart quicken, because I was fearful for my father. I didn't want to lose both parents to the dark sadness.

"I think he's sad too, but not like her. I think he's sad *because* of Mama, because she's sad and he can't stop it." I followed him into the kitchen, thinking what I was sure he was thinking too. We shouldn't leave Mama alone for too long.

Every time I lowered my cup of tea, I could

see Mama. As we sat in the kitchen I willed her to speak, or comment on any of the discussions that Sizwe and I had, mostly for her benefit. We walked in as the sun lowered, as noon turned to afternoon. It was always dry and hot here, compared to other places, but even we were feeling the chilliness of winter. It made it easier to stay indoors, invited by the fire. We sat quietly now, Sizwe and I long having abandoned our attempts to lure Mama into a discussion. I thought about how nobody had asked me about school, not even Baba. Which was just as well, because I had nothing to say. As Sizwe probed the fire, I saw a figure coming towards the door from the corner of my eye. I turned to find my father there and a slight alarm took over me. I got up, ready to receive whatever message he had to give. If he needed something he would often just shout either mine or Sizwe's name, but sometimes, if he was already outside he would just come by and give us his instruction.

At the door he met my expectant face with a weak smile and a wave of his hand. I moved aside and he walked into the kitchen, pulled up a chair and sat down. My entire reality was shaken by my father's presence in the kitchen. It looked small around him and I instantly started to see all the things that weren't in their place. The dishes were still not done, I was going to do them all after dinner. I wasn't sure if I should do them now, but then I would be standing while he sat, which was rude. Sizwe must have sensed my panic, because it was he who saved me. He took the cup of tea I had abandoned on top of the table to attend to Baba and placed it in front of the chair where I had been sitting, the chair next to Baba's. He then pulled out the chair and directed me, with his eyes, to sit. I was grateful to have a clear instruction and I sat down, wrapping my hands around the cup.

My brother was so calm, in a situation that would have made him as tense as I was before. So, I knew this had happened before. I breathed in slowly, taking it all in. If I was the new person to this new reality, then the only thing I could do, the only thing I should do was take it all in. Sit quietly and let them show me what they did. I watched my brother make my father's tea. No tray, no fuss. Just a cup on a saucer with boiling water and a teabag. He placed the sugar container next to the cup and my father proceeded to pour his own sugar into his own cup. I watched mesmerized, with the ease with which he did it. I had always imagined that if the day ever came where my father had to serve himself, that he would be both inept and unhappy to do it. I was wrong about both. He got up after a few minutes, to cut himself a slice of lemon for his tea. I was amazed that he knew where to find both the knife and the lemon. I lowered my cup to look at Mama again and found her looking at me too. At least, looking my way, our way. My presence had been negligible to her for hours, so I knew she was looking at my father.

I watched her come alive in his presence, more alive than she had been all day. I watched the way Baba made a point to talk to her, addressing a great deal of his remarks and questions to her and then answering them himself when she didn't. But he didn't seem to mind, as though he had not expected her to respond in the first place. It was strange seeing my mother react to my father in a way she had denied to me. I had not been expecting to receive the nonchalance I had seen her give him, while he received the love I was accustomed to. It felt backwards, wrong. Or maybe everything up until this point had been wrong and this is how it should have been all along?

Baba spoke to all of us, but the only person who responded was my brother. I was too taken aback by it all, that I couldn't find my voice. Baba and Sizwe filled the silence, I think, understanding where I was. I saw Mama smile and move her head from my father to my brother and then back again, like she was following their conversation. At the funny parts she let out a faint laugh, a silent giggle. The story Baba was telling was full of the funny parts, so I knew he was making it up. He and my brother built up the tale, ridiculous and full of all the people Mama knew in the village. *MaSibiya had slipped on some water and would have been hurt badly were it not for her fat stomach that cushioned the blow.* They all went like that and after Baba had established the tale, Sizwe would fill in it, adding depth, stretching out Mama's laughter. *It was lucky that there had been a wedding at the Hlogwane home the day before, and countless people had seen MaSibiya stuffing her tummy with the roasted beef. That's why it was extra cushiony when she fell and had probably saved her life. We should all eat like MaSibiya, because clearly being fat saved lives.*

Ridiculous as the stories were, it was fascinating to watch the two of them. It was even more fascinating to watch Mama, reacting to them. In the time it took Baba to drink his two cups of tea, his stories gave each of us back a piece of Mama. It was a shell of the woman we all knew and loved, a shell that didn't speak to us, even whose happiness resembled that of a small child. But it was now our only connection to her and my brother and father had managed to do the impossible and find it, and now they bravely did all they could to reach out to it. I felt an overwhelming sense of love then, for everyone in the room. As I listened to my father make up more ridiculous scenarios, I realized for the first time that he was trying too. Like my brother and like me, he was trying too. We were all trying for Mama. I looked across the cup in my hand at the woman who sat there, and I realized that she was still there. She wasn't herself, she didn't look like herself, but that *was* Mama. I looked around and realized that she was still bringing out the best in us. As we sat in the kitchen building elaborate lies for the chance to see her smile, I realized that she was still there. Even when she broke, it was in service to us, and as we tried to pick up the pieces that she had shattered into, we became a family.

I think we all knew we were on borrowed time and it penetrated its way into our every day. I found my voice in the stories Baba told and learned that I had quite the gift for elaborateness. He started staying in the kitchen longer, two cups of tea turned into four, until he started eating dinner with us in the kitchen. It was a change I adjusted to quickly, almost as naturally as everybody else. Baba came home from town one day with a hosepipe.

"So you don't have to fetch water anymore," it was an idea so simple and brilliant. He had to buy and connect two in order to reach the pump, one of us would go to connect it while the other one stayed home and filled all our containers. We did it early, before sunrise, before anyone came. It was another change that I welcomed instantly. It was strange being in the presence of my mother and father so much and it presented me with opportunities I would never have otherwise had. I saw tenderness pass between them when my mother reached out her hand and my father paused what he was doing to hold it. Mama still never spoke and I think we had all given up hoping she would. We still spoke to her and she still reacted, but she was moving further away from us.

Our entire lives revolved around my mother. Baba tried to move her back to their room, where she would at least have the comfort of the bed, but she refused. We would have continued to spend everyday at her side if she had moved, but I'm not sure she knew that. I think she re-fused because she wanted to stay in the kitchen, because the kitchen was where we were. But we stayed in the kitchen because it's where she was. Over tea the night before I had to leave, Baba asked which bus I was taking. The answer was easy for me, the decision having required no thought, but I was still shocked when the words left my lips.

"I'm not going, Baba." He turned to look at me, the large white teacup in his hand.

"Hmm?" his eyes relayed the question more than the sound did, but even they didn't push it. I think everybody knew and everybody under-stood. And whether they had thought about it before then or not, I knew they felt the same way I did. I wanted to be there, when it happened. I wanted all of us to be there together.

...

Mama didn't make it past that winter, she died three weeks later, in August. She slipped away in her sleep, so only Baba was with her. When he told us the next morning his eyes were swollen, red and tired. We wept together, in the comfortable space that now existed between us. The space that had seen so much pass between us, that tears were nothing. I felt the purity of my own tears. They weren't angry tears, or tears of regret at having failed to love her when she needed it. They were just sad tears. Sad that the person we had all come together so deliberately to love, was gone. We had all been asking for forgiveness for all our shortcomings with every second of that deliberate love. We each knew that we wasted a lot of time neglecting that duty and I think we each wondered to what degree we were responsible for pushing Mama over the edge. I think we wonder still. Somehow, in her last days, Mama blessed us with the gift of trying to make it right. I don't know if she saw everything we did, if she saw how much we loved her. If she saw how sorry we were in our deliberateness. If she felt the bond of family, that only existed because of her, and would carry us through without her. I don't know because she never said, but I think she forgave us. I don't know, because she couldn't say it, but I think in those last few weeks we began to love her like she had always loved us.

Today

"Good morning, Miss Mthethwa," I motion for them to sit. I always love how the younger ones sing the greeting. They would have my head if they heard me refer to them as 'young'. In grade five they're old enough to talk to, almost in a grown up way, but in many ways they're still just kids. In my class hangs the picture that my brother painted for me when I first went to university, the picture of Mama and I. It's framed now, and I give it a good polish every morning and every morning it makes me happy anew. Next to it is the picture from my graduation, a big smile on my face. In it Baba and Sizwe are standing proudly on my one side, with Aunty Sli and Uncle Muzi on the other. I'm holding the small pot that Mama left for me in my dorm room, the one with the impala and her calf. It made me feel like she was there, on that day and everyday I look at it. I can't help looking at it then, sitting proudly on my desk. In my wallet I carry the letter from all those years ago. Uncle Muzi had slipped it to me when he found a quiet, private moment on my graduation day. The letter that I had seen Mama give to him all those years ago, the letter I had forgotten about.

I am so proud of you, Makhosi. I'm sorry I couldn't be there, but you know I'm always with you. I'm sorry for all the things I can't explain. Just know that I never envied Sli for anything, but the love she shares with your uncle. Ma, find a love like that. Always be free, with a love like that you will always be free. And, Nana, don't forget about the

NONJABULO SANGWENI-ARAHILL

account, all of that is yours now. I would do it all again for you. Everytime.

I love you,
Mama

I had folded up the paper, tucked the piece of gold into my wallet and wept. Uncle Muzi's face offered concern and a slight embarrassment. He had read it, he knew what my mother had wanted to say to me for so long. Seeing him made me embarrassed too. The moment felt long, but it passed. I wished desperately that I could write Mama back and that she would get it. I looked up at Uncle Muzi, knowing he was the only person I could give my response to. Knowing if I couldn't have Mama, I would have to settle for him.

"I did have a love that set me free. It was Mama's." It came out in a whisper, slowly, every word deliberate. We shared the moment, another priceless one we would never speak about again. When it ended it took with it our embarrassment.

Sometimes in a moment of silence, or when I see something beautiful, or for no reason at all, I find myself thinking of Mama. Who she was and what she did for me, for all of us, and the love I have for her floods me. When I think of her death, only one thing bothers me. I wish she had stayed with us just a few weeks longer, so she could have seen the spring. Mama loved the spring.

ABOUT THE AUTHOR

Nonjabulo Sangweni-Arahill

is a South African born, U.S. based author. Being raised in a dynamic, cultural environment has instilled in her an unshakable love and reverence for the beauty of African cultures, while also allowing her a first hand look into the challenging experiences that often categorize the  various roles of women. A driving force behind her work is exploring these roles in their vast complexities, to celebrate the triumphs of women and to expose the injustices they often incur in the context of African cultures that center around male dominance. This is her first novel.

www.ingramcontent.com/pod-product-compliance
Lightning Source LLC
Chambersburg PA
CBHW051942240626
47153CB00005B/1599